SALVAGE

*'Separated for a lifetime,
searching till the end...'*

MARK BAILLIE

TIPPERMUIR
· BOOKS LIMITED ·

This first edition published and copyright 2024 by
Tippermuir Books Ltd, Perth, Scotland.
mail@tippermuirbooks.co.uk – www.tippermuirbooks.co.uk.

ISBN 978-1-913836-37-5 (paperback).
A CIP catalogue record for this book is available from
the British Library.

Project coordination and editorial by Paul S Philippou.
Cover design by Matthew Mackie.
Editorial support: Ajay Close, Steve Zajda and Jean Hands.
Co-founders and publishers of Tippermuir Books:
Rob Hands, Matthew Mackie and Paul S Philippou.

Text design, layout, and artwork by Bernard Chandler [graffik].
Text set in Plantin Std 10.2/13pt.
Printed and bound by Ashford Colour Press.

To Florence and Bing

ABOUT THE AUTHOR

Mark Baillie's short fiction has appeared in *Analogies and Allegories Literary Journal*, *Livina Press*, *Zin Daily* and *Bubble Magazine*. He has written non-fiction for *Travellers' Times* and published research in the *Journal of Media Ethics*. *Salvage* is Mark's first novel and is inspired by his own Traveller heritage. He lives in Edinburgh.

ACKNOWLEDGEMENTS

A year before he died, Bing Baillie spoke to me about his early years, going to Travellers' fairs, hawking for a living, and how life changed when he was drafted into the army. From this came the idea to write about Scottish Travellers after the war, transitioning to non-travelling life. I knew that earlier than this there was a history of authorities removing the children of Traveller families. This felt like it had plot potential until I spoke to the researcher, Robert Dawson. It turned out that anyone from a Traveller background in the early 1980s who was aiming to trace a relative from 50 years earlier would have had a virtually impossible task. This seemed like a show-stopper – then I decided to work with it. A few years and several drafts later, Dr Bob Fell provided a link to Shamus McPhee. I'm grateful to them both. Thanks also to Jess Smith, Sue McCormick, Karina, Oscar, Elliot and the Tyne and Esk Writers, Jeff Kemp and Margaret Skea in particular, for their comments and support along the way.

Mark Baillie

'A heartbreaking story of how time cannot diminish the bonds of family.'

Scotland, 1929. Without warning or explanation, council officials descend on a Traveller campsite and brutally remove a young girl. It is the last her family sees of her.

Decades later, Nash Lacklow is sick, angry and wants answers about what happened to his sister. With little time left, he enlists the help of his great-niece Emma.

Despite being warned her task is close to impossible, Emma pieces together vital clues and mounts a passionate campaign for justice as she encounters revered Gypsy elders, fiery protest groups and delusional drifters. But the search comes at a cost, uncovering painful truths and igniting conflict inside and outside the Lacklow family.

Set in 1983, *Salvage* is a gripping and heartbreaking missing person mystery, exploring family dynamics, identity and the tragic history of Scotland's Gypsy-Travellers.

LANARKSHIRE, 1929

The brothers huddled by the fire, sniffling and yawning with weariness beyond their years. A bowl of porridge and blanket between them, they ate in silence, blinking and heads nodding gently to the crackle and spit from the flames. Nine, twelve and fourteen years old. Their eldest brother was already up and gone for the day, out working with the men from the campsite.

Nash Lacklow yanked at the blanket and coughed between spoonfuls of porridge, drawing looks of disgust from Ronnie and John.

'You coming out with us?' asked John.

Nash shrugged. 'I'm *shan* the day.'

'How *shan*?'

'Proper *shan*.'

Ronnie slapped him on the back. 'You better toughen up, wee brother. I reckon you're fit to help.'

The bossing came from a wish to educate and guide Nash, and from a desire to be men. In Ronnie and John's minds, this was how to make a contribution to family life, but it usually translated into squabbles and fights.

It had rained heavily during the night and the boys' mother, Mary, was laying down waxed groundsheets on the sodden earth. She kept an eye on her sons and could tell the discussion was going the way it often did when the three of them were together.

'Enough of that,' she shouted. 'He's going nowhere till that cough's away.'

A pan of milk was heating over the fire. Mary poured it into a cup, adding sugar and a pinch of salt. She handed it to Nash then ruffled his hair. When she turned away, Ronnie teased his little brother by mimicking a baby sucking a teat. Nash elbowed him in the ribs and Ronnie jolted sideways, causing John to fall off the end of the log on which they sat.

He rolled over and sat up, wide-eyed, scanning around in cartoon confusion. He staggered to his feet, rubbing his head and groaning like he'd just fallen from a great height. Then all three burst into giggles.

After breakfast, Ronnie and John packed kindling and tinware for the day's hawking. Mary told them they'd be going out on their own. 'I'm needing to stay here with Nash and the wee one.' The wee one was Jenny, the youngest of the Lacklow children. She'd been up during the night with a fever and was now asleep inside the tent.

Nash took his terrier for a walk to the woods at the edge of the campsite. He went a short distance into the trees then took out a bag of tobacco. He'd recently started skimming off Ronnie and John's supply as payback for their teasing and bullying. But it wasn't just about getting even. These secret smokes in the trees made him feel more like a grown-up.

He lit up and took a drag, enjoying the slow drift of nicotine through his body. Grey sky broke through yellowed leaves and all was quiet except for the dog sniffing and scratching in the undergrowth. Then complete silence. The dog had frozen, its alert small body pointing in the direction of the main road. After a few seconds Nash heard it too: the faint clatter and sputter of engines in the morning air, wheels sloshing through mud, coming closer. A car and police van rolled up to the campsite entrance. He watched through the branches as three men got out of the car and straightened their suits.

He ran out from the trees and shouted a warning but nobody heard. He called out again, more urgently, but was taken by a coughing fit that had him bent double and hacking up phlegm. The men approached the tents and Nash ran behind them, wheezing, arms flailing, and calling out helplessly.

They asked Mary why her boys weren't in school.

'My husband's deid,' she said. 'I need my laddies earning money.'

One of them told her they were there to carry out a public health inspection. 'It's nothing to be unduly concerned about,' he added.

Inside the family's tent the men found Jenny asleep under a pile of blankets. They shook her and pulled off her covers. Jenny clutched a doll, crying as the men lined her up next to her brothers. They poked their ribs and listened to their chests. Hair was checked for lice and teeth for rot. The family's terrier came snuffling and licking at the children's hands, its tail aquiver.

Whispers and cautious looks passed between the officials while the police van moved closer. After inspecting Jenny a second time, the men declared she was suffering neglect and that Mary was an unfit mother. One of them handed her a letter saying they had authority to remove children. She screamed and grabbed Jenny as other women from the site ran to help, but the police came in with billy clubs and beat them back until it was just Mary left.

Ronnie and John rushed at the police, unleashing all they could muster, but were smacked into the mud. One of the policemen locked his club across Mary's throat and pinned back her arms. The authority men then marched Jenny to their car and Mary wailed as the doors closed and it pulled away.

Afterwards, Nash noticed Jenny's doll face down in a puddle. He picked it up and wiped it on his trousers, thinking he could give it to her next time he saw her but he never did.

EDINBURGH, 1983

It was always a mystery to him why they kept waiting-rooms so hot. It was like they were trying to keep all the sickness and disease in a state of suspension until the doctors got to the patients. He loosened his tie and looked around. The other men were a similar age to him. They sat with quivering jowls and heaving bellies, gasping like bloated fish. The sight of them gave him comfort because at least he'd stayed slim as he got older – a little scraggy these days, but it was nothing a suit couldn't cover up.

He'd been at his local doctor earlier that day, feeling dizzy and short of breath. The GP examined him then sent him to hospital because of his low oxygen levels. They'd taken blood, x-rays, and measured his breathing, and now here he was, waiting for the results.

The doctor appeared and called his name.

'Do you want me to come in with you?' asked Spence.

'Nah,' said Nash. 'I'll be fine.'

'You sure?'

'I want to go by myself. Wait here for me.'

In the consulting room, Nash took off his jacket and tie, and unbuttoned his shirt. He sat down and hunched over, gripping his knees as the doctor slipped the stethoscope under his shirt and pressed it to his ribs. He flinched at its coldness.

'Say 99 for me,' said the doctor.

'Ninety...' The cough exploded, sending throbbing pains up his neck and through his skull. He folded his arms around his ribs and braced his legs against the chair. It was amazing that his weakened body could produce something that vicious, with that much power.

'How long have you smoked?'

Nash looked away. 'You don't want to know.'

His chest had gotten worse in recent years. Emphysema, the doctors called it, and these days it gave him a strange sense of robustness because he'd lived with it for so long.

'Let's try again, shall we,' said the doctor. 'Say 99.'

Nash took a deep breath but it was no use. He started coughing as soon as he opened his mouth. The doctor winced at the sound of slow-shifting fluid, like a flooded engine refusing to start.

'It's been like this for about two weeks,' gasped Nash. He was slumped back in the chair, buttoning his shirt. 'I just did what I always do when my chest gets bad – switched to menthol ciggies but they didn't make any difference.'

A grim chuckle from the doctor as he held Nash's x-ray up to the light, then did the same with an older x-ray. He flicked through the test results, frowning and sucking his teeth. He was familiar with these types of men – wizened, wheezing shells who were in their sixties but looked older.

'You're quite the cocktail of industrial diseases, Mr Lacklow.'

'Oh, aye. I've got them all. A royal flush. A full house.'

The doctor took off his glasses and leaned forward, unamused. 'Mr Lacklow, if I had the amount of oxygen in my body that you have in yours, I'd be dead.'

Somehow it felt like a compliment. 'I've been living with this for years, doctor.'

'But you're not invincible, Mr Lacklow.'

The doctor brought out a device; a box with a tube and tiny cylinder at the end. There were switches and dials on the front and an air vent at the side. 'I'm giving you this to take home.'

Nash eyed it suspiciously. 'What the hell is it?'

'A nebuliser.' The doctor poured a vial of liquid into the cylinder then attached a breathing mask. He handed it to Nash and switched on the machine. 'Relax and breathe,' he said. The vapour was crisp and metallic on Nash's tongue and after a few breaths the tightness across his back began to ease. His chest rose and fell in a smooth rhythm.

'That's amazing,' he said. 'I'll be tap dancing out of here.'

'It's yours to take home. I'm giving you an oxygen cylinder, too. You'll need an hour on it twice a day.'

Nash didn't seem to be listening. He was on his feet, regarding himself in the mirror and buttoning the rest of his shirt with fresh energy. He always wore a suit and tie if he was going to see a doctor. It was like a test he set himself, the rationale being that if he ever felt too ill to dress smart then he might as well go straight to the undertakers.

The doctor handed him a prescription. 'Make sure you rest for the next week at least. Now, is there anyone else at home, Mr Lacklow?'

'Nobody. I'm on my own, doctor – and that's the way I like it.' He was still in front of the mirror, doing up his tie with fast, confident flicks, and didn't notice the change in the doctor's tone.

'How are you getting home?'

'My nephew. Spence. He's outside.'

He put on his tinted glasses, smoothed his hair, and took a final look at himself. All things considered, he wasn't bad looking at all for a man his age. He picked up his coat and walking stick but the doctor asked him to take a seat.

★ ★ ★

It was the way the phone rang the very second she sat down – not two minutes after coming in the door – that gave Emma the feeling something was wrong. She picked it up and Spence told her he was at Nash's house and they'd just got back from the hospital. 'It's his chest again,' he said. 'They were poking and prodding him all afternoon. He's knackered.'

'Dad, is everything all right?'

'It's better if you come over.'

She found Spence on the sofa, watching television, and Nash in the kitchen, filling the kettle. He told her to sit down then came into the living room with a tray of tea and biscuits.

'Well, the doctor thinks I'm dying.'

Emma's hand shot to her mouth. She turned to Spence and stared at him then turned back to Nash. He set down the tray and put his hands on his hips. 'Och, I'm not convinced. I didn't like him.'

Spence leaned towards her. 'I've been getting this all afternoon. He thinks the doctor was useless.'

'Well,' she said, 'was he?'

'I don't know. He wouldn't let me go in with him.'

'God's sake, Dad.'

She got up and made Nash take a seat then asked what exactly the doctor had said to him.

'He reckons the emphysema's got worse. It's at stage four.' She looked at him blankly so he added, 'There's no stage five.'

'Is there nothing they can do?'

Nash gestured at the oxygen cylinder next to his armchair. 'They want me to sit hooked up to this monstrosity all hours of the day. I don't see what the fuss is about. I said to the

6

doctor – I told him – I've had a bad chest since I was a laddie. Then he said to me...' He cleared his throat and put on an officious voice, '*Mr Lacklow, I need to be honest with you*...and when I heard that change in his tone I thought, uh-oh, here we go. Brace yourself, son.'

Tears welled in Emma's eyes, and Spence sighed and patted her knee. 'It's all right, sweetheart,' he murmured.

She hugged Nash and said they were there for him. Those were important words because it was just the three of them. There was no other immediate family. She held his hand and asked how long he had left.

'A couple of years tops. The doctor told me to put my affairs in order. As if I'm lord of the manor. My affairs! Christ, that'll take about five minutes.' One to two years left to live; somehow the prognosis didn't feel like a pressing concern. He didn't see how such a long-term forecast could be made with any kind of certainty. He settled back and rested an elbow on the arm of his chair. 'Anything could happen before then. A man of my age, I could have a heart attack or a stroke. Keel over in the kitchen. Get under the covers tonight, close my eyes, and that could be the final curtain. You just never know.'

'So that's it?' asked Emma. 'There's nothing you can do to get more time?'

He turned away, his eyes darting around the room, then admitted the doctor asked him to quit smoking. 'But I told him where he could stick that idea.'

* * *

The shopping list hadn't changed in years. Spence had it memorised a long time ago. There was almost no point in Nash writing it and handing it to him each week. It was just one of those odd rituals that nobody stopped to question. The list consisted mainly of tinned food and cold meat. There might be a bag of potatoes and a few apples but that was usually it by way of fresh produce. Today, though, Emma had picked up items not on the list; broccoli and spinach, whole-grain bread, muesli, and low-fat yoghurt. For Nash's weekly stew, she'd put a bag of lentils in the trolley instead of the usual mince. At the milk aisle, Spence lost patience and grabbed the carton of low-fat she'd just put in the trolley.

'Have you gone mental? He needs fattening-up.'

'Do you know what visceral fat is, Dad? It gets stored on the inside of your body. It's the worst type. It wraps itself around your internal organs.' Her hand was turned up, fingers writhing in the air as if holding jelly. 'You can be as skinny as a rake and still have it building up inside.'

Spence shrugged, examining the carton. 'But why's this not cheaper? If there's less fat than normal milk it should cost less.'

'I don't think that's how it works.'

'Aye it is. The farmers who make this are using less fat – watering it down, whatever it is they do. So it should be cheaper. Let's say I've got a piece of carpet – polyester. It's thin, it's coarse. I'll sell it cheaper, right? I'd never get away with selling it for the same price as wool. That's business.'

'But this is about Nash's health. If he isn't going to stop smoking, we need to get him eating healthier food, right?'

'Suit yourself, but he'll not be happy about all this low-fat, low-whatever, rabbit food you're getting him. It's daylight robbery.'

Perhaps Nash was just in good spirits, but he didn't seem to mind the lentil and kidney bean stew Emma made for that night's dinner. It had been a week since the hospital visit. The antibiotics had got rid of the infection and he was up and about again. Health food aside, life was getting back to normal.

Seeing the three of them together at the fold-out table in Nash's living room, there was no doubt they were family. They all had the same sallow skin and dark hair, though these days Nash's came out of a bottle. When she was very young, Emma thought he was her grandad until he explained that he was Spence's uncle, so that made him her great-uncle. She still didn't understand so he drew a family tree and told her about everyone on it; their nicknames, how they earned a living, and whether they were alive or dead. His memory was impressive, still, despite his physical decline.

After dinner, Emma opened the window to freshen the air. She wiped condensation from the glass and stood, looking across the park to the mansions on the other side. 'It's like you're on the frontier,' she said, 'with the workers on this side and the privileged class over there.'

Nash's bungalow was on the edge of a social housing estate known locally as The Scheme; a warren of pebble-dash tenements and semi-detached houses. A park with a cricket pitch was the only thing between it and a village of eighteenth-century mansions just a few hundred yards from his back door.

He looked up from the television. 'What's that you're saying, Em?'

'Being here on the edge of The Scheme, I said it's like you're on the frontier between the workers and the privileged.'

'Oh, aye. They're posh buggers across there.'

'There used to be a slave plantation owner who had a house over there.'

'Away with you. They never had any slave plantations up here.'

'No, not here. The plantation was in the Caribbean but the owner bought a house over there in the village.'

'So why didn't he want to stay in the sunshine?'

She composed her face. 'You know, getting a tan isn't exactly what this is about. We're talking about people being bought and sold as slaves, the privileged class exploiting other human beings.'

Spence was in the tiny kitchen doing the dishes and half listening. 'Wait a minute,' he called over his shoulder. 'If the plantation was in the Caribbean but the house is up here, that does seem awful far away – and a damn sight colder.'

'Would you two stop talking about the bloody weather. I'm trying to get to the point. The plantation owner had a son by one of his slaves and the son traced him back here. The story goes that when the son knocked on the door, the dad gave him a crooked sixpence and told him to get lost.'

'Well,' said Nash, 'God knows what the lord of the manor would've made of all of us riff-raff living just across the park.' He chuckled under his breath. 'Miserable sod probably would've had a heart attack.'

'That's what I'm getting at,' said Emma. 'Why'd you think they made the village a conservation area? They're just trying to keep the great unwashed at arm's length. It's disgusting.'

'Doesn't bother me,' said Nash. 'I like seeing the cricket pitch and the nice houses when I open my curtains in the morning. Those mustard-coloured walls are lovely. And those long windows – very bloody elegant. Makes me feel posh even if I'm not. If they don't like looking across here at my wee bungalow – tough.'

'I suppose this is another thing you picked up at that place,' said Spence.

Emma nodded. 'Yeah, in a lecture.'

She'd started her degree a few weeks earlier and kept bringing up facts she'd heard in classes, but Spence was yet to be convinced her going to university was a good idea.

'So what use is it, all this stuff you learn? What exactly can you do with something like sociology? I mean job-wise. You go out there after four years studying and sit down for an interview and you say – I'm a sociologist. People are just going to scratch their heads.'

'Dad, there's plenty of jobs.'

'Like what?'

'Social work. It would be nice to help people.'

'Good lass,' said Nash.

Spence rolled his eyes. 'Is there decent money in it?'

'Dad, how many times do we need to go over this? I told you, it's not about money.'

'But what actually is it? What do you learn?'

She gave him the textbook explanation she'd given him before about organisational structures, cultures and traditions, behavioural patterns, and so on, but he shook his head. It was like a foreign language.

'Think about it like this…' She turned to Nash. 'Why have

you ended up here, in a scheme, and they're over there?' She nodded towards the mansions.

'Luck of the draw, I suppose,' said Nash.

'So you think it was completely random?'

'No, not random but it was just the way things turned out.'

'Yeah, but why?'

'Beats me.'

'You don't think there were wider factors in play?'

'What, like the hand of fate?'

'The whys and wherefores don't matter,' interrupted Spence. 'We're all masters of our own destinies.'

'Nonsense,' said Emma. 'Some people are born into inequality. They'll never get away from it. That's why I'm doing sociology. So I can look into the past and understand the causes – and do something about it.'

'So it's a bit like detective work,' said Nash.

'Yeah, a little bit.'

There was a shrug from Spence as he rummaged in the biscuit tin. 'I just don't see the point of courses like that. Four years of your working life. I can tell you right now, there'll always be people at the top and people at the bottom. It's just the way of the world.' He gestured at the television, as a newsreader droned over flickering footage from a picket line. 'Look at them. Everyone wants to get their snout in the trough. End of story.'

'So don't you care about social mobility?' asked Emma.

'Something to do with everyone owning cars?'

She shook her head. 'Can people from one social class move into another? A working-class person might get rich but will they ever be upper class?'

Spence threw up his hands. 'Who cares? If they're rich, they're rich. They've made it. Fair play to them.'

'So what would you say looking at me?' Nash opened his hands to invite scrutiny. 'Have I been socially mobile?'

'No, definitely not,' shot back Emma.

A look of heavy injury descended on him. 'How?'

'You're on a low income. You've had bad health and live in

a poor area.'

'But I came up from the dirt. Our family had nothing and lived on the road. I'll tell you something; when I got the keys to this place, with that view across the park, it felt like pure luxury.'

Nash had been there for ten years, since around the time chronic back pain and choked lungs put him on the sick list from his work as a labourer. Before that, he'd moved around East Lothian, living in mice-infested digs, working hard, dirty jobs, and breathing in dust, damp, fumes – and God knows what else. But he did this to save up for the summer months when he would take what he called his holidays – touring the Traveller fairs of the Scottish borders and north of England, and catching up with old faces. Some Travellers, those who'd stayed true to the culture, might have said he'd gone *gaj* by taking the keys to a council house but there were few of the old breed left these days, and all Nash's peers had ended up with a roof over their heads either by choice or succumbing to ill health. The way he saw it, there was no romance in what was left of that way of life.

After Spence and Emma went home, he dozed off while reading a detective novel. He dreamt of searching through the lanes and alleys of his housing estate, under the street lights' amber glow. He was breathless and gripped by urgency but wasn't sure what he was looking for. He woke with a jolt, wiped drool from his chin and shook off a sharp sense of panic. Time was running out.

2

It was around the time of Emma's fifth birthday that she became curious about Nash's spare room. She was allowed to go in there on condition that she didn't touch anything. It was a bright, quiet space – the air less stuffy than the other rooms – and she liked the artist's clutter; the jars of pencils and brushes, the rolls of paper, and the sweet, oily smell that made her pleasantly light-headed. It was the place where the Lacklows' Traveller roots were kept alive, in Nash's paintings and drawings of horses, trailers and campfires, set against open fields and roaming hills. These days, she liked being in there with him, watching him at work. Perched on a stool, he'd tilt back and forth in front of the canvas, cocking his head this way and that, assessing his work from different angles.

It was obvious from how much he was smoking today that he was feeling better, the bad news of the previous month's hospital visit a distant memory. He put down the paintbrush and reached for his cigarettes.

'Don't give me that look,' he said.

'What look?'

'That one you're giving me. Smoking helps me concentrate.'

'Have you thought about cutting down?'

He rubbed his brow and sighed. 'I told you; I didn't trust the doctor. Anyway, I'm feeling better than I did. I'm on pills with names I can't even pronounce and I'm hooked up to enough oxygen to blow up the street.'

'But that's not a licence to keep smoking.'

'Why shouldn't I? What's the point in stopping?'

'You could still do something.'

'With life?'

'Of course. There's still time.'

He lit up and blew a dismissive stream of smoke towards the ceiling. 'Have I ever told you about my granny? Now there was one that smoked like a chimney. A pair of lungs on her like used pan scourers. The pipe was never out her mouth but she went on till she was in her eighties.'

'So, she was lucky.'

'More than luck. Lacklows are built to last. She was a great woman. It was her who encouraged my artistic ability – my gift, she called it. She had me going round the fairs selling paintings by the time I was twelve. She taught me about horses too. She was a respected horse dealer, actually. One of the best in the business.'

'That must have been hard for her back then. I mean, being a woman in a male-dominated trade.'

Nash slapped his knee. 'Oh, she'd be spinning if she could hear you saying that – absolutely spinning. There was one time some big shot was wanting to buy a horse from her. He was offering good money for it too. But whatever he offered, she just said no. So he said, *Right, here's what I'll do, missus. I'll offer you twenty pounds. I'm offering my hand for twenty pounds.* That was a lot of money in those days. There they were – him with his hand stretched out and her smoking her pipe, with a face on her like old milk. The crowd were loving it. You know what she did? She untethered the horse and walked away with it. She just didn't like the cut of his jib. Of course, it was said that she had the gift, and that's what made her such a good dealer.'

'What gift?'

Nash squeezed paint from wrinkled tubes onto a plate encrusted with layers of colour. 'A gift with horses.'

'How'd you mean?'

'She could look at a horse and tell if it was sick or not.'

'No way.'

'I'm telling you. See, if you were buying a horse back then, you couldn't always tell if there might be a problem. Like buying a car I suppose. It might look all right on the outside but have a bad engine. A horse might have a bad temperament or ringbone. But my granny could tell if a horse was fit or not. Folk would come to her for advice on buying one – and if she said this isn't the horse for you, they always followed her word on it, and that's the gospel truth.'

Emma's eyes widened the way they used to when she was told stories as a little girl. Then she noticed a smirk teasing at the corners of Nash's mouth. 'Ah, Jesus, can you be serious, please?'

He slapped his knee again. 'Ha-ha! Christ, I had you going there.' The sound of him laughing reminded her of the cartoon dog Muttley. It gave him a foolish quality, the way his shoulders shook as he tried to hold the rest of his body steady. Emphysema seemed an especially cruel illness for a man who loved to laugh.

Emma asked if he had any photos. He wiped his hands on a rag and went to the cupboard. As he opened it, an avalanche of junk mail and old magazines spilled onto the floor, spreading out around his feet. 'Christ! Look at the state of this.' His breathing became heavy and agitated as he rummaged through the pile. 'Need to have a good clear out. Half of this is fit for the bin.'

Emma was about to tell him not to bother when he pulled out a handful of photos and passed them to her; just a few creased snapshots, loose and neglected. She flicked through them, stopped at one, and held it up. 'Is this her?'

The old woman's mouth was open in a wry half smile as if she was cracking a joke just as the photo was taken. Nash stood at her side, smiling, young and dapper.

His face brightened and he took the photo for a closer look. 'That would've been around the start of the war. 1939, 1940 – something like that. Christ, I was a handsome bugger, wasn't I?'

Another photo fell out from the bunch and Emma picked it up. It was of a family; a mum and dad with four boys and a young girl, around three or four years old, perched against her mother's hip.

She held it up. 'What about this one?'

As Nash's eyes fixed on it, the smile fell from his face like he'd been slapped and he slumped down on the stool. 'That's me and my family.'

She'd heard from Spence about Nash's hard childhood, though she was never given much detail. She knew his dad died when Nash was still a boy, that the family were very poor, and his mum struggled raising him and his brothers – but Spence never mentioned anything about a sister.

'I didn't know...'

'That I had a sister? I did but, well, it's not a nice thing to talk about...the authorities took her off us. They took her away and we never saw her again.'

Her eyes flicked around the room, processing and reassessing what she knew of him. 'Oh God. When?'

'A couple of years after that photo was taken. 1929, I think.'

'Why? Why did they take her?'

'They didn't like having Travellers in the area. They wanted rid of us and I suppose we were a prime target, us being a big family with no dad to support us.'

He got up again and went to the cupboard and fished out an old doll.

'Do you remember this?'

Emma recalled an incident when she was much younger. She'd sneaked into the spare room, wanting to see Nash's paintings, and found the doll in the cupboard. It was an ugly thing; dirty and frayed with only one leg, but there was something about it she liked. Nash came in and found her playing with it. I told you not to mess about in here, he said, and snatched it off her. It was the only time he ever snapped at her. She'd been too young to wonder why he'd hang on to such a thing. Now it made sense.

'I picked it up from the mud after they'd taken her,' he said, and turned back to the painting. 'In my head, she was more light than dark. Sandy hair, cheeky smile. That's the main thing I remember about her, that wee grin.'

Emma patted his shoulder and said, 'Sorry, you don't need to talk about it.'

'Oh but I do. It's time I faced up to it. What I've always thought is that it was my dad dying – that was what led to it. Like a – what you'd call it – a chain reaction. He took pneumonia the previous winter and it killed him. It left my mum on her own with the five of us to look after. She couldn't

16

afford to keep the horse and cart, so took us hawking on foot, out on the streets in all weathers. My brother Ronnie was running wild too, and got into trouble with the police. I reckon that was what finally put the authorities onto us.'

He squeezed more paint onto the plate and sat down. 'I remember hearing the engines. A low rumble coming near. It was men from the Social who came for her but they brought the police, too. I tried to shout to the others but panicked and started coughing my lungs up and couldn't stop. My damn chest. So for a few seconds, it was me – only me – who knew something bad was going to happen. Obviously, there was violence. Terrible violence. My mother fought them like...I don't know what. I never thought a person could make noises like that, like an animal. Screaming and kicking. Fists, teeth, nails. She gave it everything she had but the police held her down until the officials got my sister into their car. And that was it. She was gone.'

Emma looked at the photo, staring hard at the family, fully intact and unaware of the looming tragedy. She tried to make out their eyes below the scratched print and grainy shadows, as if she could send a warning back through time to reach them. 'Surely you can't just take a child like that,' she said.

Nash swirled his brush in a jar of cleaning fluids and laughed bitterly. 'Well, they could and they did. I know that afterwards there must have been a lot of crying and sobbing but I can't for the life of me remember any of that. It's strange because there must have been a lot of it, but the memory's like a silent film.'

He couldn't remember the last time he'd spoken about it but the deep breath he let out carried relief that could only be temporary. 'I've no idea what happened to her.' He said it in a hushed voice, as if ashamed to admit it. 'Of course, it wrecked my mother. She drank herself to death by the time I was twenty. I suppose that was her way of getting rid of the pain. Sometimes I wish I could forget about it too. All the years, they've chipped away at me. My body is, well, look at it. It's all just fading away. And there's so much of my life that I can't remember. It might as well never have happened. But I'm stuck with a crystal clear memory of that day – something that lasted all of ten minutes, 50 years ago.' He looked at Emma with a child's innocence. 'Why can't time take it away – just rub it out? You know, sometimes I've gone years without thinking about it, but it always comes back.'

They were quiet for a moment then Emma asked what his sister was called. Nash paused as if he wasn't going to be able to say it. He seemed to steel himself then came out with it quickly and with a firm knit of his brow. 'Jenny. Her name was Jenny.'

Emma repeated it softly a couple of times, like an incantation giving the girl's memory currency. Nash nodded. It was nice to hear her say it. Then he added, 'We called her Wee Jenny.'

* * *

At dinner time, Spence arrived and sat picking at his food, moaning about another terrible day of knocking on doors. 'I don't understand it,' he said. 'I'm making it easy for them. What I tell them is; you can go shopping for carpet without leaving the comfort of your home. No need to wander around some big, draughty warehouse. I bring everything to them.'

Emma shrugged. 'People like going out. They like a trip to the shops and a browse. Consumer society, Dad.'

'Samples,' he shot back. 'Samples. They can sit with a cup of tea and look through my book of samples. They don't even need to get off the sofa.'

'I'll tell you what the problem is,' said Nash. 'I'm forever being offered those coupons and special deals. When I go to the department store, I get discounts shoved in my face for carpets and sofas. I get leaflets through the door for credit cards or loans offering zero percent interest. Money off this, money off that – and here's me, a poor pensioner but companies are tripping over themselves to sell me stuff, and they don't care whose money I'm using to buy it.'

Spence's shoulders sagged at Nash's breathless summary

of commercial inducements. 'I'm a carpet salesman not a banker. How am I supposed to keep up with all that?'

They ate in silence for a while then Nash said, 'I told Emma about what happened with my sister.'

This jolted Spence out of his stupor. 'You told her?'

'Aye, we had a good long chat about it, didn't we Em?'

'I can't believe no-one ever told me.'

Spence stopped eating and put down his fork. 'Well, it was a bloody awful thing. We never wanted you to know about something like that, what with her being a girl and you being a girl, too. It'd give you nightmares.'

'I think I'd like to find out what happened to her,' said Nash.

Spence choked back a laugh. 'Are you joking?'

'Why would I joke about a thing like that?'

'Because it was 50 years ago.'

'I don't care how long ago it was. Looking back on it now, knowing I don't have much time left, the years don't matter a damn.'

Spence shook his head. To him, it seemed like opening an old wound. 'Why now, though? Why rake up all that heartache? Forget about it.'

'No, I won't. And I shouldn't have waited this long to talk about it either. It wasn't right, the way they took her. She doesn't deserve to be forgotten about. She was a person, for crying out loud. A Lacklow.'

Spence turned to Emma. 'Have you been talking to him about all your human rights nonsense again?'

'No, she's not,' snapped Nash. 'This was my own decision. I can't ignore it anymore. It's like having someone following you around all the time, poking you in the back. I'm up at nights thinking about it.'

'All right. Look, you're a grown man and you're my elder so I'm not going to lecture you. But just tell me. How? How are you going to do it? Where do you even start?'

Nash swivelled his head in Emma's direction. 'I thought maybe you could help.'

'Me?'

'Why not? You're smart. You're at university. I was thinking of what you told me about your course. Looking into the past and that sort of business. Maybe you could find out what happened to her.'

'Yeah but, come on, I don't know how to go about tracing somebody.'

Nash patted her hand. 'You'll figure it out, Em. That university has the brains of the country under one roof.'

After Emma and Spence left, Nash went back to the spare room and sat at the easel, smoking and considering his painting. He picked up the paintbrush but couldn't concentrate. Moments later he was again stooping and grunting and rustling through the contents at the bottom of the cupboard. He pulled out the picture of his family and sat, staring at the faces he'd known for longer as photographic images than in real life.

3

The hall was packed and all the students had colds. They coughed and sneezed and blew their noses between scribbling notes. On stage, Professor Andrew Miller was drawing his lecture to a close. He had started at the lectern but drifted away from it over the course of the hour. Now he paced back and forth in front of the projection screen with one hand in the pocket of his flannel trousers and the other, fingers pinched round a piece of chalk, jabbing the air as he spoke.

'We're sent signals all the time,' he said. 'We absorb them. We ingest. We internalise. From before we're able to walk, even before we're able to speak, we learn behavioural expectations and social norms without knowing. Basic manners. When's it okay to leave the dinner table? When to be quiet and when to speak up. We do this just as instinctively as we learn verbal language. Yet first interactions between different societies are full of disastrous examples of the misreading of social signals. There's been wars, massacres, rebellions, even genocide – all triggered by the wrong interpretation of signals.' He gave the first-year students a sheepish smile and opened his arms out towards them. 'Love and understanding. It's vital to get off on the right foot with new acquaintances. The colonial and missionary movements descending on the African continent grossly misread and homogenised what was in fact a diverse variety of cultures with well-established belief and value systems. We – us – supposedly the great civilisers...' he gestured quote marks with his fingers, 'couldn't have made a bigger mess of it. Believe me, there are more than a few skeletons in the closet of the great British Empire. And it's that misunderstanding of cultures – and where it's led us – that will be our theme over the next six weeks.'

The hall echoed with seats slamming back into their upright positions as the students grabbed their bags and got up. Miller asked if anyone had questions but they were already streaming down the aisles and out the door. Seated near the back, Emma stayed where she was, waiting for the hall to quieten down.

Some students found Professor Miller aloof but Emma remembered the start of term when he'd told them that although he was Head of Sociology, he still liked being visible and approachable for students at all stages of their studies. He told them a lot of heads of schools gave up teaching commitments, but not him. Teaching was what got him out of bed in the morning. Regardless of his management responsibilities, he wanted students to be passionate about the subject that had fascinated him all his professional life. He added that he wanted to foster an environment where theory collided with the real world. Emma wasn't sure what that meant but she liked the sound of it, and it was one of the first things she jotted down in her notepad.

The hall was nearly empty now and Miller's start-of-term message was at the forefront of her mind as she went down to the front, where he was cramming lecture notes into a tatty leather bag.

'Have you got a minute?'

He picked up his bag and smiled at her. 'Walk with me. I'm dashing.'

She fell in step beside him and explained Nash's request.

'That's very generous of you, timewise,' said Miller.

'Well, he's very ill, actually. It's sort of a last wish.'

Miller nodded solemnly. 'Even more of a burden on your young shoulders.'

'It's because I'm at university,' she said. 'He always tells me I'm the clever one of the family. Sort of puts me on a pedestal. I don't mind, though. I want to help.'

He held the door open for her and switched off the lights. 'And your family are Travellers?'

'On my dad's side. Before my time.'

'Scottish or Irish?'

'Scottish.'

They walked along the busy corridor. Miller's eyes

narrowed and flitted around her face. 'I doubt we've had many students from a background like yours before.'

It was true that Emma didn't encounter many accents like hers around campus. Whereas most of her peers had been privately educated, she'd gone to a state school dogged by teachers' strikes during the seventies. She started university thinking this would make her an outsider but the protest spirit of the sixties was still alive and well on campus, as was proletarian solidarity. To other students, her accent alone lent weight to class discussions on social problems.

Professor Miller stopped outside his next class and pressed a finger to his lips. 'When did you say this happened?'

'Around 1929.'

'At that time a lot of children taken into care – especially those from itinerant backgrounds – would have been sent to the cities.'

'For what?'

'For labour, of course. The workforce. The Great Depression was just around the corner. The economy was going downhill. Children were cheap labour.'

'Sorry, I should have said, she was very young when it happened. Only about five.'

'So she was probably put up for adoption. Try the General Registrar's Office. Tell them I sent you.' He opened the door but paused at the threshold. 'You'll know that Traveller culture is predominantly an oral one. It's fascinating but quite a challenge from a research perspective. You're going to have your work cut out.'

* * *

An hour later, Emma was in the General Registrar's Office on Princes Street asking to see the adoption records.

'Hang on a second.' The desk clerk was studying the note she'd handed him with the details of Jenny Lacklow's removal. 'The Adoption Act didn't come in until 1930,' he said. 'If this happened before that, we won't hold anything on it.'

'Why not?'

'Because there was no obligation on authorities to keep records.'

'Wait, are you saying this was illegal?'

'No, children were still taken for adoption but paperwork was at the discretion of local authorities. If your case happened before that, it's going to be really difficult to trace this person. I don't want to say it's impossible, but...' The man's voice trailed off to a sigh.

Emma drummed her fingers on the desk. 'Are you sure? My lecturer is Professor Miller. He said you'd be able to help.'

The clerk smiled politely. 'I can give you the phone number for an adoption agency but they'll only tell you the same thing.'

'So what you're saying is there were no rules, no regulations? Is that it? The system was basically like – what? The Wild West. Just lawless.'

'Well...' The clerk paused, trying to put it the best way he could. 'It wasn't viewed that way at the time. Adoptions were handled by religious organisations and parish councils.'

'But still, they could take kids just like that, without any paperwork?'

'I'm afraid so.'

She cast her eyes over his shoulder at the rows of shelves with folders and boxes stretching back into the depths of the building. 'But this happened just before the Act. 1929. Only one year before. There might be something back there. You said some authorities did keep records.'

'But we wouldn't have collected them. If you don't believe me, you're welcome to look but I hope you've got plenty of time on your hands. There's a lot of records back there.'

She checked her watch and sighed. Her next class was starting soon.

* * *

At the end of the day, she met Kate and they walked to the South African Consulate. They arrived early but people were already there, milling around with placards and leaflets. They met a group of friends and put on t-shirts printed with the slogan 'Free Nelson Mandela'. Two policemen stood at the Consulate entrance watching the crowd grow. A photographer arrived and asked if the police could move closer to the protesters so he could get a photo. They didn't mind; the atmosphere was friendly. One of them even smiled and posed with the protesters while the photographer took a few snaps. Residents of the handsome townhouses were at their windows. Some waved and gave the thumbs-up. The anti-apartheid cause was a mainstream concern these days, with support from across the political spectrum. As reggae beats boomed out from a sound system, echoing off the Georgian facades, a man and a woman went up to the Consulate door and unfurled a banner that read 'End apartheid now!' Placards bobbed over the heads of the crowd. 'Sanctions now! Boycott now! Shame on Thatcher!'

A man with a loudspeaker climbed the steps and stood in front of the banner. 'Comrades and friends,' he shouted, 'we're here today to send a message to the South African regime, and to our own leaders. We protest peacefully but make no mistake...we're angry.' Cheers went up. The man continued. 'Yes, we're angry and we're demonstrating for the freedom of South Africa...for the freedom of political prisoners...and for a freedom that we all take for granted. We're all here for the same simple reason – because we believe in democracy, equality and justice.'

The photographer weaved between groups, asking protesters to hold up banners and placards as he took pictures. He approached Emma and Kate and they put their arms around each other and waved their placards.

They'd met during the first week of term when Kate was protesting against nuclear weapons outside the library. Emma signed her petition and took a leaflet as Kate pinned a badge to her lapel that read 'Women are disarming the world'. She patted it into place. 'There, now. It goes nice with your eyes.'

She had an impish smile and Somerset twang in her husky voice, and her multi-coloured scarf and out-of-control red hair seemed to Emma like a beacon against the grey autumn sky. They got to know each other and discovered they'd both felt isolated at school. All the lunchtime chat about boys and popstars was tedious. They each kept secret diaries. A safe space to explore thoughts and feelings – how they felt different to other girls.

There, in the middle of the protest, they kissed and said they loved each other. 'Freedom's nice, isn't it?' whispered Kate. 'Look around. Nobody cares. No-one's even looking at us.'

Emma checked over her shoulder at the photographer, still moving through the crowd. 'Hopefully there won't be pictures of us snogging in the *Daily Record* tomorrow.'

'I take it you've still not told your dad?'

'I need to think about the best way to do it.'

Kate clamped her hands over Emma's shoulders. 'So what if we're in the paper tomorrow? You've got a right to be who you are.'

'Yeah but I don't think he'd want it rubbed in his face. It's all right for you. Your parents are hundreds of miles away.'

'They already know. They've asked if you can come down during the holidays. They want to meet you.'

'Well, things are different in my house.'

Kate's eyes narrowed. 'Your dad better not give you a hard time about it.'

'Now's just not the right time. There's been a lot going on recently.'

Emma's gaze drifted over the heads of the crowd and to the man on the Consulate steps with the loudspeaker still in full flow. 'Comrades, we come together in peace but with a serious purpose – to bring an end to the oppressive apartheid state.' Protesters punched the air and yelled their support. 'We call on our government to act,' he shouted. 'Words aren't enough. Act! This regime has taken thousands of innocent lives...men, women and children.' Emma raised her fist and chanted along with the crowd as the man taped a petition to the consulate door and began reeling off the names of political prisoners.

4

Spence used to half-joke that he wouldn't allow her out the house till she was 25. He'd be watching her play and say to Fran, '25 years old. I'm telling you. She's not getting across that door.' Fran would laugh and roll her eyes and tell him not to be so uptight. Of course, it was the teenage years when she'd be around alcohol and boys that was his great fear. So it was a relief to have got through that phase without much cause to worry about either. He liked to think she'd been well brought up. But there were always new fears to plague him.

Emma held the newspaper in front of him and pointed at the photo. 'There – that's me,' she said. 'That's the top of my head.' It was a photo of the previous day's protest, with the crowd gathered in front of the Consulate. Emma was at the back and only just visible, with two policemen behind her. Still, she was proud to be in the shot. It was something to keep, to show that she'd been on the right side of history.

Spence flung it down on his lap and turned to her. 'You're just putting yourself in harm's way – and for what? For people on the other side of the world. Have you ever even met a South African?'

They were at the hospital with Nash, waiting for him to be called for a check-up. Staff and patients came and went against the administrative din of typing, phones and screeching fax machines.

'You weren't there,' she snapped. 'It wasn't just some rabble. There was a talk from a human rights lawyer.'

'I don't care if there were prayers led by Mother Teresa. It's not the protesters I'm worried about. It's the police. They're the worst for it – starting trouble.' He poked angrily at the photo. 'Look at you – did you even realise you were right next to two big, bloody policemen? If that had turned violent, you'd have been the first to be clubbed and carted off.'

'Dad, this is a democracy. We've got rights.'

Spence looked appealingly at Nash. 'Would you talk some

sense into her?' He often used Nash to echo whatever concerns he had for Emma, and it would be like two mother hens clucking over her.

Nash took off his glasses and turned to her. 'There was something on the news the other night, a demonstration in Northern Ireland. It turned violent. 22-year-old lassie, dead. She was a student, like you. Killed by a stray bullet.'

'You wouldn't know the minute,' muttered Spence, flushed and blinking in agitation.

'Oh, come on,' said Emma. 'Northern Ireland? Can we keep this in perspective?'

Nash said, 'All we're trying to tell you, Em, is people who carry guns and clubs for a living are the same everywhere. It doesn't matter what country we're talking about. It's a certain type of person that's drawn to it.'

* * *

Later that afternoon, Spence didn't look up when she came into the kitchen. He was at the table, frowning over a pile of bills and stayed like that as she made dinner. She didn't acknowledge him either. This wasn't an unusual sight. The table was more like his office than it was a place to eat; permanently covered in catalogues, receipts, household bills, and wholesaler invoices – some old, some new, most overdue. Whenever they did sit down to eat, the papers got shoved into the centre of the table, an ever-present reminder of their lack of money.

'Is everything all right?' she asked.

'It's been a bad month. Everybody's saving their money for Christmas. It'll probably pick up in the new year.' Emma had heard that one before and knew what was coming next. 'A lot of people get a bonus at the end of the year. They put big purchases on hold till January. Makes sense when you think about it.' It was an observation he made towards the end of every year as a sort of self-reassurance, part of a predictable cycle and come the end of January he would be sitting at the table, still with the stack of bills, complaining about another bad month but this time the excuse would be that everyone was still skint after Christmas.

He watched as Emma put a couple of slices of bread under the grill and poured a glass of juice. 'What time are you starting?' he asked.

'Six.'

He checked his watch. 'Better make that a quick dinner. Is it getting busy with Christmas parties yet?'

She shook her head. 'It's another few weeks before the festive madness starts.'

'Ahwell, I was just wondering because...I know you're busy with your studies but, seeing as things are tight, is there any chance of you doing a few more shifts?'

'I dunno. I've got a lot on at uni just now.'

'Give me a break, Emma. You're not going to tell me you count sitting in a library as work. I was on my feet, going round doors, twelve hours a day at your age. Six days a week. All I'm talking about here is a few extra hours.'

'Okay, I'll ask.'

Spence had suggested that she start making a financial contribution to the housekeeping a few months after Fran left. The way he'd been raised, if you were all under the same roof, one person's wage was everybody's wage. It all went into the same pot. He knew she got her student grant and the occasional cheque from her mum, but when he was short of cash he only asked if she could do extra shifts. Being financially supported by his daughter was a delicate issue so it felt better if her contributions were earned rather than coming from the government or his estranged wife.

'Hey, listen,' he said. 'While you're there; we need to have a talk.'

'Please, don't start about the protest again.'

'Not that. This business of Nash's sister.'

Emma pulled out a chair and sat down. 'Actually, I wanted to talk to you too,' she said. 'What did you know about it?'

'Not much. Only that Nash's mother was struggling with the five kids after their dad died, and that's what got the sister taken off them. Then of course, his mother turned to drink and two of the brothers went off the rails. Not exactly happy families.'

'But your dad never went off the rails, did he?'

'God, no.' Spence straightened up, offended at the mere thought of it. 'He had a lot to shoulder at a young age. He was the oldest of the brothers, you see. He had to step up and be the man of the family. Off the rails? No way. Your grandad had a good head on his shoulders. It was the middle two who got themselves into trouble. Ronnie and John.'

'And Nash?'

'It's complicated. After his sister got taken, that made him the youngest, if you see what I mean. His mum wrapped him in cotton wool. Well you would, wouldn't you, after losing one child.'

'You've never spoken to him about any of this?'

'Of course not,' he said. 'It's one of those things, isn't it?'

'You keep saying that. *One of those things*. One of what things?'

'Well...painful, unpleasant. Not to be brought up. Which brings me to the point – what I wanted to say to you. Don't look into it, Emma. It's not a good idea.'

'He can make his own choices, can't he? Like you told him, he's a grown man.'

'Look, I don't blame him for thinking about the past. The poor man's been told he's dying. He's going back over his life. Taking stock. I get that. But this – wanting to dig it all up – this is silly.' Spence held her eye and nodded as if he'd already convinced her. Injecting vigour into his voice, he declared, 'We need to focus on the here and now. Looking after Nash. Work. University. Paying the bills.'

'So why don't you speak to him? Tell him you think it's silly.'

'Well, I did. You were there, remember.'

'So speak to him again.'

'Right now, the easiest thing is if you tell him you're going to look into it, but just sit on your hands. Don't do anything.

He'll forget about it soon enough.'

She got up and rinsed her plate in the sink. 'I don't think that's very nice. I'm going to do it.'

'You're just done telling me how busy you are with your studies. Why not tell him that? You wouldn't be lying. The last thing he'd want is to distract you from university.'

She wondered if this was all just an attempt to reassert authority after he asked for help with paying the bills. 'I'm interested,' she said. 'And I want to help. So I'll make time for it.'

'You've never asked about our history before.'

'You never talk about it.'

'I would've – if you'd bothered to ask. You never ask me about hawking. You haven't been to a fair since you were wee.'

'Look,' said Emma. 'The bottom line is, I can get interested in our family history any time I want.'

'Oh aye,' muttered Spence, 'something else to get on your high horse about. All I'm saying is, I think you should wait and think about it.'

'Actually, I've already started. I spoke to my lecturer. He gave me some tips.'

Spence absorbed this with a few slow nods then a sigh. 'Tips? Nash's been told he's dying and you're taking our family's private business and giving it to strangers?'

'Dad, the man's a professor. He's an expert on this type of thing.'

'An expert on our business?'

'You know what I mean.'

'So these tips, did they help?'

She looked away and shook her head.

'See what I mean?' he said. 'It's silly. It's never going to lead anywhere. All this...' He grabbed the bills and waved them at her. 'This is real life. These are real problems. Things that actually need to be dealt with. All those professors wouldn't last five minutes out here, but they think everybody's problems are theirs to solve. It's none of their business.'

'Doesn't what happened bother you?'

'No, because life is tough and the way to deal with it is by getting over it and carrying on. If you cry about it, you've already lost and the bastards have won.'

'I don't see it like that.'

'That's because you're young. You've got a certain way of looking at the world. I respect that but sometimes a parent needs to give advice. Nash is a sick old man. As your dad – your father – I'm asking, don't turn him into one of your causes. Leave him be.' He searched for the word he'd heard her use many times before so he could hold the argument on the same intellectual level as her. Then it came to him and he lowered his voice. 'Emma, you'd be exploiting him.'

'Holding on to hope makes people live longer,' she said. 'Do you know that? There's been studies done on it. They've looked at different groups of people living in really shitty situations all around the world, and the thing that makes a difference in the long run is hope. You do it yourself – that spiel you give me about how business will pick up in the new year. You say that every year.' She gestured at the pile of bills. 'If there's no hope, everything else goes down the toilet. Health, happiness, even the will to live. But if people have hope, they hang on. Right now, he's got hope. Do you want to take that off him?'

This was the latest in a string of arguments she'd won. It was an uncomfortable feeling and she didn't want to acknowledge that she found it hard to take his strenuously expressed opinions seriously anymore and could pick them apart without much difficulty. He couldn't get away with acting worldly in the same way he could when she was a child. His stubbornness and pride were masking the fact that, when it came down to it, he was a little ignorant of things beyond his limited experience.

Arriving late for work, Emma went in through the kitchen and picked up a tray of cups and saucers on her way to the restaurant. They weren't needed for anything other than to create the impression that she was mid-task and couldn't possibly have just arrived.

The manager, Mr Tate, appeared behind her as she pushed through swing doors into the dining room. 'Emma, love, nice of you to join us,' he said. 'Margaret will be pleased. She's been covering your tables for the last twenty minutes.'

The restaurant at the racing track often held functions – work nights out, as they were called – with long tables of men who had enjoyed an afternoon at the races followed by the ritual of mass drunkenness. Like some debauched mediaeval court, they smoked and jeered and banged the table when Emma arrived in her white blouse and black skirt. The familiar questions weren't long in coming. How old was she? Did she have a boyfriend? One man asked if she liked older men, another if she'd give him her phone number. She'd worked there since she was sixteen and had heard it all before.

Amongst them was a young lad who looked not yet old enough to drink but was pink-faced and slurring and muttering to himself. The older men beside him laughed and lined up more drinks in front of him, a game to see how drunk they could get him. The lad's shirt was untucked, his flies undone, and he seemed helpless against the situation. As Margaret and Emma were clearing the plates, a man next to him smacked Emma's arse then offered his friend a tenner if he'd do the same to Margaret. Emma pretended not to hear but when she returned to serve coffee, she placed the cup and saucer on the very edge of the table. She filled it to the brim, then, as she moved away, caught the edge of the cup with the coffee pot, knocking it into his lap. The man screamed and jumped up, slapping at his steaming crotch but moments later he was laughing again, along with the rest of his drunken friends.

At the end of the night, Emma went to Mr Tate's office in the festeringly warm basement. He sat under a spotlight, against a bare brick wall with pipes overhead. He looked up at her. 'Emma.'

'I was wondering if I could pick up more hours?'

'What's the matter? Have you spent your student grant already?'

'No, I just...'

'I'm teasing. Ignore me.' He leaned back, looking puzzled. 'You've got great timing, asking for more shifts the same night you come in late.'

'Sorry about that.'

'What happened at that loud table tonight?'

'Somebody spilled something,' she said. 'They were pretty drunk.'

'Ah, the lads. Letting off a little steam, were they?'

'Yeah, just a bit of harmless chauvinism.'

'Margaret would keep them in line though. She's tough as old boots. What were they saying?'

'The usual stuff.'

'That's right. It's only banter, isn't it?'

'Yeah.'

'How long have you been here now?'

'Coming up for four years,' she said.

'And you're still fresh as a daisy. It's good to have a young thing like you on staff. The punters like it. Margaret's an old warhorse but...' Mr Tate lowered his voice. 'I'm not blind. They laugh at her. They tease her. It's embarrassing.'

'So have you got any extra hours?'

'That depends. I can't have you turning up late.'

'It won't happen again.'

He gestured at a pile of papers on the desk. 'This is how I spend my time. When I'm not out there, I'm in here, planning rotas. There's prisoners who see more daylight than me. I think I've got – what do you call it – vitamin deficiency.'

Rotas were pinned to the notice board in front of his desk. Seven-day grids marked up with red biro and highlighter pens. Entries were crossed out. Names underlined. Dates circled. He pointed at it. 'Do you think this is easy?'

'Not at all,' Emma replied. 'I'm sure it's a lot of work.'

'You've got no idea. You can't learn this in a textbook, sweetheart. It's like a military operation. If one person phones in sick or doesn't turn up or needs a day off to take their cat to the vet, the whole thing crumbles. I need reliable people.

Do you get what I'm saying?'

'I do.'

He sat back, fiddling with his pen and staring at her. 'How many years of university have you got left?'

'Three and a half.'

'And you'll still be as fresh as a daisy.' He grunted and picked up the rotas.

5

The path was covered with ragged leaves that squelched underfoot. They tramped over them towards the entrance where the trail thickened into a dark organic heap that seemed to prop open the old gate.

'Have you got them there, aye?'

The flowers were plainly there in Emma's hand – vivid pinks and purples in the December grey – so she got the impression Nash was nervous and asked only to break the silence as they walked from the car. The cemetery was on a hillside, overlooking treetops and pylons. Tucked away in the corner, a council van was parked with two workmen inside, one sleeping, the other reading the paper. On the path ahead, a man strolled while his dog sniffed around the headstones.

Nash stopped to catch his breath. He grimaced at the cold and looked around the cemetery. It had been 40 years since he'd been in Carluke, and he couldn't remember the whereabouts of his mum's grave. 'I think it's up here,' he said, and set off up the hill.

It took a few minutes to find the headstone but when they came to it, he remembered how all his family could afford was the smallest, plainest type, with the minimum of engraving: Mary's name, the year she was born and the year she passed away.

The afternoon air had a dank, heavy feel about it, like the day had never properly got started. Nash cleared his throat, took a few puffs of the inhaler, then laid down the flowers. 'That's better,' he said, then straightened his jacket as if to make himself more presentable. They stood in silence for a while then he said, 'It came on slow and got a hold of her.'

Emma turned to him. 'What did?'

'The drink. She'd never been a drinker till after everything that happened.'

'When did you notice?'

'Not for a while, anyway. A few years. Things were normal at first. Well, not normal. Nothing was normal.'

'Did you carry on living at the campsite afterwards?'

He shook his head. 'The authorities closed it down. But they needn't have bothered. No Traveller would have stayed there after what happened. There was a taint on the place, like a taint of bad luck – and it was on us, too, I suppose. On the family.'

The police withheld the assault charges against Mary on condition that she left Carluke. They especially wanted rid of her two sons, Ronnie and John. So she took what was left of her family and moved around Lanarkshire, trying to find work but by the time Nash was in his teens, Mary had given up on life altogether and was slowly drinking herself to death.

'That whole time she was torn between wanting to do something to get Jenny back and looking after me and my brothers,' he said. 'The problem was that if she kept pestering the authorities that would keep us on their radar – mark us out as troublemakers – and that might lead to them removing more of us. I was a sickly wee runt, too. I had pneumonia twice. Got hospitalised with it the second time. The doctors said I might not make it. That wasn't long after my sister was taken. Imagine my mum's worry. If the authorities came back, maybe they'd have taken me away. It was a hell of a position for her to be in – keep your head down and hang on to what you've got or kick up a fuss and fight for what's yours.'

Drinking helped Mary forget but it wasn't enough to stop her from occasionally turning up at Carluke Town Hall and demanding the return of her daughter. 'Every couple of months,' Nash continued, 'she'd be banging on their door and causing a scene. Sometimes the police turfed her out on the street. Sometimes she got a night in the cells. I think they ended up feeling sorry for her.'

'At least she had some fight in her,' said Emma. 'I like the sound of your mum.'

Nash burrowed his chin into his collar and stared at his mum's headstone. 'Oh, aye. She did her best.' He cast his eyes upwards at the sky, wrinkled and smudged grey, like wet newsprint. 'Oh, aye,' he said again, very softly.

'Dad told me you got mollycoddled.' She said it with a derisive snort, as if she didn't take the claim seriously.

'I was well looked after, let's put it that way. But the thing is, it wasn't any comfort because I could see my mum was slowly falling apart, and I felt like an imposter in my own family, filling the shoes of someone else – soaking up love and attention that should have been going to my sister. Anyway, for a few years after what happened, mum wouldn't let me out of her sight. She could see the way Ronnie and John were going and wanted to protect me. Mollycoddled?' He turned to face her. 'I was more like a salvage job.'

The phrase most commonly used for Ronnie and John Lacklow was that they had gone off the rails. Aunts and uncles, distant cousins, they all used it as a polite shorthand for the complexities of lives lived in violent desperation. Nash had heard the expression so many times in relation to Ronnie and John that he came to associate it exclusively with them. If he heard it on television, they came immediately to mind and his thoughts would drift into the past, recalling grim news, worrying rumours and depressing facts of his brothers' troubled lives. Off the rails. It made him picture them careering into some awful abyss. Yet part of him wondered if there might be something positive in it too. Off the rails. It could mean escape or breaking away. Freedom from constraint. Perhaps it was wishful thinking but, whatever the details, he had rarely seen or heard from Ronnie or John. Of course, the odd story got back to him but he never knew exactly where they were or what they were doing, whether it was by choice or if they really were out of control. What he did know for sure was that he'd been too well looked after to do that – to go wild and rage his way through life.

'I don't blame them, mind,' he said to Emma. 'I felt sorry for them. After what happened to my sister, they were bound to hate authority. But the problem was, they got on the wrong side of the wrong people. Ronnie went down to London. He got involved in gangs and was killed in a fight in the early fifties. John was a dogsbody at amusement fairs around the north of England and in and out of jail for years.'

On hearing of John's death in a Newcastle homeless shelter in 1976, Nash wondered if that made him the last of his siblings or if Jenny was still out there somewhere. He lit a cigarette, took a drag. 'I've been thinking about her a lot since then.'

Back in the Ford Anglia, they drove a long stretch of road to the east of the town centre, looking for the turn off to where the campsite had been. Nash couldn't remember the exact location and the town had changed a lot in the intervening years. They stopped at a junction with a petrol station and a Mace supermarket.

'I'd swear it was near here,' he said, rubbing his chin and scanning around. There was something familiar in the bend and dip of the road ahead, and the view beyond the fields to a thick stand of trees on the horizon, with a gap before another, thinner cluster. He twisted around, looking back at the supermarket. 'Surely not,' he muttered. 'Turn around, Em.'

She spun the car around and into the car park. Nash's eyes traced a line back and forth between the entrance and the railway embankment behind the supermarket. 'This is it. They've built a fucking Mace on it.'

'Here? This is where the campsite was?'

'Aye, I see it clear as day now. This is it.'

They got out and circled the car. Crying kids trailed out from the store behind their frazzled mums. A vacant-eyed lad in a crumpled Mace's uniform rattled trolleys across the tarmac. Nash thought about the feel of the old land. He never realised back then that it was only temporarily graced by nature. Seasonal beauty could be blocked out or forced to share space with brick, steel and signage that got worn down and damaged but never renewed itself.

'I knew it wouldn't still be a campsite,' he said, 'but I wasn't expecting this.' He gestured as if to thrust the sight away. 'I thought it would just be wasteland. Stupid idiot. Of course it's changed. Everything does.' He put a hand to his brow and stretched the other towards the embankment, tracing a horizontal line. 'The trailers and tents were along there and apart from the railway, there was nothing around here. Nothing. Just trees and fields. We could keep to ourselves.'

The campsite had been there for generations, a handy stopping place between Glasgow and Dumfries. There was plenty of farming work nearby and a degree of tolerance towards Travellers from the landowners. Nights of music and stories by the campfire were scant. Nash's memories were of people who went to bed early and moved around in the cold morning as if slowed down by the weight of clothes they were wrapped in. They lifted and mended, packed for journeys, cleaned and cooked, all in the pale, fresh light.

Emma rested her hands on top of her head and sighed. 'Well, what do you want to do? We've come all this way. Do you want to take a minute while we're here?'

'How do you mean?'

'Do you want a few moments to yourself? For private thought.'

'Em, we're in a Mace's carpark. This doesn't lend itself to quiet reflection.'

'But we're standing on the site where she got taken. I feel like we should mark the moment.'

'I'd have been better off bringing my bloody shopping list.' He waved the surroundings away and got back into the car. Emma waited to see if she could divine a connection to her ancestors, a feeling of humble dignity lost to the ages, buried under the tarmac, but it was no use. She couldn't ignore the reality of her surroundings.

A weak light settled on the streets. The sunshine of early afternoon gave way to patchy clouds and drizzle. They drove to Carluke Town Hall, where Nash brought out his grainy family photo. He uncrumpled its edges and laid it eagerly on the counter, like a gambler handing over an old betting ticket. He explained to the receptionist the reason for their visit and asked if she held any adoption records. 'They'd be old,' he said. 'From a long time back.'

'All our records went up to Glasgow years ago,' she replied.

'It's all about centralisation these days. It's more efficient – so we're told. Those bigwigs at the regional council are stripping everything away from the town councils. Money, power, jobs – it's all going up there.' She flicked her chin towards the door.

'What do they do with it all?' asked Nash.

She shrugged. 'Call them and ask.'

It was a small, wood-panelled room stinking of damp and old carpet. Behind the desk, a bucket caught drips from the leaking roof. Emma imagined Mary Lacklow there, causing a scene; banging on the desk, screaming for her daughter and being carted off by the police. 'So what do you do here?' she asked.

'Allotments, public loos, parking – and the library.' The woman's composition was glum and brittle, like she'd been there for years being whittled down by administrative tasks diminishing in quantity and importance, till all that was left was the tedious and unglamorous rump.

'You're sure you don't have anything that could help?' asked Emma. 'We've come from the east coast. It's been a big trip for him.' She gestured at Nash, hunched and wheezing, resting a hand on the desk.

The woman was sorry but couldn't help. Nash tugged at Emma's sleeve. 'Come on,' he said. 'Let's go. I'm tired.'

On the way out, Emma stopped and turned back. 'What about Travellers' sites,' she said. 'Are there any left in the area?'

A troubled look came over the receptionist. 'Why would you want to go there?'

They found the campsite at a disused coach depot on the outskirts of Carluke. It was quiet and stark, with a handful of vans and caravans sitting on damply glazed concrete behind a high mesh gate.

'It looks deserted,' said Nash.

He'd been expecting a field or forest clearing but this was nothing like the campsites from his youth. There were no campfires, mucky-faced children running wild or grazing horses.

'It's worth a look,' said Emma.

Driving in, they saw a woman sweeping aggressively at puddles on the concrete around her caravan while, inside, children huddled at a window, pulling faces at the two strangers in the stuttering Ford Anglia.

Sun-bleached and ragged bits of plastic, concrete and twisted metal were heaped into piles to mark the site's boundaries. The lines of a nearby railway crisscrossed scratches into the grey winter sky. They stopped near a long, cream-coloured static caravan. It was bigger than the others, with lace curtains in the windows. A length of burgundy carpet was laid down over the wet concrete leading up to the door. A man came out and stared at them. He was a similar age to Nash, wearing a grey suit and mustard cardigan. Nash wound down the window as the man approached the car.

'Ye lost?'

'Is there anyone here that remembers the old campsite at Whiteshaw?'

'What's it to ye?'

Nash showed him the old family photo. 'I used to stay at Whiteshaw when I was a laddie.'

The man leaned in for a closer look. 'What's yer family?'

'The Lacklows,' said Nash.

'Oh aye. I've kent a few of ye here and there.' He came closer, eyes narrowing, then he shook his head. 'But yours isnae a face I ken.'

'Well, you wouldn't. I've been settled over on the east coast for years. My travelling days are long behind me.'

'Cannae say I feel much like a Traiveller maself, these days,' sighed the man. He gestured wearily at the surroundings. 'The Social's had us stuck here for years. It's like a bloody prison.'

Nash forced a smile and nodded. 'Not like the sites from the old days, eh?'

'Aye, well, yev come a long way for nothin, pal. Whiteshaw's not there anymore.'

Nash explained he'd been at the site's location earlier. 'I barely recognised the place. All that concrete and steel they've put up – it took me a while to get my bearings.'

'So what brings ye back?' asked the man.

'My sister – she got taken off us by the Social. Long time back. We were staying at Whiteshaw when it happened.'

'My old ma lived there,' said the man.

Nash's face brightened. 'Ah – did she tell you much about it?'

The man straightened up and jabbed a thumb over his shoulder. 'Ye can ask her yerself. She's inside.'

The caravan's interior was pristine, with polished glass and chrome surfaces glinting under the lights. Around the seating area, high shelves were lined with Crown Derby Bone China. Everywhere Emma looked there were horse-themed trinkets. Even the tea caddy had a horse's head lid handle and miniature stirrups hanging from the sides.

The man was Patch Andrews and he explained he'd acquired his nickname after being kicked in the eye by a horse when he was a boy. The eye in question – the right one – was glazed and sagged down on his cheekbone, the muscles supporting it all gone to shot. His accent was a blend of Scottish and Cumbrian, but there was also something faintly Irish-sounding in the dipping and drawing out of the vowels and in the rise and roll of the Rs.

The three of them huddled around a table and drank tea as they waited for Patch's mum to wake from her afternoon nap. He enquired what it was like hawking around Edinburgh – 'the posh toon,' as he called it – and Emma told him about

43

Spence and made out that he made a good living from it. 'Specialising in carpets,' she added. This prompted a story from Patch about hawking in the Borders when he was much younger, going village to village, pulling a pony and cart over fields and hills. 'I'd have given ma eye teeth for proper roads back then.' He looked Emma up and down as he slurped tea. 'And what about yerself, young miss? Did yer ma raise ye well?'

'I'm at university,' she said.

An air of grave concern came over Patch. 'But look at you. A full-grown lassie. Ye'll be past your prime before ye turn yer hand to raising a family.'

Nash leaned across the table and said quietly, 'Her mother was *gaj*. She's never travelled.'

'Never mind,' laughed Patch. 'Get yerself married to an honest Traiveller laddie. That'll sort ye out.'

Emma asked how long they'd been at the site and Patch said they'd stopped travelling about ten years earlier. 'The final straw for me was the last time we went down to Appleby,' he said. 'We'd settled for the night at a regular stopping place near Carlisle. But at ten o'clock, we had two police at the door, telling us to shift. Caravan Act, one of them says to me. Never heard of it, I says to him. It's the law, he says. Nae stopping here.' Patch jabbed at the air and his voice went up a notch. 'Listen, I says, I've been coming here since I was a lad. My faither, too – and his faither before him. We respect the land and we leave the place just as we found it. Caravan Act or no Caravan Act, yer no telling me I cannae stop here. I even told them that my old ma was settled in for the night.' He shook his head in disgust. 'They didnae gie a damn. They told us to shift or they'd turn our caravan out on the roadside.'

From the other room, came three thumps on the wall and Patch gulped down the last of his tea. He went into the room and after a few minutes of stirrings and low murmurings stuck his head out and signalled for them to come in.

Nell Andrews was propped up, resting heavily on an abundance of pink frilly pillows. She had bulk and a healthy colour. Her hands were meaty and swollen, resting on the quilted duvet. Nash introduced himself then said, 'Your son told me you lived at Whiteshaw.'

There was a nod and slight movement of the mouth from Nell Andrews, but she didn't speak. She looked sleep-glazed and confused by her visitors. She gestured for him to pass a glass of water from the nightstand. She sipped at it, then, in a voice that was barely there, said, 'The bairn. You're here about the wee bairn.' She told him she remembered his mother and his granny, too. 'A fine woman.' Nash smiled and nodded as she took his hand, as if to reaffirm an old acquaintance.

He asked if she heard much about what happened on the day his sister was taken. The old woman cleared her throat and her voice was thick and sticky-mouthed. 'Hear about it? I was there. I got myself a night in jail and ten stitches for trying to help your poor ma. I don't need to tell you how she fought. Not nice, seeing a woman in that state.'

'I want to find out what happened to my sister,' he said.

'You better get your skates on. No offence, son, but you're no spring chicken.'

'Don't I know it.' He took off his glasses, laid them on his knee, and massaged the bridge of his nose with his thumb and forefinger. 'I'm dying. The doctors think I've got one, maybe two years left.' He nodded towards Emma. 'The lassie here's helping me. She's the brains of the family; goes to university in Edinburgh.'

The old woman was unimpressed. 'You'll need a miracle, not brains.'

'I know the odds are long,' he said. 'I'm not expecting a reunion with her, like something out of a film. She could be on the other side of the world. For all I know, she might be dead. But I'd settle for knowing what happened to her. Where she ended up. What sort of life she lived. Em's made a few enquiries but we need more information, something to get us started. I'm not even sure what year it happened. I think it was 1929 but wouldn't swear to it.'

'You're not wrong,' said Nell. 'It was in the autumn, after all the fairs had finished for the year. September or October. I heard they took your sister to St Augustine's Children's Home.

Then I daresay she'd have been settled with some *gaj* family.'
Nell watched Emma scribbling in her notepad. 'How are you
going to do it, Miss smarty pants?'

'We'll write to the authorities.'

'The authorities?' The old woman let out a chuckle. 'Look
at you. You're just a wee lassie yourself. You're forgetting who
it was that did it.' She dug her elbows into the mattress, trying
to sit up. Her eyes strained with effort but she moved nowhere
until Nash propped her up. Her voice rose and hand shook as
she pointed at Emma with a preacher's fervency. 'They're not
to be trusted. Never. Of all the things they did to us, taking
the bairns was the worst of it. The very worst of it.'

'There was more of it?' asked Emma. 'Kids being taken.'

'Plenty more,' said Nell. 'There was never any warning.
Just like what happened to your sister. The Social would turn
up with the police and they weren't messing about. It made
families scared to settle anywhere for too long. And that was
the idea. Fear. Parents wouldn't let their bairns out of their
sight. They'd warn them – never talk to the *gaj* or you might
be snatched. You'll never see your family again.'

'Bastards,' muttered Nash.

Nell placed a hand over his and patted it. 'I can understand
why you're angry, son, but it'll do you no good.'

Nash seemed not to hear. Sitting there, perched on the
edge of the bed, took him down a particular passage of
memory. He was 22 years old and in a one-bedroom flat in
Carluke. His mum was dead and his brothers had left town.
'You know, I used to sit like this with my granny,' he said,
tracing a finger along the quilted pattern of the bed cover.
'The Social gave us a wee flat after her health went. That was
the first time either of us had lived in a house. It was a real
shoebox but it was warm, dry, and she had her own bedroom.
It's strange how the same people who did that for us could
take a bairn like they did. Sometimes I feel ashamed we didn't
tell them to shove their flat.' He came back to himself with a
sniff and a taste of salty wetness on his lips. 'You're bloody
right I'm angry – and I want answers.'

7

Spence had done the routine thousands of times. First, he offered to take his shoes off at the door. That showed the prospective customer he cared about their home as much as they did. His hawking suitcase was bulky, so he always put it down on the doorstep and crossed the threshold first, then lifted it in. He didn't want his entrance to look clumsy and certainly didn't want to risk chipping paint off the doorframe. He'd made that mistake only once. First impressions last, and his entrance was designed to show he was considerate and could be trusted to pay attention to detail. Now, here he was sitting down, opening his battered case of carpet samples.

'This one is Apache Flame,' he said, with a twist of panache. 'It's very popular.'

He had the case open on his knee, and Mrs Green, a past customer, sat next to him, sipping tea. He'd fitted linoleum in her kitchenette and bathroom the year before and now had his sights set on a bigger sale.

Mrs Green leaned over and ran her hand across the sample's soft, thick fibres. 'Oh aye,' she said. 'I like that. It's got a nice feel about it.'

'That's deep shag. Like I say, it's one of our most popular lines.' He always referred to a collective – we, us, and our – as if there was more to the business than him. He gestured at Mrs Green's living room carpet. It was decades old, with a dense yellow and green pattern of nauseating intensity. 'What you've got there is lovely, but is showing its age, if you don't mind me saying. How old did you say it was?' Mrs Green hadn't, but the trick was to get people talking. That was what his dad taught him.

'Twenty years,' said Mrs Green, then, with a twist of her lips, revised it to, 'Maybe closer to fifteen. I'd like a new one but it's convincing him that's the problem.'

'And how is Mr Green?'

'Fine, I suppose.' She flipped through a few more samples then came back to Apache Flame.

Spence beamed a wry, neglected smile. 'This is the one you like. Well it must be fate, Mrs Green, because I happen to have a roll with me today. It's in the van. Like I say – very popular.'

'Really?'

'It's outside right now. In fact, I was en route to drop it off at the showroom, but...' he broke into a chuckle as if the thought had just come to him. 'Perhaps you can save me the trip.' Of course, there was no showroom. The carpet had been in the back of his van for months. A wholesaler who was going to throw it away had sold it to him for a knockdown price because of a stain in the corner. Spence got the stain out after shampooing it several times and had been trying to sell it ever since.

'I can bring it in if you want to see it. Now, it was £9.99 per square yard but we recently took it down to £7.99.' He took the measurements of the living room and gave Mrs Green a price. He laid the sample on the floor next to the fireplace then looked at the room, angling his head and considering the rust-coloured curtains and cushions. 'It would go nice with the rest of the decor.'

Spence saw the frustrated eagerness in Mrs Green's eyes. 'You need time to think about it? No problem. I can come back later. When works for you?' His voice was light and breezy because people could pick up on tension. That was another thing his dad drummed into him. Customers sensed it and it could change their frame of mind from positive to negative in a heartbeat. Moods go up and down hundreds of times each day. An old song on the radio makes someone think of their first love then a news headline reminds them of their dire finances. Certain foods, a stain on the wall, a particular date, a faulty cupboard door they've been meaning to fix for months. They all influence subtle shifts, not causing ecstasy or despair, but moving emotions up and down within the mid-range. So Spence tried to be a feel-good presence. Open your door to him. Let him into your home and for half an hour, he'd be your best pal.

Mrs Green sat back and took out her cigarettes. 'I better not, son. I'm sorry.'

The slump across his shoulders came instantly and was instantly corrected. 'Did I mention it's made with a special stain resistant treatment? Don't ask me how they do it but it works a treat.'

'I'm sorry, I really can't.'

'Maybe I can sharpen the pencil on that price.'

She shook her head. 'We just don't have the money right now.'

'Absolutely not a problem, Mrs Green.' He put the samples back in his suitcase and clipped it shut. 'I'll try you again in the spring.'

She stopped him at the door and pointed at his suitcase. 'I'll take some hoover bags if you've got any.'

Fran walking out didn't affect him the way that might be expected. He didn't fall apart, turn against the world, or himself. If anything, he became more disciplined. Up at six every morning, he did exercises on the living room floor before porridge and a cup of tea. Then it was into the van and out to the streets. Physically, he became not skinnier, but leaner. At 46, Spence's creased, leathery skin didn't make him look old but gave him a firmness, like he'd stood up to a great test.

After Mrs Green, he drove to a nearby supermarket and took the van to the far end of the car park. He sat for a while, giving serious consideration to whether he was losing his sales touch and if he should just go home for the day. A brown Ford Cortina pulled up next to him and a man got out, stretched, and came over to the van. Spence wound down the window and the man peered at the roll of carpet in the back.

'What've we got?'

'Apache Flame,' said Spence, a little deflated. 'Deep shag.'

'Very nice. It might be the right size for a mark I've got. She's just a few streets away.'

'Please don't say Mrs Green.'

'Jesus, not her. I'm talking about a real prospect, Spence. A sale.'

Pursed lips and a nod indicated that Spence had heard him, but no more than that. The man was Archie Matthews, another long-time hawker and Spence's on-off partner since the late sixties. As far as Archie and Spence knew, they were the only old-style carpet hawkers left in East Lothian, most of their peers having given up the previous decade. But not them. They held on, partly in the belief that less competition meant a larger market share for them. The size of that market and whether it might be shrinking never occurred to them.

'What size is it?' asked Archie, pulling his coat tight around his body and shuffling from one foot to the other, trying to keep warm. Spence gave him the dimensions and Archie grinned, jabbing a finger into his shoulder. 'Ideal. I'll get it sold for you no bother.'

Theirs was an uneasy partnership, born of necessity. Door-to-door carpet sales around flats and tenements was back-breaking work, so they helped each other with the logistics. Their partnership's commercial aspect was trickier still. It depended on who had the goods – the carpets, rugs and curtains – and who had marks – sales leads where customers said they were on the lookout for certain items. Rarely these days was Spence lucky enough to have the goods and a mark at the same time, so he partnered with Archie when he was desperate. Although the aim, of course, was to do anything but give an impression of desperation.

Archie drummed his fingers on the van as he stared at the carpet. 'That looks cosy,' he said. 'I'd guess it's been sitting there for a while, no? How long have you had it, Spence?'

He tried for a nonchalant shake of the head and shrug of the shoulders. 'That thing? Oh, not long.'

Archie squinted at him. 'You've had it for a couple of months, I can see it in your eyes.'

Spence laughed and lied that he had plenty of interested customers. He was taking his time, warming them up, finding out who'd pay the best price. Archie screwed up his face and shook his head, as if avoiding an unpleasant sight. 'Come on, Spence. Why do we have to play these games? You've got that old suitcase of hoover bags sitting next to you. You're struggling right now. You can't kid me.'

'I'm telling you; I'm not needing a mark.'

'Come on, Spence. The woman's only around the corner. She's after something just like it. Where's the harm in letting her see it?'

'Thanks all the same, but I'm going to pass.'

'The mark would love it, absolutely love it,' said Archie. 'She's one of them *nouveau riche* types, you know – wanting to impress the neighbours. How about, right...' He stepped back, rubbing his knuckles, then came forward. 'How about, if I get it sold for you, we'll split 50–50?'

Archie was puffy and dishevelled and dressed like it was still the seventies; a kipper tie and Cuban heel boots like little hooves sticking out the bottom of his flares. He was also stooped, with an impressively brisk step for a beer-bellied, twenty-a-day smoker who'd recently had a heart attack.

'Even split?' gasped Spence. 'No way.'

'Stop being so proud. I swear, that's the same piece of carpet you had last time I saw you.'

'You're imagining things. I'd think about doing a 70-30 split.'

Archie spun on his heels and walked back to his car. 'Nice seeing you, Spence. Same time next month?'

'It's my carpet,' Spence shouted after him.

'And it's my mark.' Archie dug out his keys and opened his car door.

'60-40,' said Spence.

'Am I a good salesman? Just give me a yes or no.'

'Course.'

'What if I told you – made you a promise – I could get 200 for it?'

'You'd have my interest.'

'Well that's what I'll do,' said Archie. 'I swear on my mother; 200. But we need to split 50-50.'

A pause and a sigh. 'All right, then. But that's only because we've got a history.'

They drove to the flat and found the woman at home. Sure enough, she was interested in the carpet but needed the okay from her husband who didn't finish his shift till six. 'You'll need to come back after his tea,' she added, 'so he winnae be in a bad mood.' She gave them a deposit and they left her with the carpet and said they'd come back later. It was already after four so they went to a local pub and killed time at a pool table. 'Come back after his tea so he won't be in a bad mood,' groaned Archie. 'Jesus Christ, why's it always got to be so complicated?'

When they came back, the woman's husband stood in the door and offered them £100. Spence said they'd agreed 200 with his wife but the man laughed and said he'd given her a smack in the mouth for that. He told them there was one person in the house who brought home a wage and they were speaking to him. He was much bigger than them and explained that if they wanted their carpet back they'd have to come past him. Spence looked at Archie, who gave him a shake of the head that said: please, no. It's not worth it, not six months after a heart attack.

In the van, they sat by the dashboard light and split the money. It didn't look like much. Over the years, Spence had come to notice how small amounts of money were counted out slowly, as if it would somehow make it seem a larger sum.

★ ★ ★

It was no surprise that Spence never had high expectations of hawking. On what he regarded as his first official day as a hawker – his fourteenth birthday – his dad patted his shoulder, pointed him at a house and said, 'Get yourself up to yon door and see if you can keep the *gaj* talking for a minute. I'll time you.' There was no mention of selling anything; just the challenge to keep whoever answered talking for 60 seconds. His dad insisted that Spence went empty-handed to the door. It was part of the challenge that he wasn't allowed to show the prospective customer what was for sale. He was quietly outraged by this. He was a man now and expected to be told to go forth and sell, not be given some silly game. But his dad was serious.

Spence's indignation turned to panic. 'But what am I supposed to say? Can't I take something with me, something from the cart?'

'Talking comes first,' repeated his dad. 'It's the most important part. Learn to talk and you'll learn to sell.'

Time seemed to slow on the walk to the door. He cleared his throat and knocked on its faded brown paintwork. It was answered by a spindly woman with washed-out eyes.

'You needing anything, Mrs?'

'Needing what, son?'

'My da's over there with his cart. Is there anything you're needing for the house, like?'

'You'll need to tell me what you've got, son.'

'Eh, we've got rugs, tinware. Baskets. Eh...pots and pans. Lots of things.'

'Any fire wood?'

'Aye, plenty of it.'

There were footsteps behind her and a low mumbling. She stepped back and was replaced at the door by a small, stone-faced man. Spence was wondering whether he should start his spiel again when the door slammed shut and he found himself staring once more at the faded brown paint.

Back at the cart, his dad asked, 'Was it a man?'

'A woman first, then a man.'

'He's a miserable old git, isn't he?' His dad laughed and shook his head. 'He never lets her buy anything. I never bother with that door anymore.'

'So why did you send me there?'

'I wanted to see if you could bring us a bit of beginner's luck. Never mind. You managed 30 seconds. Not bad.' His dad broke into a whistle and took the cart up the street. 'Come on, son. There's plenty other doors.'

Over the next few weeks many more doors were slammed in Spence's face but slowly he found his voice and edged closer to his first sale. It happened on the 26th of July 1951. It was a Hall's cooking pot, and the woman who bought it for seven shillings said he'd knocked at just the right time because the handle had fallen off her old pot. 'Must be your lucky day,' she told him. Afterwards, his dad patted his back, shook his hand, and said well done, he was getting to be a good hawker.

'Better than Uncle Nash?'

His dad winked. 'Don't tell him I said so.'

'Better than you?'

'Don't get carried away.'

It would have been a cigar moment – if they had any.

'Now, watch me at this next door,' said his dad. 'If you see me stepping inside you'll know I've got a mark for the rug. Keep your fingers crossed.'

His dad had brought the rug home a few weeks earlier. It was Oriental. Very high quality. He'd cleared a space on the floor and put a dust sheet down before unrolling it to show Spence. He ran his hand over its smooth fibres then invited Spence to do the same. 'See that, that's a lovely piece of carpet.' He explained how to judge the quality according to fibre density – counting the 'face weight' of the yarn per cubic inch – and how cheap carpet had thicker matting to compensate for thin fibre density. Afterwards, Spence helped wrap it in a sheet before tying it up with string. They would take it to a well-to-do town, said his dad, and sell it for a lot of money.

So here they were. Spence stood by the horse as his dad heaved the rug onto his shoulder and carried it to the next house. A woman answered. His dad doffed his cap and launched into his pitch, gesturing as best he could at the rug while trying to keep it balanced. Eventually, she nodded and waved him inside. His dad turned and smiled at him.

Spence waited and watched and thought it must be going well because it was taking a while. Just as his dad told him, he crossed his fingers and muttered wishes of good luck. The horse snorted and flicked its tail when the door flew open and the woman came rushing out and ran to a house a few doors along. Spence stared at the door, willing his dad to appear. The woman returned with a neighbour and hurried back into the house.

The horse reared and shook its head, unlocking his grip from the halter. He crossed the street and went into the house. Frantic voices and the hurried scraping of furniture being moved came from a room down the hall. The walls seemed to close around him, enveloping him, bringing him to the door of the room. 'He's not breathing. Oh God. He's not breathing,' a woman said. He peered round the door but stopped when his dad's legs came into view, splayed out on the floor. Later at the hospital, the doctor told him and his mum it was unusual for a fit, working man. He was sorry for their loss.

8

It was a filthy callbox strewn with fag stubs and crumpled bus tickets. The faint whiff of stale urine caught in Emma's nostrils as she stepped inside. She wedged the door open, dialled the number for Strathclyde Council and explained why she was calling. After a pause, the switchboard operator's voice came crackling down the line. 'Is this about the hippies camping up at the green?'

'No, I mean Travellers like Gypsy Travellers, from a while back.'

'We don't have a department for that, love.'

'No but what about something like social work?'

'When did you say this happened?'

Emma repeated the details.

'Nah, not for a case that old,' said the man. 'There was no such thing as social work back then.'

'That's the problem,' said Emma. 'I don't know which department would deal with this.'

'I'll tell you what, I'll put you through to the records department. Hold the line, please.'

She let out a long sigh and looked around at the dried lumps of chewing gum stuck to the windows, to the phone, even on the ceiling. The surfaces were densely graffitied with names, obscenities and threats. She'd learned from her studies that even here, in an industrialised city at the tail end of the twentieth century, these were tribal markings put there as acts of faith, that they would be seen and interpreted, that they would mean something to the wider world.

A lorry thundered past, rattling the callbox, as a faint voice came on the other end of the line, a hesitant office junior struggling with the complexities of her enquiry. Again, Emma went over the details.

'I'm just the filing clerk,' said the lad.

'That's what I'm asking about,' said Emma. 'Files. Old ones.'

'I'd need to check.'

'That's the idea. The office at Carluke said you've got them.'

'Not me. I've only been here four months.'

She sighed and scratched her neck. 'I don't mean you personally, I mean...look, this is important. My great-uncle doesn't have long to live and he's asked me to look into this. Is there maybe someone more senior I could talk to?'

He put her on hold and went to check with his manager. The beeps sounded and she fired more coins into the slot. Back on the line a few moments later, the lad told her to send a letter with all the details.

'But I've just told you everything. Can't you take notes?'

'My boss says it's the procedure. We need something in writing – for the records.'

'Come on, mate. This is urgent.'

'Sorry, that's what he told me.'

'Okay, okay, I'll write. Who do I address it to?'

'Richard Ash – Mr Richard Ash.'

Later, Emma sat down at a projection booth in the National Library. A flick of the switch and the booth flooded with light. She blinked and adjusted to the glare. Dust particles glinted in the air and a low hum came from the projection machinery. Next to her, the librarian teased a delicate roll of film from a small cardboard box. 'Did you ever help your granny with knitting?' she asked.

'I never met my grandparents.'

'Well, this is no different from a wool spinner,' she said, attaching the film between two spools and positioning it under the spotlight. 'The management weren't going to train me on this. Old dog, new tricks is what they were thinking. But I showed them.' She adjusted the controls and slowly brought the scratched and blotchy film into focus until the front page of the *Lanarkshire Gazette* was projected, crisp and clear, inside the booth. 'There we have it. All the hot gossip from 1929.'

Judging from the headlines, life in Lanarkshire back then was dull and much-maligned. There were adverts for backache pills and stories about parish council meetings. Half a page was dedicated to the retirement of a local minister and below that, an advice column on how to wear hats.

'What is it you're looking for?'

'A wee girl who got taken from her family.'

'Oh God bless her. I hope it wasn't one of those horrible kiddie snatcher cases.'

The phrase put Emma in mind of a Disney film she'd watched as a young girl. Fran and Spence had taken her to see it at the cinema – a special day out – and she was enjoying it up until a scene where children were lured into the back of a trailer by a sinister man offering sweets and cakes. The appearance of the child catcher briefly transformed an otherwise family-friendly film into the stuff of nightmares. Watching the spidery man in the crooked top hat made her palms sticky and she left the cinema convinced that such pantomime villains were out there, preying on children. The reality, she now knew, was more complex. It was men with badges of authority who brought the nightmare to her family.

'No,' she said. 'It wasn't one of those cases but it was still horrible.'

'You never used to hear about kids being taken,' muttered the librarian. 'It's all the sex and violence on television that's twisting people's minds, making them into perverts. You could understand that there'd always be some men who'd be that way inclined, towards bad impulses, but maybe they'd never act on it if it weren't for all the muck they're seeing on screens, you know. The government's right to clamp down on it.'

The librarian got up and left Emma to scroll through the pages. There was a hypnotic quality about it, cocooned from the world, watching the columns of news spin past under the squeal of the film and clack of the spools. The projector was a cumbersome thing to use. One button spun the film so quickly it was impossible to control where it stopped. The other moved it at a snail's pace and kept jamming. Yet she combed every edition of August, September and October. Headlines of court cases jumped out at her: two vagrants jailed for sleeping in a brickworks; a miner charged with reckless handling of explosives; and a drunken bus driver had crashed into a bridge. Still, there was nothing about trouble at a Travellers' site. Perhaps Nell Andrews was mistaken about the time of year? Maybe it happened earlier? She checked but there was nothing in the June or July editions.

Two hours had passed by the time the librarian came back to say they were closing in ten minutes. 'Did you find anything?'

Emma drummed impatient fingers on the side of the booth and shook her head. 'Nope. It doesn't look like it got reported.'

In frustration, she pressed the scroll button, letting the reel spin wildly for a few moments. When she released it, the columns tumbled to a stop on the first edition of November. There it was, starkly lit and sharply rendered:

29th of October, 1929
Five Tinkers Arrested After Police Assault

Arrests were made at the Whiteshaw tinkers' encampment last week after police and public health officials were attacked while carrying out their duties. Three tinker women will appear in court on Friday charged with assault. A police source said officers were assisting the Town Hall officials with an inspection of sanitary conditions when a young child was found and judged to be suffering neglect. A number of the site dwellers, including the child's mother, turned on the officers with a vicious assault and had to be restrained while the child was removed. The attack only confirmed to officials that the child was living in a dangerous, savage environment, and strengthened their resolve to discharge their duties. The young girl, believed to be around five years of age, was placed into care. Dr Robert Banks, Public Health Officer for Carluke Town Council, said: "We have had grave concerns over sanitary conditions at the site for a number of years, especially with regard to the welfare of children. I'm pleased to report that the site has now been cleared of tinkers and we hope to make it inaccessible to their kind on a permanent basis."

Dr Robert Banks. The name went down in her notebook. Alongside the article was a photo of the campsite, with distant figures clustered around horses and trailers. She ran a finger over her mouth, leaning in for a closer look at the photo. This was it, the place where it happened. She stared into the tiny dots of newsprint that made up the image and tried to picture the exact spot where Mary threw herself on top of Jenny and had to be wrestled off. Nash's violent narrative ran in her head, giving life to the yellowed image. She pictured the scene: spit and blood in the mud. Mary's punches and kicks delivered with primal fury. Screaming. Crying. Snot and tears. The men with clumps of hair pulled out, Mary's fingers gouging at their faces, and at the end, Nash picking up his sister's one-legged doll from a puddle.

She reached into her bag and took out the doll. It had been in there since Nash gave it to her. She ran her fingers through its hair. Dirt and tiny bits of stone were ingrained in the woollen strands. The thought struck her that these were probably from the scene itself when the doll fell in the mud. The idea seemed incredible – specks that had been part of the earth for however long until the day they became caught in the doll's hair and the Lacklows' torrid history. She read the article again, seeing more than words on a page; bodies thrashed, fists lashed out and a woman and a child cried out for each other.

* * *

When it came to the telling of history, truth was a complicated business. Those were the words of Professor Andrew Miller from a class a few weeks earlier. Emma flicked back through her folder and found her notes. She'd written that it was usually the voice of those with power that went into the official record of events. The perspectives of the weak, the defeated, and the vanquished were distorted or ignored. But more than this, Miller made a distinction between factual truth and something more murky, which he called 'accepted forms of truth'. Here, assertion could be just as compelling,

just as strong, as facts. 'It all depends on who owns
medium,' he'd said. 'Who holds the power. Compet
perspectives can be reduced or completely ignored, as if th
didn't exist – washed out of existence like a stain on fabric.

'Emma, are you okay?' Kate nudged her. 'You look li
you're miles away.'

She was in the pub with friends but in her head she'd nev
left the projection booth at the library. 'Sorry, I was ju
checking something.' She closed her notes and took a sip o
the beer she'd been nursing for half an hour. Her money had
run out and her friends were buying rounds. She'd already
taken one strategically timed trip to the bathroom to avoid her
turn to buy drinks and didn't want the embarrassment of
doing it again. It was another ten minutes before Spence
would be outside but she decided to go and wait on the street.
She gathered up her coat and bag.

'I'll walk you out,' said Kate.

'It's all right. I'm fine.'

'I want to meet your dad.'

'Another time.'

'I thought you said he's protective,' said Kate.

'So?'

'So he'll appreciate me walking you to the van.'

'All right,' said Emma, 'but we're just friends, okay?'

At the van, Kate shook Spence's hand and told him she
was from Bath.

'You're a long way from home,' he said. 'What family have
you got down there?'

'Mum and dad. I don't see them much.'

He seemed troubled by this and insisted that Kate come
for dinner soon. On the road home, he said to Emma, 'Your
pal seems nice.'

'Yeah, Kate's nice.'

He nodded and patted her knee. 'Good, I'm glad you're
making friends.'

9

Kate tried not to be snobbishly curious about all the pubs, betting shops and hair salons. It wasn't just that she'd never been outside Edinburgh since coming to university, she'd never even been beyond the student district, with all its bars and cafes set among beautiful old buildings that she no longer noticed.

Tranent was bigger than she expected, with a long high street punctuated by boarded-up shops. Emma and Spence lived a few streets away in a semi-detached with a lane and row of garages at the back. She took high ceilings and bright, spacious rooms for granted so the size of their house was a shock.

'It's lovely,' she said.

They sat at a table, squeezed in behind the sofa, eating vegetable lasagne with garlic bread. Nash was there too, curious about Kate and dressed to the nines. They spoke about government spending cuts and Kate said how much she hated the Tories, assuming she was in like-minded company.

'Oh, I don't know about that,' said Spence. 'They've got the right idea on a few things.'

'Like what?' asked Kate.

'Helping businesses.'

'That's just helping the rich get richer.'

'No, I saw it on tv. They want to help small businesses. People like me.'

Earlier that week, Spence had seen a government minister on the lunchtime news talking about plans to revive the economy. 'This fellow said the country needed more, what was it, people with the guts to work for themselves, building up businesses from scratch – entrepreneurs. And I thought, that's me. I'm an entrepreneur. I'd never heard it before but then it hit me – I've been an entrepreneur all my life. I'm from a line of them. Lacklows have always worked for themselves. It's in our blood. Anyway, the government's launching

a scheme. Loans for small businesses.' He pursed his lips. 'I reckon I fit the bill.'

Spence had always talked about money but it was usually from the begrudging perspective of a down-at-heel slugger who had none and knew he probably never would. Now here he was, brimming with optimism, talking the language of aspiration and capitalism, and sounding like he really could make it.

Emma said, 'Dad, you're not going to start voting Tory, are you? They're shutting down industries, putting thousands of people out of work. It's devastating communities.'

'I'm not saying they're getting everything right but they're doing a better job than the last mob.'

'Dad, what are you talking about? Unemployment's doubled since they came into power.'

Kate turned to Nash for a change of subject. 'Emma tells me you're trying to trace your sister.'

'We're trying. Not getting very far.'

'What happened sounds horrendous.'

'That's why we don't really talk about it,' interrupted Spence.

'Sorry, I didn't mean to stick my nose in.'

'No, it's fine,' said Nash. 'I don't mind. You see, back in those days, the authorities thought Travellers weren't much better than animals. They probably thought they were doing the right thing by taking our kids away.'

'Have you had any yourself?' asked Kate.

'Kids? No. Maybe what happened with my sister put me off. I never married, either. There was a lassie once but it never worked out.' He noticed Spence and Emma exchange looks. 'I've never told you?'

'First I'm hearing of this,' grumbled Spence.

'I must have told you.'

Spence shook his head. 'I'd remember.'

'It's how I got my nickname.'

Emma said, 'I always thought your nickname was to do with your teeth.'

'My teeth?'

'Your grin.'

'No, no, no. Nash. You know? Cant for running away from something. That's what I did. I ran away from getting married.'

'Who was the girl?' asked Emma.

He paused and looked up, recalling his fiancé's name. 'Eleanor – that was it – Eleanor Wilkie, from Jedburgh. I'd been working in the Borders over the summer, laying tarmac on the road between Kelso and Jedburgh. We'd been going steady for a while, me and the girl. I'd met her family and got the nod from her parents. Set a date and I was putting away money for the wedding. But that road was a hell of a job. Killer on the back. Braw summer, too. Maybe I'd gone a bit doolally with the heat because when we finished, I got the bus up to Edinburgh. I was feeling good that I had all that money in my pocket and was going somewhere different. I don't know why I did it. Maybe I just needed a change of scene but, anyhow, I did what I did.'

The others stared at him. 'Come on,' said Emma. 'Out with it.'

'When I got to town, I went and got myself a suit – not a wedding suit. A nice suit. Dapper. New shoes. Trilby hat – the works.' He smiled at the memory and ran a hand over his hair. 'I checked into the Balmoral Hotel. Had a bath to wash off the smell of the tarmac. I'd had it on me for months. It got up your nostrils, in your eyes, in your hair – awful stuff. I got my suit on and went downstairs to the restaurant and ate dinner like I was a posh bugger. I just wanted to live the high life for once. So that's what I did – and I blew the wedding money in two nights. A visit to the casino. A trip to the racetrack. It doesn't last long.' He coughed and cleared his throat. 'It was a queer thing to do, right enough. Anyway, I couldn't go back to the Borders. Her family wanted to have a word with me, if you catch my drift, her father and brothers in particular – and I didn't fancy going back to Carluke, so I washed up over here on the east coast. That's where my name came from – because I did a runner from getting married. I was a *nasher*.'

10

Richard Ash didn't just sit down at his desk, he positioned himself at it, straight-backed, with his arms resting neatly on either side of a leather folder. He brought out Emma's letter, frowning and clearing his throat as he read it.

'Okay,' he said. 'Going back a fair bit here.'

'54 years.'

'Before my time – just. Definitely before yours.' He smiled at her, taking in her appearance. She had what he regarded as a boy's haircut and wore a man's oversized pinstripe suit jacket, with rolled up sleeves and bangles on her wrists. He squinted at the protest badges on her lapel. They were all there. CND, the Anti-Nazi League, the Anti-Apartheid Movement, and others for causes he hadn't even heard about. 'You're a student?'

'At Edinburgh.'

He held up the letter. 'And this is your family?'

Emma ignored the barely disguised tone of disbelief that someone from such a background would be at university. 'Like I said in the letter, we're trying to trace an old relative. Jenny – Jenny Lacklow. We think she was forced into adoption.'

'Forced? Dear, oh dear. What a world. Forced by whom?'

'By the authorities.'

He checked the letter again as if he might have missed something. 'They must have had a reason to do something like that, don't you think?'

'That's what's so terrible about this – they had no good reason. None whatsoever.'

'How old are you, Miss Lacklow?'

'Nearly twenty.'

'And this was 50 years ago. How can you be sure what happened?'

'My great-uncle told me about it. He was there.'

'Must have been very young.'

'But he still remembers it,' said Emma. 'It traumatised

him. He asked me to look into it. It's not been easy but I've managed to find someone else who was there. She remembers it just the same as he does.' She brought out a print of the old newspaper story from the *Lanark Gazette*. 'And I found this at the library.'

'You've been doing your homework.'

'I'm getting there, thanks.'

'It sounds to me like she was kidnapped,' said Ash. 'Have you contacted the police?'

'No.'

'Well, if you want to be thorough about this, it strikes me that they'd be the best people to contact.' A quick, confident nod. 'Leave it to the professionals.'

Emma said, 'The police were there when she was taken. They helped the officials who did it.' She pointed to the story. 'The police beat the women.'

Ash picked it up and looked more closely at it. 'It says here the police were assaulted.'

'That's the media for you.'

His eyes widened in theatrical bafflement. 'But you said there was no good reason for them taking her.'

'That's right.'

'Forgive me, Miss Lacklow, but that seems like quite a length to go to if there was no good reason.'

'I'm not asking you to make judgements.'

'I just want to be clear on the details so we know what sort of records we'd be looking for.' He picked up a letter opener with a decorative handle and swatted it gently against his palm, waiting for her response.

'I don't know what sort of records,' Emma eventually said. 'That's the point. You're the ones who took her.'

The chair creaked as Ash leaned back and cocked his head. 'Well now, that's quite a thing to say.'

'Those are the facts.'

'I'd love to share your certainty but I'm not sure we can justify a wild-goose chase for 50-year-old documents that might or might not exist. This local authority is being cut to the bone right now. Public services are not in a good state. An enquiry like this would take a lot of time.' It could also open a can of worms, he thought. 'I need to consider taxpayer value. People don't like to see their money wasted.'

Emma stared at him, incredulous. 'This is a publicly accountable organisation,' she said. 'I'll look into my rights if I have to.'

He wondered how long it would be before she mentioned her rights. These types always did.

Richard Ash stood up and straightened his suit. He liked to think people could tell he was ex-military just from the way he held himself. What they saw was a certain calibre of man; standards and discipline in a well-pressed suit. It was that simple. A friend had lined him up with the role as head of records when he came out of the navy. What he didn't know about public services was beside the point. It irked him that the pinnacle of his military career coincided with what became known as the decade of national decline. Great Britain on the skids in the 1970s. Terrorists and power cuts. A government taking the begging bowl to the International Monetary Fund. Public servants on strike right down to the bin men. Britain had grown lazy and slow, and was allowing all sorts of types to leech off it, sucking it dry. Ash saw himself as part of the recovery effort.

He smiled politely at Emma and went to the filing cabinet. 'I didn't say no, did I?' He took out a form and handed it to her.

'What's this?'

'An information retrieval request.'

'But my letter,' she said. 'I told you everything.'

'We still need an official request. As much detail as you can, please, and don't forget to sign and date it.'

* * *

It was the slow-moving queue he stood in on the last Monday of every month. Always, there were gripes and grumbles at the counter. It annoyed him that people were never able to pay their rent quickly. His attention drifted up to the squint ceiling panel above the desk. It had been like that for years, a few degrees off, revealing a dusty pipe and the darkness of the ceiling cavity. That sort of carelessness bothered him. He'd never get away with it in his line of work. Good God, if he fitted carpets a few inches off the skirting boards, he wouldn't get paid. Simple as that. The queue moved forward until he was directly below the offending panel. He wondered what workman could have been in such a rush that he didn't have time to move it back fully into place.

'Doesn't that bother you?' Spence asked the lady at the counter.

'What?'

'Up there. That panel.'

'I've never noticed.'

'You know, it wouldn't take two minutes for a janitor to nip up there and shift it back into place.'

'I suppose so,' she said.

He half-joked about bringing a set of ladders next time and going up there himself to fix it. 'Would that qualify me for a discount?'

A withering smile as she stamped his rent book and passed it back to him. As he turned to leave, a poster on the wall behind the desk caught his eye. It was for the government's business support scheme he'd heard about on the news. He pointed at it, the woman gave him a leaflet, and he wandered back to the van reading it. Successful applicants could get a loan for capital investment to grow their businesses, to be paid back at 0% interest over ten years. If he was turning a profit, he'd barely even notice that.

'We could get premises,' he said to Archie later. 'Display racks for the carpets. Imagine a showroom.'

'I tell you what else,' said Archie, slapping the van's rusted metal shell. 'You could get rid of this piece of crap. Get a new van with our names on the side. Print some business cards. We'd be a class act.'

'We need to be honest with ourselves – hawking is a dying

trade. People don't want to be bothered by us when they're at home. They're trying to watch the telly or make dinner, and I don't want to spend the rest of my life having doors slammed in my face.'

'Me neither,' said Archie. 'It's not good for our self-esteem.'

'We've been hawking the streets for decades now.'

'I could use a rest.'

'You'd get it,' said Spence. 'A wee office with a kettle.'

'Tin of biscuits.'

Spence asked, 'How many miles do you think we've racked up between us?'

Archie puffed his cheeks. 'It's the stairs and the lifting I struggle with.'

'I've told you how my old man popped it.'

'Ah, don't remind me,' said Archie. 'The clock's only ticking in one direction.'

'All these years, Archie, I thought I could stay on top with willpower and hard work, but I see it now – I've got to move with the times.'

Back home, Spence fixed himself a sandwich and sat down to watch television. As he settled back on the sofa, something dug into his backside. One of Emma's textbooks stuck out from under a cushion. She'd been in a rush that morning and must have forgotten to pick it up. He looked at the cover – *Contemporary and Classical Sociological Theory and Practice*. It was a psychedelic design, with coloured circles overlapping. He read the back cover. It said the book provided valuable insights on the causes and consequences of human behaviour over the centuries, covering everything from established patterns to calamitous upheavals. Below that, a black and white photo of the author. Fancied himself as a serious thinker by the looks of it; furrowed brow and bearded in front of a bookshelf. He read the man's biography. Never a day's real graft to his name, of course. This was the irony; someone professing what makes society tick but utterly removed from the real world. The tip of a bookmark stuck out from the middle pages. Let's take a look and see what this eejit has to say that's so special. Opening it, he saw that the bookmark was in fact one of those slim photobooth strips; five glossy, black and white pictures of Emma and Kate. They cuddled up next to each other and posed differently in each shot. Clowning and pulling faces in one, big grins in another, alluring and serious in the next. Then, in the final picture, Emma cupped the back of Kate's head, pressing tightly into her hair as they kissed with their eyes closed and mouths wide.

He blinked and scratched his mouth then looked around as if there might be someone else to share his shock. He recalled two occasions when he'd been in a photo booth – once with mates, all piled in and pulling silly faces, and once with Fran, as cosy young lovers. He remembered never knowing quite when the flash would go off and it always caught him off guard.

11

Early February, and the previous week had brought three days of heavy snow. A stagnant, damp cold clung to the place. Trees and bushes were laced with it and the cobbled street was quiet except for the occasional car hissing by, spraying slush on dirty mounds of ice along the pavement's edge. They walked at a leisurely pace, taking in the grandeur. Every so often, Nash would stop and lift his walking stick, pointing out a mansion and telling Emma who owned it and what he'd heard of their line of business. It always amazed him that so much wealth was a stone's throw from his back door.

'This is all inherited,' said Emma. 'Hard work's got nothing to do with it.' She held out her arms and turned around on the spot. 'Privilege. That's all I'm seeing here. Generation after generation of privilege. Those houses should be requisitioned by the government and turned into flats. You could fit five families into one of those.'

They ambled past wrought iron street lamps and high, ivy-topped walls, then turned down a lane into a yard, where stood a small building of mouldy red brick. A stooped man in a pork pie hat led a horse around the yard. He looked over at them. 'Long time no see, Nash.'

'I've been out of commission. The chest again.'

'On the comeback trail now, are you?'

'I'll be going ten rounds by the summer.'

The old friends burst into cackles that startled Emma.

'It's not looking good for this one.' The man patted the horse. 'Laminitis comes and goes. It plagues him. He had a bad spell last week but he's been better this week. I'm not sure what to do.'

The man was Jockey White, and Nash had known him since the fifties when Jockey was in the mix of horsiemen – the trainers and handlers who worked at East Lothian's race tracks. He'd come close to making a name for himself at one time but these days he was the stable manager for the estates of the village.

'How old's he?' asked Emma, reaching up to pat the animal.

'Twenty-odd years now,' said Jockey. 'I'm just giving him a trot to be sure, you know. Before I make a final decision.'

'You're going to put him down?'

'Probably.'

Nash nodded and rubbed the animal's mane. 'Poor bugger,' he said. 'The pair of us, we're both fit for the knackers yard aren't we, boy?'

'Here, sweetheart,' said Jockey, offering the rope to Emma. 'He seems all right today. Take him into the field for a quick trot.'

'Are you sure? I don't want to hurt him.'

'He wants to run, I can tell.'

She led the horse through the gate and went slowly at first, keeping it on a short rope.

'Go on,' Jockey shouted. 'He's looking steady. Let him pick up a bit of pace.' Emma jogged and fed out handfuls of slack from the rope, all the while clicking her tongue in encouragement. The animal stirred and shook its head. A flock of birds flew from a tree as it broke into a gallop.

'That's it, sweetheart,' yelled Nash. 'Let him run if he wants.' The horse was going at a pelt and Nash craned his neck, gripping the fence, willing it to continue.

Its shoulders dipped and rolled as it cut around the field in wider and wider circles. Horse and handler brought defiance and grace to the wintry landscape. Then something shifted in the movement of the horse's withered flanks. Its head hung down and the rise and fall across its back became jagged. Emma carried on but the animal slowed and started to limp.

'Keep going,' shouted Jockey. 'Let's give him a chance.'

It went on for a few moments longer but, by now, the animal was snorting constantly. It limped with a sideways gait, straining away from the rope, frustrated with its failing body. It wanted to break free and run – to cover distance.

'Ah, fuck it,' shouted Jockey, slapping the fence. 'Bring him in. I've seen enough.'

'Aye,' sighed Nash, 'it's a shame, so it is.'

Emma brought the horse back, its tail agitating the air and its head flicking from side to side. She left it with Jockey and joined Nash at the fence. They were silent for a few moments, staring at the empty field. Snow was cast in pockets of blue and gold and the hills caught the soft, low sunlight. Winter had made a wraith of the land – the bare branches, the miserly blue sky, and the odd cawing crow to break the silence.

Eventually, she said, 'I got a letter from Strathclyde Council this morning.'

'I knew you had something to tell me.'

She brought it out and showed him. It was short but he read it a couple of times, rubbing his brow and sighing. He looked like he was about to say something then crumpled it and tossed it in a puddle.

He asked, 'What was he like, this fellow you met?'

'Pen-pusher. I knew he'd say no. I don't know what to do now.'

'You've done your best.'

They walked in stops and starts, following the crooked fence along the field's edge.

'There must be another way we can do this,' said Emma. 'There must be.'

Nash shook his head. 'I've told you everything I remember about it.'

'What about before?' she asked. 'Do you remember much from before it happened?'

'Bits and pieces. Moving around. Fairs. Villages. All different places. We must have covered a fair amount of mileage but it all blurs into one. I do remember the Dumfries Fair, though. That one stands out.'

'Something special about it?'

'It was the last fair we were at before my dad died. I must have been about seven. He'd taken my brothers down to the riverside where the Travellers did their horse-dealing. I was too young to go with them and got told to stay put at the campsite with my mum and Jenny. I wasn't too happy about that so I snuck out after dinner and went looking for them.

I went through the crowds at the town centre and found my way down to the riverside. That was quite a sight; men riding up and down the road with others running along behind them, cheering and slapping the horses. One laddie came riding, showing off, going too fast on a horse too big for him. He lost control. Went into the crowd and one man fell in the river. All along the street, there were men standing in wee groups. Dealing, you know. Getting business done. And whenever a deal was settled, one man would hold his hand right up in the air and then – smack!' Nash raised his hand and brought it down with a hard slap into the palm of the other. 'Anyway, there was no sign of dad so I carried on through the crowds, down to the end of the road, where there was another bunch of men. I pushed to the front and saw two lads. Stripped to the waist, very pale. One was slim, maybe about fifteen, sixteen. The other was older, with a bit more weight on him. Men were gathered around them, whispering and patting them. Then they moved back, opening a big ring around the lads – but one man stayed with them. He stood between them and reached out, touching their arms, like that...' He stretched his arms to the sides, recreating the scene playing out in his head. *'That's it lads*, he said to them. *Step in. Move in. That's it.* They circled around each other and the men were all shouting, *Go on, boys, move in boys, step in.* That's what I remember – those words; move in, step in. It was the older one who went first. I'll never forget the sound of the punch when it landed on the other lad's face. Not like you might think. Not a hard crack, but a sort of soft, slapping noise – *PAP*, like that. *PAP*.' Nash drove a fist into the cupped palm of his other hand. 'The crowd went mad, shouting their names and cheering, but the lads didn't seem keen to fight. They kept drifting apart but the referee would touch their arms to bring them back towards each other. *Go on boys*, he'd say. *Step in. That's it.* It was a funny thing; he was sort of gentle with them, you know, like he cared about them.'

Nash picked splinters from the fence and flicked at lumps of moss, as if this was helping him uncover the memory.

'It was the older, beefy lad who ran out of steam first. His shoulders were down and he was breathing heavy. But it went on. They could barely keep their arms up. Blood. Sweat. Dog-tired, the pair of them. But I could see it was the older one who didn't care about winning anymore. He just wanted to stop. That's when the referee stepped in and held up the younger lad's arm. Dad must've spotted me in the crowd. He came over and clamped his arm around me and pointed at them and said – *That'll be you one day. We're going to train you up. You'll fight and be a champion.*' He turned to Emma and asked what it was called when people went through an event, like a ritual.

'A rite of passage,' she answered.

'Aye, it was something boys were expected to do, but after seeing that I was scared, and I remember sending up a prayer or a wish – please, please, don't let me ever be in a fight.' He lit a cigarette. 'Dad died a few months later and then Jenny got taken. After that, my mum was so scared about something happening to me that she hardly even let me cross the street. So that was me off the hook. I got my wish. I never did have a fight.'

'How do you feel about fighting now?' asked Emma.

'It depends what sort of fight we're talking about. I'd be up for it if it was the right sort.'

* * *

It wasn't a fight Spence had to contend with that afternoon, but all week he'd been going about his preparation with something of a fighter's mindset. He'd been for a haircut and dug out a shirt and tie from the wardrobe. He'd got a book from the library on how to strike business deals and spent the morning memorising tips on using body language to project confidence and make people feel at ease – not that he felt he needed help, but he wanted to get this right.

'I hope everything was in order,' he said to the lad across the table. He had Spence's loan application in front of him.

'Eh, yeah,' said the lad. 'You completed everything we

needed. No worries there, Mr Lacklow.'

'Good. So it's all there? Everything you need?' This was called the "positivity loop", a conversational technique from the business handbook. It involved asking questions to elicit positive responses from the decision maker, then repeating their answers back to them.

'Sure,' said the lad. 'We got all we needed to make a decision.' He closed the application and moved it to the side. 'You sell carpets, is that right, Mr Lacklow?'

'I've been at it since I was a boy. My dad sold carpets. And his father before him.' This was another tip from the book – share a personal story to make the decision maker feel invested in you. If they feel like your friend, they're more likely to say yes.

'And you're looking for premises?'

'I started off selling from the back of a cart, then graduated to a van and that's been how I've sold carpet for the last 25 years.' He chuckled and added, 'I reckon it's about time to move up a league.'

'Whereabouts have you got in mind?'

'I'm still looking at options.'

It was a tiny office, with barely room for the table and chairs. Next to his skinny leather tie, the lad wore a badge with a cartoon graphic of a fat rocket taking off and the name of the support scheme – Britain's Business Booster.

'Have you always worked for yourself, Mr Lacklow?'

'You might say I'm a born entrepreneur. I like to think that it's in the blood.'

'And the reference you included from...' He checked the application. 'From Archibald Matthews; what's your relationship?'

'He's a business partner.'

'But you said in your application that you're a sole trader.'

'I don't mean he's my partner, like, in an official way. We just help each other out here and there.'

'We needed a reference from an employer or customer.'

'Well Archie's sort of both, I'd say. We've done business over the years. He's scratched my back, I've scratched his.'

'But the application is just for you, as a sole trader?'

'Absolutely. 100 per cent.'

After a pause, the lad clasped his hands and leaned forward, as if going into prayer. 'Unfortunately, your application hasn't been successful.'

Spence felt the weight of his body on the chair. He rubbed his calloused hands and sighed. 'How? What was wrong with it?' He pulled the application back to the middle of the table.

The lad paused as if to plead – *do I really have to say it?* 'Mr Lacklow, you have a criminal record.'

'But that was over twenty years ago. I got a suspended sentence.'

'A criminal record's a criminal record.'

'Look, I could give you chapter and verse about what happened but you'd be here all day. The bottom line is – that conviction wasn't fair. It was my partner's fault.'

'Your partner?' The lad raised his eyebrows. 'Mr Matthews? Your reference?'

'No, not Archie. My partner before him. We weren't together long. I can't even remember his name to be honest with you. He got hold of some radios. I didn't know they were stolen. I don't think he knew either.' Spence knitted his fingers and tapped his thumbs together. 'That was a hard lesson in due diligence.'

The lad shrugged. 'We need to carry out checks. Having a criminal record disqualifies applicants.'

'Everyone's got a past, mate.'

'I'm sorry.'

'Come on. Twenty years ago. Were you even born?'

'They're not my rules.'

'I keep records religiously these days. Everything's goods-receipted. I could show you.'

'There's nothing I can do,' said the lad.

'But I saw this on the news.' Spence picked up the application and waved it at him. 'Look, son, the government wants to help people like me. I'm ideal for this. Please.'

The lad slumped back and looked towards the window as

if he wanted to be out there, with the birds on the snowy rooftops. He turned back. 'Look, you seem like a decent man and everything, but it's not my decision. Those are the rules. It excludes anyone with a criminal record. It doesn't matter how old it is.'

Spence opened the application and scanned it as if he might find some detail that would reverse the decision.

Afterwards, he went to the bathroom and stood looking at himself in the mirror. He took off his tie and leaned on the sink, letting his head hang down. He looked again and reminded himself he was still his own man. But the longer he stared, the more he had to pretend to be looking at himself with pride.

12

It was a new one on Peter Franks, and that was always welcome to a hack who'd been at it for as long as him. He tucked the phone into his neck and flicked open his notepad. 'Uhu, okay,' he said through a mouthful of sandwich. 'How long's he got left? Less than a year.' He scratched his chin and considered what Emma was telling him, condensing all the elements into an imagined headline. 'And the council won't lift a finger?'

'No,' said Emma. 'They said it was too long ago and they can't justify the resources. Very little chance of finding anything – blah blah blah.'

Franks switched the phone to his other ear and cocked his head at his notes – dying man, long-lost sister, authorities won't lift a finger. 'It's got potential,' he said.

The last story he'd covered on Travellers was when a local campsite had been granted funding to build a toilet block and refuse area. The nearby residents had been complaining for years that it was a public health hazard and bringing down the value of their houses. So the council came up with £50,000 for an upgrade and the next thing was that the same people who'd been complaining were up in arms about the outrageous waste of taxpayers' money, and how the new site was going to be like a Butlin's holiday camp for the lazy gypos who lived there. Of course, it was Franks who'd told them about the costs and suggested the line about it being like a holiday camp. That was a nice touch, he thought. It really got their blood up and their tongues flapping. He'd long since given up caring about ethics in his line of work. Still, there was something about Emma's story that captured his attention and stirred up memories of why he'd wanted to be a journalist in the first place. As they said in the trade, her story had human interest.

'You know what else?' said Emma. 'I think the official I dealt with was prejudiced.'

'What did he say?'

'Nothing. I just got a feeling.'

'I'd need more than a hunch to put something like that in print.'

'Okay, fair enough. So what do you think?'

Franks asked about Nash; how long he'd lived in East Lothian, what he did before he got sick, and what sort of man he was. 'Proud,' said Emma. 'He's very proud.' Franks scribbled notes and wondered if he could sell it to one of the nationals.

'Ach, I'm not sure,' he finally said.

'Why?'

'It's about Travellers and it's a long time ago. No offence, but our readers won't care.'

'Fine, maybe I'll call one of the Glasgow newspapers. I really need to get this out into the world.'

'Hang on a minute.' He checked his diary for the next day. There was a death knock scheduled for the afternoon. He hated death knocks. He was at a point in his career when he could do without distraught relatives of the deceased lunging at him. Sometimes the neighbours came out too and joined in. He'd been spat at and shoved up against walls and told he was the lowest of the low. Yes, he decided, he'd give the death knock to the cub reporter – let the ambitious little shit earn his stripes the hard way.

'I tell you what,' he said. 'Don't call anyone else. Let me speak to him. Would he be available tomorrow afternoon?'

Franks arrived with a photographer the following day and got straight down to business. 'Would you say you've been unfairly treated, Mr Lacklow?'

'In what way?'

'By the authorities.'

Nash cast a furtive glance around the room then leaned towards him. He lowered his voice. 'They're not going to turf me out of this place, are they? If I go on record about what I really think and you print it, they can't put me out on the street?'

Franks shook his head. 'That would be a hell of a story, but there's no chance of that. It's not even the same local authority.'

'Aye, but they're all the same though,' said Nash.

Emma patted his shoulder. 'That would be against your human rights. They can't do that.'

'That's right,' said Franks. 'Freedom of speech. You can say whatever you want. Please, don't hold back.'

Nash gathered up his thoughts. 'It doesn't seem to me like too much to ask. I just want them to have a look in their filing cabinets. I mean, I've never worked in an office, but – a big organisation like that, with a lot of staff – it can't be too much of a stretch. The woman at Carluke told us Strathclyde Council took their files away – centralisation, she called it.'

'Were you surprised that they refused to help, Mr Lacklow?'

'Like I say, I thought they'd at least have a look. But they said we've not given them enough information. What information are they expecting us to have, for God's sake? They never told us a damn thing when they took her. According to what Em's told me, they never bothered keeping records back then.'

'The Adoption Act,' said Emma. 'They took her the year before it was introduced.'

Franks chewed his pencil and frowned at his notes like there was an offensive drawing there. 'So why bother?' he asked.

'There's still a chance,' said Emma. 'There might be records. That's the point. We won't know until they look. Before the Act it was up to agencies whether to bother with paperwork. Some did and some didn't.'

'Still, though,' said Franks, 'I wouldn't lay any bets.'

'And here's the thing that really bothers me,' said Nash. 'The man Em spoke to acted like she was making the whole thing up. She went all the way to Glasgow to get fobbed off. She's found an eyewitness and newspaper stories, for Christ's sake. We've got proof. What more do they want?'

'Sounds like they're stonewalling,' muttered Franks. 'Do you think their refusal to help might be down to prejudice, on account of your Traveller background?'

'They've gone into arse-covering mode, is what I think,' said Nash.

81

Franks laughed. 'I won't quote you directly on that.'

'You can quote me how you like. They're scared. Why would they want to help? None of this shows them in a good light, does it?'

Franks asked how common it was for Traveller kids to be taken from their families.

'You speak to any old Traveller and they'll tell you. They knew. It was drummed into them from a young age. Keep clear of the *gaj*, their parents would say. Don't talk to anyone. Don't tell them your business. Your name. Your age. Don't say anything about yourself or your family. Imagine living with that fear, that any moment you could be taken away. It was your worst nightmare. Family means everything to Travellers. Whatever they have in the world is built on it.'

Franks chewed his pencil. 'Did you say *gaj*?'

'Aye, *gaj*. It's what Travellers call outsiders – non-Travellers. But what that means to me is a man in a suit or a badge, you know. Someone with authority.'

'They weren't to be trusted?' asked Franks.

'More than that.'

'They were a danger?'

'Of course. Don't get me wrong. I'm a fair-minded man and I've tried giving them a chance. During the war I got called up, put on a uniform and got sent down to England. I was ready to do my bit for the country, like we were asked. But the problem was that it had got around my unit that I was a Traveller and every day I was being called a filthy pikey or dirty tinker or thieving gypo. If anything went missing, I got blamed. It was dog's abuse. All that was to be expected, but there was incompetence at the top. Lack of equipment. We were given rifles from World War One. World War One! Training exercises were going wrong. I wasn't about to put my life in the hands of those idiots. Suits, uniforms, badges, medals – whatever. You just can't trust them.'

Emma shared the information she'd gathered from Nell Andrews and the National Library.

'She's been doing all the legwork,' said Nash proudly.

Franks closed his notepad and slipped it back into his jacket. 'What would you say to your sister if you were reunited?'

Nash thought about this for a long moment. 'It wouldn't be about what we said. The important thing would be that we did it; beat the system, beat the odds, beat the bastards that took her away and wouldn't tell us a thing.'

The story was published the following week and looked not out of place next to news of sky-rocketing unemployment and miners' strikes.

East Lothian Reporter
21st February 1984
Dying Man Takes on Establishment in
Battle for Truth over Long-lost Sister
By Peter Franks

Terminally ill Nash Lacklow wants to trace his little sister after she was taken by the authorities fifty years ago, but stubborn officials at Strathclyde Council have refused to help, saying there isn't enough evidence. Doctors have given Mr Lacklow a year to live but the plucky patient is determined to use what time he has left to uncover the truth. He's demanding to know what the authorities in Carluke did with his sister after she was removed from his family in 1929. The sixty-four year old Musselburgh man is from a gypsy-traveller background and believes authorities took his sister due to prejudice and as part of efforts to deter travellers from the area. Assisting Mr Lacklow is his great niece, Miss Emma Lacklow, nineteen, a student at Edinburgh University, who believes officials at Strathclyde Council may be deliberately suppressing records for fear of similar cases being uncovered.

In the accompanying photo, Nash held his sister's one-legged doll. He sat bolt upright, without a breathing mask or oxygen cylinder in sight, his hair immaculately Brylcreemed and jaw grimly clenched.

Calls started coming in to Franks a week later. There was a man who'd been taken into care in the sixties. His family's tent had caught fire and he and his siblings were taken to hospital with smoke inhalation. The man's youngest brother died and the authorities removed the rest of the children. Another call came from a woman who'd spent a long time in care in the fifties. By the time she got out and retraced her family, her parents were dead. Franks was very sorry for their troubles but was just a local journalist and had given up aspirations to win a Pulitzer Prize a long time ago.

* * *

A group of golfers were teeing off, chatting and joking in spotless beige trousers and diamond pattern jumpers. Spence sat in the van, watching them. He'd always thought of the game as the preserve of toffs, but in the past few years he'd found out there were people who lived on his street who had memberships – a plumber and electrician who'd done well for themselves and could come and rub shoulders with doctors and lawyers – or that was how Spence imagined it at least. Maybe this was what Emma meant when she talked about the curse of upward mobility. Apparently, having a successful business and making money wasn't enough anymore. You had to want to move from one class into another; abandon your roots, develop more sophisticated interests and move in higher social circles. The house and street where you lived, your kids' school, the supermarket where you did your shopping, those weren't good enough anymore. You had to want to move up.

There was an old tweed jacket he kept in the van for situations like this, when hawking occasionally took him into more stratified social settings. He put it on, ran a comb through his hair and went into the clubhouse.

Well-turned out men gathered in twos and threes at the bar and around the tables, in jovial conversation. He told the barman he was interested in becoming a member and asked if the manager was around. There was no point in admitting to being a cold caller. A few minutes later, a stout man in his sixties appeared, all florid cheeks and vowels jumbling around in his mouth. He wore a three-piece suit with a silk handkerchief in his breast pocket – not pressed and folded like the military types, but messily arranged so it puffed out like a flower. Spence stepped forward to shake hands and wasn't surprised to catch the whisky whiff off the man's breath. Good, he thought. A posh drinker.

The manager showed him around – the bar, the cosy lounge and the dining room. Upstairs, there was a large function room. Spence took mental note of the square footage.

The manager asked about his line of work.

'Carpet sales. It's a family business.'

'Ah, really? We're getting ready to redecorate this place. Fresh lick of paint and a new carpet. Needs it badly.' This, Spence knew already from a neighbour.

'How old did you say the club was?'

'We go back over a hundred years.'

'That's something special,' said Spence. 'You should be proud.'

'We are indeed.'

'I don't know what you've got in mind for the carpet, but I'd recommend something traditional. Some people might tell you to move with the times – modernise. But not me. Go with tartan. Trust me, the Americans will love it.'

The manager stopped and looked at him afresh. 'That's right. Americans. We're getting more Americans coming over. They play all the courses along the East Coast. The money they spend – you wouldn't give it credence.'

'Well, they come all that way for a game of golf, afterwards they want to sit down for a drink somewhere that feels authentic.'

'Authentic, but not too authentic, if you understand me.' The manager tapped the side of his nose. 'We have a budget.'

Spence fiddled with his cuff. 'I don't mean to be forward, but I could speak to my suppliers. I guarantee you wouldn't get a better price from anyone else.'

He bated his breath, waiting for the manager's eyes to narrow and scan him more closely but they only brightened.

'The important thing is, we don't want to be closed for too long. How quick would you be?'

'In and out in two days. You'd barely even notice us.'

Back in the van, he scribbled figures on a scrap of paper, working out how much carpet he'd need. He visited his wholesaler and haggled them down on price. Next day, he phoned the manager with his quote and was offered the job. It was going to be the most money he'd ever made in one go. What he didn't have was the logistical capability or money to buy industrial quantities of carpet – but he'd work on that.

Later, Archie stared at him, incredulous. 'The golf club. That's huge. Spence, how did you find out about it?'

'I've got connections.'

'You must have priced it keen, am I right?'

'Is my pricing ever anything else?'

'And they'll want the job done quick-smart, to cut down on disruption to business.'

Spence feigned ignorance. 'Two days. That's what I told them. Two days. That's what they were happy with.'

'Let me get this straight. All you want from me is a bit of lifting and laying? Is that what we've come to?'

'Don't be like that. I'd give you a decent share.'

'Ten years working together, Spence. Ten years.'

'If it had been your mark would you be acting any different?'

'I have to hand it to you,' said Archie, 'that's the job of a lifetime. What's the square footage?'

'The square footage is all taken care of. All I need you to do is help with the practicalities.'

'I'm not just a dogsbody, you know.'

'You're no prime cut, either.'

'I see the way you've set this thing up. You've brought me in late on purpose so you can take the lion's share.' Archie came closer, scrutinising him with a hard stare. 'I wasn't born yesterday. You need me on this.'

'I don't, actually. Emma's got two friends from university looking for weekend work – a pair of strapping lads.' This was a lie, of course, but it had the desired effect.

Archie fidgeted with his cigarettes. 'Tell me this – how'd you get the money for all that carpet? Because there's no danger the wholesalers would give you credit, not for that amount.'

'All you need to know is that I'm sick of playing in the small leagues.'

* * *

They arrived at the clubhouse the following Monday and took an hour just to unload the van. They heaved roll after roll of underlay onto their shoulders and became pink and breathless carrying them across the carpark. Spence checked his drawings. If his calculations were right, there would be very little wastage. His plan was based on achieving maximum efficiency.

They worked through lunch, getting the underlay down, then drove back to the wholesalers and loaded the van with carpet. Knees unfit to grace rugby fields trembled under the weight, and Archie's face took on the hue of raw mince.

By evening, they weren't halfway finished and Spence's panic had given way to a foul mood. 'Jesus,' he gasped, 'I've put years on my back today. I'll be an inch shorter after this. I'm needing to get another two decades out of my body.' He was on his hands and knees, fitting carpet around a fireplace. Intricate work, with a knife, ruler and piece of chalk.

'You couldn't have roped in Emma?' asked Archie.

'To help?'

'Aye.'

'Her ladyship'll be busy breaking sweat over a pile of books.'

'How's she getting on?'

'You should hear some of the nonsense she comes out with. I had an argument with her the other night about her wanting to go to a party in a warehouse in Leith.'

'No danger,' said Archie. 'Don't let her go anywhere near Leith.'

'It was in a squat run by art students.'

'A squat?'

'My thoughts, exactly. I said to her, that's fine, Emma, you can go to the party but I'll tell you what – I'll be driving you there and I'll be waiting outside and you'll be coming home at 10.30. You should have seen her face. She turns around and puts her hands on her hips and says to me – *This is just another example of patriarchal repression.*'

'What the hell is that when it's at home?'

'God knows, but I said to her – the only thing this is an example of is your dad wanting to keep you safe. She forgets, I was young once. I know what it's like at parties. I know what goes on.' Spence's hair was sweat-matted and beads of it tickled his cheeks as he cut along the carpet. He threw down the knife, got up and rubbed his back. 'Patriarchal repression. Look at me! On my knees, breaking my back, trying to make a living. Patriarchal fucking repression. Am I being unfair, Archie?'

Archie seemed exhausted by the onslaught of parental frustration and fished out his bag of tobacco. 'The last thing you want is some druggie laddie getting her up the duff when she's only just started university. Keep the horny little bastards at bay for as long as you can.' He laughed and grimaced slightly, then coughed and smacked his chest as if to dislodge something. He walked to the window and plonked down on a roll of carpet. Dusk was settling over the golf course, turning the fairways a cool purple.

Spence returned to cutting the carpet. 'Well, it's funny you mention that because I don't think I need to worry about boys. She's not interested – if you know what I'm saying.' He took a breath then went over the details of the morning he found the photo-strip of her and Kate. 'I've never mentioned it to her, of course. I just tucked it back inside the book and left it where I found it. Not that I'm nervous about saying something. It's just a lot to take in. Especially right now. On top of everything else. If this is the way she wants to live her life – fine. I'm not going to stop her. But has she thought about what this means for me as I get older? My wife's gone, and now I'm looking at an old age without grandkids. A proud family name dying out. I don't know if I should say something or wait for her to bring it up. And what do I say? How am I meant to act? Her bloody mother should be here to deal with this. This sort of thing, it's her department, not mine.'

He finished cutting, sat up, then began chalking the next section of carpet. Having something practical to focus on helped him get his thoughts in order and put them into words. 'The funny thing is, I was always scared of her getting to an age where she'd bring boys to the house; some spotty wee shite at the door asking to take her out for a ride in his car – or on his motorbike, God forbid. I knew there'd be arguments because I knew how I'd act towards them. But there wouldn't have been any other way because I'm her dad. The boys would be wanting to take her to the pictures or to parties. And I'd be having to shake their hands, look the scruffy bastards up and down, and warn them to have her back by eleven. They'd nod and say yes sir and not to worry and that they'd take care of her, but I'd see the look in their eyes. That smirk on their lips, and I'd know what they were really thinking because I've been that age myself. I know what I was like. I know what we were all like. She's spared me all of that.'

Archie hadn't said a word the whole time and Spence assumed he was just giving him space to get everything off his chest. He got to his feet and turned around. 'So what do you think? Should I speak to her or just wait?' There was no response. 'Archie, are you listening?' Still no response. He took a few steps towards him. Perhaps Archie was just fed up listening to him? But he remained unresponsive as Spence shouted again and there was a pronounced heaviness to the slump of his head and shoulders. Approaching at a wide angle, he walked up behind him and saw a string of drool hanging from Archie's mouth. The frozen, downward stare held Spence's attention for a long moment. Eventually, he worked up courage to give the lifeless lump a poke. 'Archie?'

13

There are people behind every decision and action. People with power or influence, putting plans into action and affecting lives. It was listening to Nash talk continually about 'the Social' as if it was some mindless machine – a depersonalised system of the state – that made Emma curious about the men who took Jenny Lacklow. So far, she had one name – Dr Robert Banks, the public health official quoted in the article from the *Lanark Gazette*.

She'd since looked him up and discovered he was an eminent public health physician noted for his part in plans for the demolition of Glasgow slums in the early 1900s. She'd also found an article he'd written for a medical journal on eugenics, the school of thought that society could be improved by preventing those deemed to have undesirable characteristics from reproducing. It led to experiments in forced sterilisation of the mentally ill and persistent criminals. The Nazis took an interest, too, as a way to rid themselves of unwanted ethnic groups and achieve a pure Aryan race.

Emma pushed through the heavy double doors of Carluke Town Hall and approached the desk.

'Back again,' said the receptionist.

She thought of Spence, and what he said about hawking – always project confidence. If you don't believe in yourself no-one else will. She flashed a smile and her student badge, and said she was carrying out research on the history of Carluke. 'Between the world wars. 1920s and 30s. It's a fascinating period – so much upheaval for families. I'd love to see records of meetings from then.'

The receptionist took her into the council chamber behind the desk, where there was a long mahogany table, slick with polish and surrounded by sturdy, leather-backed chairs. The atmosphere was starched and dried-out, and orange tinted plastic hung on the inside of the windows. 'Stops sun damage,' said the receptionist. Black and white portraits lined the walls;

memories suspended in the undisturbed air.

'It's nice to have someone take an interest,' beamed the receptionist.

More than you know, thought Emma.

Inside a cupboard in the corner were shelves lined with folders. The receptionist ran her hand across the neat rows. 'Every set of minutes from every council meeting. They're labelled by year, from the sixties back to 1800 and whatever. You won't have any bother.'

'Why weren't these centralised?' asked Emma.

'We had to hang on to something. This is our history. I like reading them if it's a quiet day. It's nice to look back and see what was going on years ago.'

'It certainly is.'

The receptionist went back to her desk and it took only a few minutes for Emma to find the period in question. In minutes from March 1930 she found agenda item 76.15 – Public Health Response to Vagrants and Tinkers. It detailed how the councillors agreed to the permanent closure of the Whiteshaw campsite and to sell the land to a commercial developer. She checked back through previous minutes, looking for references to standing order 76.15. Eventually, she found its original entry.

Carluke Town Council meeting, 20 January, 1925.
Agenda Item 76.15: Public Health Response to Vagrants and Tinkers.

Chairman: *As you know, we've had an increasing number of complaints about tinkers coming to the area in the last few years. I know that many of our elected members have had constituents writing to them with concerns and I fear we've arrived at a point where we can't ignore the issue any longer. It's only fair to acknowledge that most of the tinkers are looking for work, but they come with a lot of mouths to feed – and we can't favour them over our own decent citizens – and we certainly can't give them jobs if there are no jobs to* *give. We've had reports of them scavenging rubbish, occupying land, and leaving a mess behind after they leave. We've got business owners and property owners worried about theft. They're rightly concerned about undesirables and, gentlemen, they look to us to do something about it.*

Secretary: *Mr Chairman, I'd go further. If I may speak frankly?*

Chairman: *Please.*

Secretary: *There's a feeling among constituents that this is an invasion, getting worse by the year. If we make ourselves accommodating, where's it going to lead? Other regions are doing something about the tinker problem, so we don't want to be seen as a soft touch.*

Chairman: *Not on my watch.*

Secretary: *If we don't act, we'll end up swarmed with them. We've already got residents in some towns who feel under siege – in their own homes. If I might be bold, tinkers need to be not just deterred – they need to be vanquished. This calls for more than light measures.*

Chairman: *I thank Mr Secretary for his comments. His concerns are noted and, I think, shared by us all. If I may now invite the view of our public health officer, Dr Banks.*

Dr Robert Banks: *Thank you, Chair. You'll not be surprised that my chief concern is for public health. Tinker sites are unhygienic – and what does a tinker do but travel? They go from region to region, from town to village – and they spread their muck and waste and, ultimately, this is what creates disease. Their campsites are nests of filth – and we must eradicate them. The question is – how? Mass evictions create considerable public order challenges for the* *police and clog up the courts. However, there is another solution. I have been in contact with public health officials in other regions and, certainly, one option that tends to have the desired effect is the removal of their children. The justification in law would be public health and child welfare. There is of course a moral consideration – the sanctity of the family. But we must ask ourselves what prospects a tinker child has in an environment of such poverty and degeneracy – compared to the prospects if a child is taken into care or adopted, and educated to become a proper member of society. Gentlemen, I have weighed the matter up and feel confident in saying that, not only is it the right thing to do, it is the Christian thing to do.*

The motion was carried and the council instructed the Town Clerk that measures be taken under the Public Health Act to disperse and deter Travellers from the area. Emma was still reading when the receptionist appeared behind her.

'Anything useful?'

'Some interesting discussions,' she said.

'If you're looking to put faces to names, the twenties and thirties are up here.' The receptionist pointed to a wall crammed with group photos of successive councils. Rows of unsmiling men in suits. Another wall was lined with individual portraits of office-bearers and senior officials.

'It's like a museum,' said Emma.

The receptionist blushed. 'Keeps me out of mischief.'

The portraits were arranged in chronological order. Emma scanned the labels and stopped at one. It was a head and shoulders portrait of a man in his fifties; side-parted hair, neatly slicked back, chin up and with a middle-distance stare – the stuff of empires. Dr Robert Banks was halfway handsome but had a thin, slightly squint mouth, like a worm writhing across his face. It was impossible to know if he was smiling or not.

Before she knew what she was doing, she had the portrait down off the wall and felt the weight of its dense frame in her hands.

'Careful with that,' said the receptionist, taking a step forward.

'How much do you want for it?' The question surprised Emma as much as it surprised the receptionist. It wasn't just that the man's image didn't deserve to be held in any form of esteem, she wanted to own it, to have the power to throw it away, destroy it, or put it in a jumble sale so it would end up somewhere unknown and unpredictable, just like what happened to Jenny Lacklow.

The receptionist's puzzled eyes flicked across her face. 'You're asking to buy it?'

Emma nodded. 'Yeah. How much?'

'What are you talking about?'

'Money. How much do you want for it?'

'Nothing. I mean, you can't. It's not for sale.'

'But can't we work something out?'

'Work something out? This is part of our records – our history. It's important. I'm not going to sell it to you.'

If she couldn't own it at least she could reduce his memory, his elevated status, to this tawdry little transaction. Spence came to mind again. Project confidence. 'Look, I'm a collector of old history. I won't bore you but I've got a personal interest and I'm doing a project. I mean, this guy...' she tapped the portrait's glass covering, 'he wasn't like the mayor or anything that important. Would anyone really notice if he disappeared?'

The receptionist took the portrait from her and hung it back on the wall. 'You need to leave – now. Or I'll call the police.'

* * *

The phone rang a few minutes after she got home. Emma picked it up, half expecting it to be some official from Carluke, calling about the earlier incident. But it was a rough voice, high-pitched and urgent.

The man said, 'You only get one chance with Mikey Thomson.'

'Sorry?'

A pause then he said, 'You only get one chance.'

'Who's this?'

'I'm a warning.'

'Mikey Thomson? Is that your name?'

'I said you only get one chance with Mikey.'

'Who's Mikey?'

'I'm sending a warning from him.'

'I think you've got the wrong number, mate.'

She was about to hang up when the man said, 'Spence Lacklow?'

'That's my dad. Who is this?'

'Tell your dad he's late. He only gets one chance with Mikey.' Then the line went dead.

When Spence got back she told him about the call and he explained that, because of Archie dying, there was a delay in getting paid for the job at the golf club. Things had become complicated. There were issues about liability and insurance. The coroner's office was involved, and the club's lawyers. Then he told her that he'd got a loan to pay for all the carpet.

'From the bank?' she said.

'No, a company.'

'What sort?'

'A proper one. A loan company. They've got an office. Not a big one, but – still – an office.'

'Who are they?'

'I don't know. Just a couple of guys. Entrepreneurs, like me.'

'Ah, Jesus.'

Jabbing a finger slow and hard into his chest, he raised his voice and said, 'The government wants more people like me. We're good for the economy.'

14

The people at the table behind Emma were in a hushed yet heated conversation. It was a man and a woman – Emma assumed they were married – speaking to the man's mother. It became apparent she had racked up a lot of debt because of a relationship with some man. 'He's a fucking scumbag,' hissed the son, over and over. Emma liked to do this – eavesdrop on other people, and this here was a belter. She wondered what their lives were like and how they got to this point in time, with this particular problem – and why talk about it in a cafe? 'He's sucked you dry,' the man continued. 'Dad would be turning in his grave.' There was no response from his mum as far as Emma could hear. She went up to the counter to order another coffee and looked back towards the table. The old woman was wispy and vacant-eyed, sipping tea and seemingly oblivious to her son's rage.

Emma was a little disappointed when they got up to leave just as she came back to the table. She watched the brutishly thick back and neck of the angry son as he stomped to the door. He scowled at the floor yet still held the door open for his mum and wife. As they left, a woman came in. She was in her thirties and wore a long, patterned skirt with lots of bracelets and necklaces. Emma waved and the woman hurried across the room and hugged her.

Her name was Maria. She was fair-haired and spoke with a Midlands accent, though Emma couldn't pin it to a particular region. There was no trace of Lacklow family resemblance in her pale skin and pinched features. She had with her a copy of Nash's newspaper interview. She brandished it proudly then put it on the table.

'I'm so glad the journalist got in touch with you,' she said. 'When I saw this, I knew. I just knew. It sounded exactly like everything mum told me about her life. That's what I told the man at the newspaper, and I said – promise me. Promise me, you'll pass on my message.'

'Where is your mum?' asked Emma. 'Can I meet her?'

Maria looked out the window. Fat ribbons of condensation ran down the glass, distorting the view of the street. 'She died a few years ago.' She turned back, reaching across the table to clasp Emma's hand. 'It's good to meet you, though. We're family. We've got the same blood.'

Emma asked if her mum ever talked about being taken by the authorities. Could she remember much about it? Maria said it was just like what Nash told the journalist but offered no further detail.

'Don't take this the wrong way,' said Emma, 'but how can you be sure? I mean, that we're your mum's family?'

Maria leaned in and lowered her voice. 'I've got proof. Letters that my mum kept.'

'Letters?'

'Yeah. I've had them for years.'

'God, that's amazing. I've been trying to find something concrete for months. It's been such a struggle.'

'Well, I've got what you're looking for.'

Emma sat back and smiled. 'Those letters will mean a lot to Nash. Can I see them?'

'I don't have them with me.'

'What's in them?'

'Proof,' said Maria, her eyes glinting. 'Exactly the proof you need.'

Emma leaned in, earnest and urgent. 'She had a good life, did she? I mean, ups and downs, sure – but overall, did she have a good life? A happy one?'

'She did.'

'He'll be so relieved to know that. It'll be a comfort.'

They drank coffee and chatted. Maria's own life sounded chaotic but she said her mum had been a stabilising influence, and that after she died Maria drifted around the country, staying at campsites and squats. 'The place I'm living now isn't far from here,' she said.

They finished their drinks, got into Emma's car and headed out of town. They drove for half an hour into the countryside, through farmland and forest, and the air turned cool and still. The horizon was a mess of thuggish clouds, threatening a gothic downpour. They turned off the road and came to a farmyard with a row of cottages and a half-moon of caravans and campers outside. A dog on a rope barked as they went into one of the cottages. Two women and two men huddled on the sofa of a living room hovel. They smoked and chatted in the stench of incense, hash and coffee. They looked up and grunted as Maria entered. There were no enquiries about who Emma might be.

On the walls, posters overlapped and peeled off at the corners – Ban the Bomb, the movie *Easy Rider*, and Chairman Mao. Maria brewed herbal tea and brought out a box of photos. At the kitchen table, she showed Emma pictures of her at music festivals and campsites over the years.

'I've always travelled,' she said. 'It's in my blood. I belong on the road.'

'What about the letters?' said Emma. 'Can you show me, please?'

'I don't have them right now.'

Emma blinked and took a breath. 'But I thought you did. That's why I came.'

'I did have them.' Maria rubbed her head, pressing heavily into her furrowed brow. Her skin went a yellowish white then red as she removed her fingers to fidget with the pile of photos. 'I thought I did. But I forgot, they're somewhere else. I mean, they're still mine. I own them but someone else has them. I'll try to get in touch with him. The problem is, I don't have a lot of money right now.' She sounded as if she might cry.

Somewhere, Emma felt pity but not enough to temper her response. 'Waste of my time.' She got up and put her cup in the sink.

'I'm not trying to mess you about or anything. It's not me. It's him – my ex. Fucking nightmare. He has the letters. He moved out and took a lot of my stuff. He's trying to get money from me any time I need something. But I want to help you, I swear.'

Maria went out of the room with the box of photos and Emma remarked to her house-mates that she had an interesting accent. 'Does anyone know where she's from?'

'Lincoln,' said one of the women.

'No, no, no,' said one of the men, a long, hollow-faced fellow in a woolly hat. 'I took her under my wing in the sixties. She thinks her mum was from Lincoln, but her dad was from Sheffield. She never knew much of either of them. Lost soul, that one.' He turned to Emma. 'Was she showing you her photos?'

Emma nodded.

'Aye,' he said, 'she always does that.'

15

It was the loneliest week of his life going back to finish the job at the golf club. It spooked him being back in the room where it happened, and he tried to avoid the spot near the window where Archie suffered a massive heart attack while he'd been too busy spilling his guts about Emma to notice anything was wrong. After all the delay and impact on business, there were grumblings from the golf club manager about breach of contract but it now looked like he would be paid – a couple of months late.

He was still coming to his and Archie's meeting spot at the back of the supermarket carpark. He was there today, having lunch and listening to the radio. He poked around inside a bag of salt and vinegar crisps, gathering up the dregs then sucking his fingers clean. He tipped the last crumbs into his mouth and wiped his hands on his trousers.

A brown car with its stereo blasting pulled into the space next to him. He looked across, half expecting to see Archie but it was two men. He felt a tug of sadness. Despite all their years meeting in this spot, Spence still wasn't sure if their partnership had done much to benefit either of them. But they'd never had a real falling out either and that had to count for something.

He realised he was still staring at the car and that the man in the passenger seat was staring back, really fixing him with a hardman glower. Spence turned away and caught his reflection in the rear-view mirror. He was doing that tight pursing of the lips he always did when he was tense. He hated to see his face like that. He never realised he was doing it until he caught sight of his reflection. God forbid he did it in front of customers. It could kill a sale stone dead. He rubbed his face and stretched his jaw, trying to relax the muscles. The inside of the van was a mess. He'd let it build up again; dried tissues, faded parking tickets, crisp packets, Styrofoam cups. He stuffed it all into a bag and opened the door to go to the bin. As he was getting out, the car passenger got out too and grabbed him by the collar. 'Mikey wants his fuckin money,' he screamed, all bad breath and spittle.

'I don't have it yet,' shouted Spence. 'They've not paid me yet. My partner died but I'll get it. I promise, I'll get it.'

'Fuckin liar,' the man shouted, and punched Spence in the stomach.

He then pushed him back against the van door and head-butted him. Spence's head smacked against the frame and his knees gave way. The man pulled him up again, gripping his collar and choking him. The man let go, punching him again and again in the side of the head as Spence collapsed sideways into his van.

'We're no wantin excuses. Give Mikey his money.'

'All right,' gasped Spence. 'It's coming. On my life, I'll get it.'

Still, the punches came down, on the back of his head and back of his neck. He tried to protect himself by wedging his head and shoulders farther into the van's footwell. He wanted to curl up completely and cocoon his whole body into that small space. The man then slammed the door on him as if to force him on his way. 'The next time we'll break yer fuckin legs,' he shouted. 'Pay what ye owe, scumbag.'

They drove away, leaving Spence with his face pressed against the pedals, panting and breathing dust and grime off the van's floor.

* * *

Late afternoon and Nash was all creased brow and muttering lips, scribbling, revising words – and didn't notice they had arrived. 'Ladies and gentlemen, I want to tell you about a terrible injustice that happened to my family...a terrible injustice that befell my family.' He turned to Emma. 'Is that right? Befell? Would you say something befell you?'

'You don't need to give yourself airs and graces. Just be yourself.'

'I'm asking you – is befell the right word?'

'Sure, you could say it.'

'But would it be befell on my family or just befell my family?'

'Just befell.'

'Because I want to strike the right tone, you know.'

'I can see.'

'And should I say ladies and gentlemen or boys and girls? How old are they?'

'Look, it's not the Oxford Debating Society,' said Emma. 'Call them whatever you want but we need to go.'

Kate was waiting at the door. She came towards them, waving and tapping her watch. 'Everything all right, Mr Lacklow? It's starting in a minute.'

'Have I got time for a quick smoke to calm the nerves?'

'No,' Emma and Kate said in unison.

He got out and looked up at the building. The late afternoon sun reflected off three storeys of elegant windows. A row of small, fat pillars ran along the roof's edge but down at street level the sandstone was grimy and the entrance plastered with posters for gigs and protests. 'I never imagined I'd be speaking at a university,' he said. 'I wouldn't know an A level or an O level if it came up and bit me on the arse.'

Inside, he stopped at a poster for that evening's meeting. His face hardened and he turned to Emma and Kate. 'I'm not looking for anybody's sympathy.'

'What's the matter?' asked Emma.

'Society for Solidarity with Oppressed and Marginalised People?'

'That's right.'

'I'm no poor case. I've got a house. I get sickness benefit.'

'You need to look at the bigger picture. Think about it; why are you on sickness benefit?'

'Because I knackered myself doing hard labour.'

'Without decent pay, without decent rights, in hazardous environments.' Emma counted off the points on her fingers.

'It was work,' said Nash. 'That's what it was like back then. Hard graft. Everyone had it that way.'

'Not everyone.' Emma turned the palm of her hand out in

a gesture of reasoning. 'And did you ever think about why you turned away from travelling?'

'Because it was a rough life.'

'But why was it rough? Look at what happened to your sister. Would that have happened if your family lived in a house?'

Below his tinted lenses, Nash's eyes softened and flickered.

'See what I mean?' said Emma. 'You've been surrounded by so much prejudice and hardship that you didn't even see it. It was the norm.'

They carried on into the building but Nash stopped as he became alert to a babble of voices coming from a room at the end of the corridor. He was expecting a handful of students gathered round a table in some pokey room, but he could hear this was a hall with a lot of people.

Up on stage was an arrangement of seats and a lectern, with a hand-written banner on the wall with the society's name – Edinburgh Students for Solidarity with Oppressed and Marginalised People. There was a stall with leaflets, protest badges and magazines. From portraits on the oak-panelled walls, long-dead professors glared down, morose and disapproving, as a smoky haze drifted over the heads of the audience.

Kate was one of the committee's longest serving members and had grown up on political debate around the dinner table. There'd been a few Conservative politicians on her father's side of the family, but her eldest sister caught the tail end of the hippy era. She became the family rebel and got into strikes and protests in the seventies. This went down badly at home, with father and eldest daughter frequently butting heads over family meals. Kate listened and absorbed these debates and now felt it was her turn to change the world – and cause consternation at home. But at recent committee meetings she'd raised concerns about the fact they spent most of their time supporting high-profile international causes. Of course, she was all for helping to free Chile from the grip of General Pinochet and showing solidarity with the African National

Congress, but there was a new buzzword on the scene: localism. The philosophy was that activists' power to influence and make a difference was greater if they tackled smaller issues. After all, lots of small changes could add up to something big. In this spirit, she suggested that the committee direct some of its efforts to causes closer to home. Cue Emma and Nash.

They joined the committee members on stage and the hall settled as Tristan Anderson, the committee's chair, strode to the lectern. 'Comrades!' he shouted, with a fist-pump in the air. 'Thank you for joining us. The fight for freedom and equality goes on. We're here to debate, learn and draw strength from each other.' He wore a Che Guevarra beret, an earring and waistcoat over a baggy white shirt. 'We have a very special guest speaker on this evening's bill, and I hope you'll all get behind him with a motion of support. First, though, we have a few standing items to discuss.'

He handed over to one of the other committee members for a discussion on the finer points of an alternative curriculum to be delivered during campus occupations. Then there was the issue of the Basque separatists who supplied beer to the student union bar. They had raised their prices three times in the last year. Although the committee supported the fight for freedom in the north of Spain, it wasn't made of money. What to do? The matter was put to a vote. No majority was reached so it was held over till the next meeting.

Nash's gaze drifted across the audience and he was struck by all the pristine faces, keeping dull adulthood at bay with plans to change the world. Around his own streets, he was used to seeing only two types of young people – those who were unruly and those who walked already with the weight of work, marriage, and kids bearing down on them. But the students in front of him now were in full command of youth, with their soft mouths and bright eyes.

Tristan Anderson signalled for hush and introduced the main item. 'Comrades, when he was only a boy, Nash Lacklow witnessed the authorities snatch his sister from the Traveller campsite where he lived. It's been 50 years since it happened, but Mr Lacklow has never forgotten that day. He wants answers and would love to trace his sister. But...' he held up his hands to focus attention, 'surprise, surprise, the authorities are refusing to help. I hope he won't mind me telling you, Mr Lacklow is in serious ill health but he's here tonight despite that, to share his story and ask for our support in holding those responsible to account.'

Nash remained seated, his walking stick in one hand and his notes in the other. He cleared his throat and began his story. The audience made not a sound till he'd finished. 'At the end of the day, the way they took her – the violence of it... it was just so quick – ten minutes and she was gone. I can't forgive them for it.' He looked across the audience. 'I don't know what you can all do about it but I see there's a lot of you out there and I appreciate you taking the time to hear me out. Emma said I should come and talk, that you might be interested, so there you have it. I've said my piece.' He tucked his notes away and sat back.

There was a brief delay as if everyone was still absorbing what they'd heard, replaying his last words, then applause rose up and swept across the hall. Some got to their feet, whistling and punching the air. It went on and all Nash could do was nod and mouth thank you.

Emma stood up and took out her copy of the story from the *Lanark Gazette*. 'You've heard what happened. Now here's how it was reported by the establishment.' She read the story. 'Doesn't it make you sick? It's like they were more interested in the police taking a few punches than a little girl being taken from her family. What parent wouldn't fight in a situation like that? When I went to see an official at the council about it, you know what he told me to do? Call the police. *Call the police?*'

From the back of the hall, someone shouted, 'Fascist pigs!'

Some booed and jeered. Tristan Anderson turned to Nash and Emma and opened his arm in a proud sweep towards the crowd. 'You see the strength of feeling this has aroused. We're with you all the way. What can we do to help you get justice?'

'We need you to write to the council,' said Emma. 'The newspapers, too. Do whatever you can, but please make a noise about this. We could be scratching at the surface of something big – a scandal.'

Some in the audience clapped and a girl in the front row called out, 'More power to you!'

A sniffy lad in the front row raised his hand. He wore a brown corduroy jacket, a wispy beard, and had a slab of dark hair pasted across his brow. 'Not that I'm trying to delegitimise this in any way,' he said, 'but it was fifty years ago. If we want to have impact and relevance, surely we need to support more contemporary causes? Awful as this is, it's just another tragedy of history. It would never happen these days.'

Emma brought out a copy of Nash's newspaper interview. 'The journalist who wrote this told me he'd had calls after it was published. People saw it and phoned him with similar stories – but from the fifties and sixties. So this wasn't a one off. There are more cases like this, we just don't know how many. It was a policy – planned and orchestrated by the authorities.'

Tristan Anderson bristled and boomed as he walked the stage, waving his long arms. 'Brothers and sisters, I think we've heard enough and I want to thank our comrades for speaking to us. This is just another example of the ingrained prejudice and injustices faced by so many oppressed peoples. The brutal capitalist order...,' he smacked his fist into his palm and raised his voice, repeating, 'The brutal capitalist order, they're stealing freedoms and stamping out traditional cultures all around the world. So I say – it's time to send a message.' He set his jaw and raised a fist. 'Committee, who's with me?'

* * *

The house was quiet when Emma got home. In the kitchen, Spence's brown jacket lay crumpled on the table. It looked like some awful piece of roadkill. The pile of bills that normally occupied the centre of the table were scattered on the floor.

She picked up the jacket and examined dark stains on the collar and shoulder. Halfway up the staircase, she heard running water coming from the bathroom. She knocked on the door. 'Dad! Are you all right?'

'Fine, sweetheart. Fine.' Spence's voice was muffled and unconvincingly upbeat.

'Your jacket – is that blood on it?'

'A wee bit. I had an accident but everything's fine. Just go back to bed.'

'Bed? I just got back.'

'I mean just go downstairs. I'll be out in a minute.'

She banged the door again. 'Come on, I'm worried. What's going on?'

The lock clicked and Spence stuck his head out. Emma cupped her mouth at his bruised and swollen face. There was dried blood around his nose and under his ear.

'I'm all right,' he said. 'I got mugged but I'm fine now.' He forced a smile that gave his blotchy and bloodied face a foolish quality, like a pathetic clown.

She lifted her hand halfway to his face but held back, scared to touch it. 'Oh my God. What happened?'

'Just a couple of yobs.'

'It's to do with that phone call, isn't it? About the money.'

She was expecting him to be defensive and say he'd take care of it, but he slumped down against the bathtub and held his head in his hands.

'I don't know what to do,' he cried. 'I don't know what to do.'

16

The office was tucked away at the end of a basement corridor but still Emma was nervous of being seen. 'Come on,' she muttered, checking her watch. The appointment was supposed to start ten minutes ago. From inside, she heard muffled voices and chairs shifting then the door opened and a student hurried past without meeting her eye. A man popped his head out and invited her in. Posters on the walls carried supportive slogans – 'We're here to help' and 'You're not alone'. The student support officer was a man in his fifties, with beleaguered eyes behind thick-framed glasses. He introduced himself as Rick and his heavy brow wrinkled as he read her hardship grant application.

'You're still at your family home?' he asked.

'Just me and dad.'

'You live with your dad?'

'That's right.'

'That's okay. I understand these things are complicated.' There was well-practised delicacy in how he said it – just the right words said in the right way to encourage her to open up.

'My mum's not around,' she said. 'My dad's been struggling for work and we're behind on rent.'

'That's nothing to be ashamed of,' said Rick. 'Times are tough. A lot of people are struggling for a lot of different reasons. We get staff coming here, too, you know. They don't know where else to go. Sometimes they just need to speak to somebody.' He waited, elbows on the desk, hands clasped.

'My mum left us just over a year ago. It was more or less out of the blue. There'd been a few ups and downs between her and dad but nothing major. Then it was, like, suddenly she just wanted something different – and she moved up north. She's living what I suppose you'd call an unconventional lifestyle – staying in a commune with loads of other people.'

'I've heard of lifestyles a lot more unconventional than that. How's your dad coping?'

'Okay, I think.'

'And is your mum happier?'

'She better be. They're very different from each other, my parents.'

For most of her life, the only thing Emma remembered her mum expressing regret about was not finishing university. Then, shortly after Emma's sixteenth birthday, Fran – short for Francesca – decided all of the last sixteen years was a regret. She never said so directly but Emma was smart enough to join the dots. Her mum simmered with malcontent and unpredictability, manifesting in comments and observations on life. Youth had gotten away from her. Experiences had been missed. Chances gone by. Sacrifices made for family life coalesced around her until she was drowning in regret and had to make a change or else she didn't think she could carry on.

'Ah, families,' sighed Rick.

She didn't go into all the details but said their old house was owned by her mum and she'd sold it when she moved out, leaving Spence and Emma to move into social housing.

'Your mum's far away,' said Rick.

'That was her choice.'

'Do you have any other family nearby?'

'Just my dad's uncle but he's very unwell. He doesn't have long to live.'

Rick nodded and shuffled his papers. 'Do you need to get away from your dad?'

Emma frowned. 'He's a very decent man.'

'Sorry. Certain things, I need to ask.'

She couldn't decide if being there made her complicit in, or even supportive of, her dad's behaviour. By applying for a hardship grant, she was welding herself to his failings, encouraging him in risk-taking and unrealistic ambitions. Because the other option was that she could just leave – she knew this. She could be like her mum. She could move in with Kate and leave him to it.

When the money came through a week later, Emma left it on the kitchen table without a word. The next day, it had gone but it was another few days before Spence mentioned it.

'You'll get every penny back, I swear.'

'Dad, you know, it doesn't have to be like this. If you spoke to a lawyer about your rights...'

'Enough, Emma.'

'Just talk to someone. Get some advice. That's all I'm saying. She's got money. Find out where you stand legally.'

'Your mother's got nothing to do with this.'

'Maybe you're owed some sort of settlement.'

'A man can't go begging because his wife ran off with someone else.'

'Dad, we need money. If she were a man it would be different. She'd have to pay.'

'Well she's not,' he shouted. 'I'm the man. I'm the man.'

★ ★ ★

The security guard had just opened his lunch box when the receptionist gave him a nudge. There was a bunch of kids outside and she didn't like the look of them. He sighed as he rewrapped his sandwich and went outside. Pasty youths with placards milled about on the pavement and more of them came off beaten-up vans and an old coach.

They were eager to get things started and wore a sheen of the day's dense and persistent drizzle. They felt the dampness on their clothes and in every breath. Someone prompted Emma and she went halfway up the steps then turned to face the crowd. The guard was just behind her. She didn't care. It would look good in the photos, her standing up for justice in a grey and hostile environment.

The idea for a protest had gathered momentum after Nash's talk to the Edinburgh Students for Solidarity with Oppressed and Marginalised Peoples, and soon there seemed an inevitability about it. People would mention it to her around campus. When's it happening, they'd ask. Count me in, they'd say. We'll show them. She'd written an article for the student newspaper and there'd even been correspondence with the Glasgow Student Union to help organise today's event. The

110

result was a large and mixed turnout; a little restless in the wet, but nonetheless ready to send a message. They smoked and chatted and shared tins of beer. Many of the faces she knew from university but there were others, too, who didn't look like students. A little older, a little rough around the edges.

It was a mix of grassroots activists: anarchists and communists, and splinter groups of each. There were hippies, and punks and white Rastas. It wasn't until the placards were held aloft that Emma noticed they were for a patchwork of causes: 'Right to Roam', 'Free Festivals', 'Squatters' Rights' and 'Anti-eviction'. But there was no obvious link to the core issue – getting Strathclyde Council to look for information about Nash's sister.

A man with spiked Mohawk hair put a small amplifier on the steps next to Emma. He plugged in a microphone and handed it to her. As she raised it to her mouth, it crackled and whistled at such a high pitch that she winced and so did most of the crowd. The man with the Mohawk fiddled with the amplifier and the whistling died down. She raised the microphone again. 'Thank you all for coming. We're here to show solidarity with a lost little girl,' she called out. 'A relative of mine who was denied freedom because of the family she was born into. Her family were denied information about where she went. And we're still being denied it today.' People going past on buses turned to stare. Office workers across the street were at their windows. She pointed behind her at the council headquarters. 'They say it doesn't matter. It was a long time ago. Why bother? They say there's no record of it, like she didn't exist, like maybe we're making it up. Well, we say it does matter. She mattered. Her name was Jenny Lacklow. I wrote letters and filled out their forms. I asked them nicely. But it seems that they still don't think Travellers matter very much.'

Someone shouted, 'Shame!' and others echoed.

'What are they hiding?' shouted another.

Emma raised the microphone again. 'If they won't look

into it, then this is what they get.'

The traffic along India Street slowed to a crawl. Car horns blasted through the fumes. Officials joined the security guard on the steps. They bristled and whispered to each other. The crowd moved forward and grew more vocal.

'Cover up!'

'Freedom! Freedom to roam!'

Three riot vans pulled up at the roadside. Police got out and began to circle. The crowd stirred, booing and hissing like the villain had just walked on stage in a pantomime.

Someone shouted, 'Fuck the pigs! Fuck them all!'

'Fascists!' shouted another. 'Look at them. Itching to have a go at us.'

A banner was unfurled at the back of the crowd. It bore the slogan – 'End the Evictions' and showed a cartoon drawing of a businessman with devil horns poking out of his bowler hat. A thin lad with a skinhead climbed onto a bus stop roof and sat like a grinning imp, leading a chant. At first, Emma couldn't make it out but it grew louder and clearer: 'Wipe the grin off his face – take over empty space! Wipe the grin off his face – take over empty space!'

It drowned her out and she tried to regain the crowd's attention. 'All we're asking...what we need... what we're demanding...' It was no use. She'd lost them.

'Wipe the grin off his face – take over empty space!'

A bottle smashed against the building and the police moved in. They pulled out truncheons and blows came down on heads and hands. Some in the crowd scattered. Others laughed and taunted the police.

They pinned people to the ground then hauled them up and dragged them messily towards riot vans. Once in their grip, protesters went limp and heavy against the tense, jagged movements of the police trying to march them away. Handcuffs flashed. Insults flew from the depths. Police helmets fell off mid-scuffle. Emma saw three police jostling with a single protester. One lost his balance then the whole group collapsed in on itself in a tangle of limbs and aggravated faces.

Meanwhile, a photographer moved through the crowd, stooped protectively over his camera, capturing the action. The comic wrestling and violent intimacy.

Protesters surged towards the building. Emma tried to avoid them by jumping down off the steps but was too late. She got caught at the front. Three lads broke away from the main group and ran, laughing and whooping, into the building. There was shoving and grappling as the police moved in, pinning protesters against the wall. Emma was trapped, crushed against jagged stone cladding. An elbow pressed into her throat. A placard smacked into her head. She pushed towards the steps. She was dizzy and something warm and wet ran down her face. The doorman grabbed her jacket and lifted her up so that she was teetering on tiptoes. He shouted to the police that he had the ringleader. The photographer was there, in front of them, crouched down and taking shots.

Richard Ash stood and watched the chaos from his fourth floor window. He was on the phone to a friend in the police. 'Thanks for sending your men down to clear up the scum,' he said. 'Yep. I'm watching it now. They're bringing it under control. It was the girl I told you about. The family's name is Lacklow. That's right...Lack-low. Like they are lacking and low – low down. Lacklow. I'll give you her address. Check out the dad. See if you can nail him on something.'

17

Frank O'Grady sat on the bus and read the *Evening Times* headline: 'Callous Council Accused of Cover Up'. A photo showed a frightened and petite young woman, blood running down her face, being manhandled by a large security guard on the doorstep of the council offices. Her fringe was matted with blood. The guard had her by the collar and looked like he was lifting her off the ground.

O'Grady looked around him at the crowded seats, at the faces of his constituents, wondering what they made of it. He was up for re-election soon. Stories about Travellers were usually negative; crime and antisocial behaviour. But this was different; a tenacious young woman battling the authorities, wanting to trace a long-lost relative.

At the office, he called Martin Scott, a journalist he'd known for years. 'You know me,' said Scott. 'I've been at this long enough not to get carried away but this story is a gift. It's all there. Some poor wee lassie. Heartless officials. The dying wish of an old man. And that photo – the brave girl – it's a belter. It looks like a cover up.'

'Come on,' said O'Grady. 'It's no cover up.'

'Doesn't matter. The point is, you've got to look into it now. It would look bad if you didn't.'

'We do, don't we,' groaned O'Grady.

'Because otherwise everyone's going to think you've got something to hide. How many old records do you have?'

'Jesus, I don't know. Could be tens of thousands. Maybe more.'

'Well, you were the ones who wanted to centralise.'

'Don't remind me. Look, help me out. What would you do?'

'You're asking me, a man who sells newspapers, to stop this turning into a bigger story?'

'I'm asking for a bit of friendly advice,' said O'Grady.

'And I need to make a living.'

'I'll give you someone under the bus.'

'You better,' said Scott.

'I'll haul the bastard in front of a committee.'

'Okay, okay,' said Scott. 'My advice is to get in front of the story.'

'You mean on top of it.'

'No, you don't suppress it. You let it run – but you guide it. Shape it. Investigate yourselves before someone else does. Anticipate questions and answer them before they're asked. If you find something nasty lurking in a file, you hold it up and say – *'Forgive us father for we have sinned'*. You don't want a government minister on your back saying this is another example of inefficiency in local government.'

'No, we bloody don't,' said O'Grady. 'Not this close to an election.'

'The most important thing is, do exactly what this girl is asking. Bring her in for a meeting with one of your family people. Give her warm words and a sympathetic ear.'

At a council meeting the following week, O'Grady issued an apology to the Lacklow family and stated for the record his profound regret about the way the matter had been handled. Then he turned his attention to Richard Ash, sitting alone at a table in the centre of the room. It was a spot traditionally reserved for the grilling of officials and used so often for their public lambastings that councillors had a nickname for it – 'The Stocks'.

'Let me understand this...' O'Grady had a copy of the newspaper in his hand and was flapping it around. 'We had a young girl – a university student from a disadvantaged background – asking you to look up a file for her grandad...her terminally ill grandad.'

'I believe it was her great-uncle,' interrupted Ash.

O'Grady scowled across the room and the distance between him and Ash seemed only to increase the intensity of his unblinking eyes. Secretarial staff fidgeted and a few throats were cleared. 'Grandad. Great-uncle. Nearest and dearest. Whoever he is. The point is you said no.'

'I judged that the request wouldn't be a good use of

departmental resources.' Ash nodded to the row of councillors facing him. 'This administration has directed department managers to make budget savings.'

O'Grady looked at his colleagues in disbelief then turned back to Ash. 'I'm sure we all appreciate your concern but I hardly think you digging out a few old files is going to break the bank.'

Stifled laughter rippled around the committee room.

'I was concerned about the staff hours involved,' said Ash. 'Having met Miss Lacklow, I felt she may be quite persistent in her requests for us to investigate the matter.'

'As is her right,' said O'Grady. 'As is her right. And didn't it occur to you that by saying no it would look like we were being evasive?'

Ash shuffled his papers. The desk was tiny, with barely room for a file binder and cup of water. 'It's possible my response may have been misinterpreted as a little uncaring. But the incident she was enquiring about was over half a century ago.'

O'Grady hunched forward and slapped the desk. 'It doesn't matter when this took place. Things like this can't be swept under the rug. And because of what you did we're in the middle of what might or might not be a national scandal of the state stealing kids from their families.'

A light sweat was visible on Ash's brow. He collected himself and gave the only response he could. 'I followed the department procedures. Everything's been properly documented.'

'It's been documented, all right.' O'Grady flapped the newspaper again, almost shaking it to bits. 'A great big photograph of that wee lass, blood pouring down her face, being flung around by our security guard. Do you understand me? This is sitting at our doorstep. Literally.'

The public gallery was packed with journalists and O'Grady knew this had to be a hit job. But it was a tricky issue, requiring political dexterity. Fight the corner of the down-trodden Travelling community without giving concern to swathes of suburban voters who like to keep immaculate lawns and wouldn't want a Travellers' site anywhere near them.

O'Grady put the newspaper to one side and picked up Ash's personnel file. He flipped it open and pursed his lips. 'Before starting in this role, exactly how much experience did you have in local government?'

Ash puffed his chest. 'I was an officer in the Royal Navy.'

'So none, then,' came O'Grady's cold response. 'Let's try our luck with records management. How much records management experience did you bring to this role?'

Ash was flushed and fidgeting with his pen and notepad. 'Well, as a naval officer I was in charge of some very sensitive and highly confidential materials. There were strict protocols to control access.'

'Mr Ash, we're talking here about giving access. Handling legitimate information requests from the public. You seem to have a policy for most things so I'm assuming you do have a policy for that?'

Ash blinked and opened his mouth but it was a moment before he spoke. 'I didn't know I needed one.'

Turning to his fellow councillors, O'Grady said, 'I think we might be coming to the root of the problem.'

Afterwards, O'Grady phoned Nash to give him a personal apology and tell him the matter had been referred to the head of children's welfare. He also promised a full review of the records department, starting at the top. A few days later, a letter landed on Nash's doormat – an official apology from the leader of Strathclyde Council. 'This is victory,' he said, waving it at Emma. 'Whatever happens, this is victory. You've put the bastards on the hook.'

18

Spence couldn't remember the last time he sold so much as a toilet brush or cleaning rag on Shade Park Crescent. You're losing your touch, son, he thought as he lugged his case of scrubbers and dusters back to the van. He was still deciding whether to try his luck on a different street or just give up for the day when he noticed two men, a big one and a slighter one, in long coats, looking in the back window of his Ford Transit.

'Hiy! You two, get away from there!'

The little one turned and smiled at him, while the big one carried on looking through the window.

'Are you deaf? I said get away from my van.'

'That's some old banger,' the shorter one shouted. 'I was just saying to my colleague it must cost you more to run it than the damn thing's worth. Road tax, insurance, garage bills.' He slapped the side of it and shook his head. 'It all mounts up, doesn't it?'

Spence slowed down. 'It's none of your bloody business, pal.'

The big one turned around and showed Spence his police badge. 'Detective Stokes and this is Detective Barnes. That looks like a nice bit of carpet you've got in there. I might be looking for a bit about that size. How much do you want for it?'

'It's not for sale.'

'Not for sale?' His eyes flicked towards his partner in amused disbelief. 'You sell things don't you?'

Detective Barnes pointed at a car parked farther up the road. 'We've been over there watching you for the last half hour,' he said. 'You've been going round the doors with your suitcase.'

'So what?' asked Spence.

'The people around here don't like hawkers. It brings down the tone of the neighbourhood.'

'What's in the suitcase?' asked Detective Stokes.

'Look, lads, what's this about?'

'You know you need a traders' licence for the way you make a living?'

'I don't have it with me,' said Spence.

The two detectives smiled at each other and Stokes smacked the side of the van again.

'Not in the glove compartment alongside your insurance, no?'

'I keep it at home,' said Spence.

'Ah, of course you do, son. Quite right to keep it somewhere safe. Fair enough.'

Barnes came and stood in front of him as Stokes went round behind, looking him up and down.

'How long have you been at this game, then?' asked Barnes.

'Hawking? A long time.'

'Should think so,' said Stokes. 'Don't see many of your kind about these days.'

'Started when you were a lad, I bet?' said Barnes.

'That's about right.'

'Your old man show you the ropes, did he?'

Spence nodded.

Barnes came a step closer and looked up at him, grinning. 'I'm going to stick my neck out here and take a guess that you're a gypo. Am I right?'

'I'm a businessman,' said Spence.

'Of course you are. My apologies.'

'Why are you insulting the man?' said Stokes. 'Look at him – he's a professional.' He turned to Spence, clamping a fat hand on his shoulder. 'Aren't you, son?'

'Where'd you get the carpet from?' asked Barnes.

Spence told them he got it from a wholesaler.

'Got a receipt?'

He picked up his suitcase and walked past them towards the van. 'I've got to collect my daughter, so if you'll excuse me...'

They followed him to the driver's side.

'We're going to need a look in the suitcase,' said Stokes.

'Why?'

'There's been a few robberies in this area recently. You fit the description of the suspect. And here you are, going round the doors with a large suitcase. Open it up.'

A woman in a dressing-gown sat out on her balcony, doing her makeup. She took her time about it and Spence could tell she was watching to see if he got arrested. He opened the suitcase and Stokes crouched down and picked through the assortment of dusters and cleaning rags. 'What a load of shite,' he said, tossing them onto the road. He looked up at Spence. 'Is this really how you make a living?'

'That's just for upselling,' said Spence.

'Up-what?'

'Upselling. I sell carpets and curtains then offer cleaning products for extra sales. People like to look after their homes.'

'Call it what you like – it looks like a load of crap to me.'

'Well,' said Spence, 'I daresay it proves I've not been choring anything.'

Barnes walked up and placed a finger on his chest. 'Don't get smart. I don't like the look of you. My gut tells me you're lying to us. I think we need to turn this piece of shite van inside out. I want to see your papers. Insurance. Licence. Everything.'

'This is harassment,' said Spence.

'Oh, here we go with the rights,' said Stokes, laughing and shaking his head. He took out a notepad and opened it. 'You wouldn't be the same William Lacklow – aka Spence – given a suspended sentence in 1960 for selling stolen goods? Radios, I believe it was.'

Spence gathered up the clothes and dusters off the street. He brushed off the grit then bundled them back into the suitcase. 'That wasn't my fault. My associate picked those items up by mistake.'

'Associate?' said Barnes. 'Now we're getting fancy.'

'See, it was very confusing when we were looking into this,' said Stokes, 'because there's a few Lacklows with criminal records. I do apologise if you find the questions an inconvenience but we're following what's called a process of deductive reasoning. We have to eliminate the other Lacklows.'

'It's not a common surname, that,' said Barnes. 'Strange one, too – Lack-low. You're never going to go anywhere with a name like that.'

'What is it, is that a pikey name?' asked Stokes.

'You don't need to look so pissed off, son,' said Barnes. 'Wasn't us who gave you that name. It was your mum and dad.'

'This isn't going to work,' said Spence.

'Where were we?' asked Stokes.

'Deductive reasoning,' said his partner.

'That's it. Deductive reasoning. We have to eliminate the other Lacklows. We have to establish which of the criminal bunch we're dealing with. So let's go through them. Now bear with me because it's complicated. There's another William Lacklow residing at Lewisvale Crescent.' He looked up from his notepad. 'That's just a mile or two down the road from you. He must be a relative of yours, surely.'

Spence stared hard at them, trying to control his twitching hands.

'It's all right,' said Barnes. 'We can fill you in on the details. He was a serial deserter during the war. A coward. So that's obviously not you. You're too young.'

'You're a pair of bastards,' said Spence. 'That's my uncle. He's dying.'

'And we found records for another Lacklow who's got a charge pending for breach of the peace. Resides at the same address as you, actually. Miss Emma Lacklow. Nineteen years old.'

'Following in the family tradition,' said Barnes. 'You must be very proud.' He came up in Spence's face again and smiled at him. 'Maybe we should speak to your girl, too? I heard she's been causing trouble recently. Started a full blown riot in Glasgow. Banging on about her rights – same as you – annoying decent people. What she needs to do is remember her place.'

Spence stepped towards him but Stokes grabbed him and threw him against the van. 'You people are scum. We're watching you.'

They took down the van's registration and told him he'd be arrested if he came back to the area again. Then they let him go. He fished his keys out of his pocket and got into the van and watched them drive away. He looked in the rear-view mirror and saw he had the tense mouth on him again.

* * *

It was one of those rare spring days for dropping everything and going outside. Students swarmed around the park. Smiling couples walked hand-in-hand. Solitary wanderers wore headphones and sunglasses. There were cyclists and jugglers, and friends in clusters on the grass, smoking, eating or knocking a ball about. It was like a painting you'd see on the wall of an art gallery cafe – the backdrop to scones and coffee; someone's vision of a world without trouble or conflict.

Emma and Kate were heading for one of the benches when a Hare Krishna monk stopped them. He stood in the middle of the path, smiling, and handed them a leaflet for a yoga class. It was on that night, offering a discount for students.

'Your journey towards spiritual enlightenment starts here,' he said.

'I could do with a bit of that,' said Kate. 'Do you fancy it?'

Emma cocked her head, squinting at the leaflet's picture of a hippy man and woman contorting their limbs into unfathomable angles.

'Jesus, I couldn't do that.'

'You'd be surprised,' said Kate. 'It's really good for you.' She stopped at a bench and broke into a wide-legged pose with her arms pointing up in a steeple shape. 'It's just stretching and balance, see.'

'I can't tonight,' said Emma. 'I promised to get Nash's shopping.'

Kate crumpled the leaflet and slumped down on the bench.

Emma stared at her, wide-eyed. 'What's the matter?'

'What?'

'Your sour face.'

'Are you going to sit down?'

'Kate, I'm not sitting in the sunshine with you in the huff because I can't go to a yoga class that we didn't even know about till two minutes ago.'

'It doesn't matter.'

'So stop acting like a four-year-old.'

'You're always doing things for your family – or working.'

Emma shrugged. 'So what? We're close. I like to help.'

'You help a lot. Like, *a lot*. That's all I'm saying.'

'You're saying you're getting fed up.'

'I'd like to see you more.'

'Well, I'm not going to apologise for helping my family.'

'It's not just how much you help. You're distracted by them. You talk about them all the time.'

They sat in silence for a moment then Emma took the leaflet out of Kate's hand and uncrumpled it. She stared at it for a while. Her expression hardened, then she said Spence had got himself into bother with money and she'd been helping him.

Kate placed a hand on her knee. 'How much?'

'My grant money and then a hardship grant on top of that.'

'Jesus, Emma.'

'It's not as if he's drinking and gambling it away.'

'Still, he's taking advantage,' said Kate.

'He's my dad,' said Emma. 'And he's skint.'

'So why doesn't he work nights in a restaurant?'

'He made some bad decisions recently. That's all.'

'That money's supposed to help you through university.'

Emma gestured around her. 'He's not interested in any of this. He never asks about it.' If he was there now, seeing the hordes of students lounging on the grass, he'd have a few choice words about work ethic and life in the real world. 'I think he'd prefer me to drop out and get a job.'

Kate turned to her. 'Has he said that?'

'No, but I can tell.'

'What about your mum?'

'She's not here.'

'But what does she want you to do?'

Emma shrugged and folded her arms. 'I don't care. I've had enough of being caught in the middle. You know, they argued about me coming here – to university. They'd been at my school for parents' night – I was about sixteen – and the teachers all said I was doing really well and that I should think about applying for uni. Dad said we'd need to discuss it privately as a family – fair enough – and when we got home he let rip that he wasn't going to have a load of strangers tell him what was best for me. He said I already had all the education I needed. I think he thought extra years of studying would make me soft or work-shy, or something. He didn't see the point when I was already old enough to start working and earning.' She picked at the bench's flaking green paint. 'But mum was having none of it. And it's strange because she always talked about being an individual and cutting free from conventional thought. Didactic institutional whatever it was – but when it came down to it, she really wanted me to go to university. She said it would make me more cultured, more rounded – that I'd learn about the wider world – that sort of thing. You know what dad did? He asked us if we knew why Persian rugs contained tiny, deliberate mistakes in the pattern.' She turned to Kate. 'Well, do you?'

'No idea.'

'Because the makers believed that only Allah could make something perfect. They did it out of respect – and dad knew this amazing fact but he'd never mentioned it before until he used it to win the argument about why I didn't need to come to uni.'

'What did your mum do?'

'She threw a pot of mince at the wall. Doors were slammed so hard they just about came off their hinges, and she put a suitcase open on the bed. That was the first time I realised something wasn't right between them. So here I am – but she still left him in the end.'

After lunch, Emma went to the National Library and sat with a stack of textbooks, trying to write an essay on ethnographic research and the Scottish diaspora. The afternoon ticked by slowly. She flipped her notebook shut and tapped a pen against her teeth. The last few months had been like a crash course in the history of her family, and here she was in the country's great depository of knowledge. There was a certain inevitability about it that she was up at the desk a few moments later.

'You don't have anything on Travellers, do you?' she asked.

'Travellers, like explorers?' asked the librarian.

'No, like gypsies,' she said. 'Romany Travellers.'

The librarian flicked through a couple of card indexes but found nothing. He took a large, cloth-bound volume from the shelf and traced his finger down the headings. He tapped the page and looked up. 'We do. It's an old one. 1845. It's in rare collections. Through the doors on the other side of the main reading room.'

The rare collections room was as dim and fusty as the name suggested. A handful of people sat with disconcerting stillness, hunched over books and notepads. She filled in the requisition form then took a seat in the corner. The room was big, its carpet threadbare. She imagined telling Spence about the state of the floors in, of all places, the National Library of Scotland. His eyes would light up at the prospect of another big sales opportunity – however much of a long shot. After the golf club incident, she wouldn't put it past him to turn up at the entrance, sample book in hand, and try to talk his way past the front desk.

The librarian brought a small wooden box to Emma's desk. Inside was the book, with ornate lettering embossed on the cover: *A History of Scottish Gypsies by Charlotte Harris*. Alongside it was a pair of white gloves and an old cushion. She found herself leaning closer and breathing in the sweet smell of the leather-bound jacket. It had a pleasant, cloying thickness that settled in her throat.

The librarian coughed as if to remind her she was still there. 'Please use the gloves to handle it and keep it on the cushion,' she said. 'I'll leave you to it – we close at six.'

The first few yellowed pages spoke fondly of a golden age

when gypsies moved in and out of royal courts as messengers for the kings and queens of Europe. Gypsies were thought to have descended from the Pharaohs and were known as the Lords and Earls of Little Egypt – later shortened to gypsies – but somewhere along the way they fell out of favour with the authorities and within a few years were being hanged, drowned and nailed to trees by their ears. Emma winced and fingered the tip of her ear, wondering how that was even possible.

It was a long book, meticulously detailed with sections on customs, traditions and Traveller Cant. She read how Cant still carried several words of Hindu and this was why experts thought gypsies were descended from India. She tutted at the outdated language in accounts of outlawing and persecution of what the book called the swarming and swarthy Saracen Race. An ugly feeling rose in her stomach as chapters told of hangings, enslavement, deportations and of children being ripped from mothers' arms and sent into slavery in the Americas. It was real, she had to keep reminding herself. It's a wonder my family's here at all.

The pages lamented how those who survived were a miserable scattering of wretches, beggars and petty thieves. I came up from the dirt, Nash frequently told her. Now she understood. She understood the silk ties and good suits. One chapter concluded:

'There can be no doubt in any right thinking person's mind that the task of bettering the standing of gypsidom in Scotland would be an undertaking of considerable difficulty'.

She flicked on through the pages, then a chapter heading caught her eye.

The Rise of Queen Lacklow

Queen Lacklow travelled on well-bred horses, dressed in silk-embroidered cloaks, jangling with gold and silver. She could quote readily from the Bible and Shakespeare and was a composer of fine poetical verses that held all listeners in her thrall. As well as Gypsy Cant and Saxon English, she was said to be fluent in Spanish and Latin and could hold her own in discussions on any matter among people of high breeding.

She read how Queen Lacklow emerged as Scotland's gypsy leader in the early 1700s, mobilising a large and loyal following who held sway over much of southern Scotland and restored something of her people's past glory. For a while at least, things were like the golden age again.

By the time the librarian returned to say they were closing, Emma had filled her notebook and was shaking off a cramp in her hand from all the writing.

19

Dinner was finished. A few bottles of wine had been drunk, and Kate's flatmate, Brian, brought out a video tape sheathed in a discreet, plain cover and asked if anyone was in the mood for a scary film.

Emma had heard about 'video nasties' and how the government wanted to ban them. Still, she wasn't prepared for what followed. Two hours of blood and gore flashing relentlessly on the television screen. Howling demonic faces, up lit and white-eyed. Screams and cheap yet startling sound effects of splatter and possessed voices. All made for small, flickering screens in dimly lit rooms. It was terrifying on a visceral level, and the first time she'd found herself in agreement with the Tories.

The film was about teenagers terrorised by a demon who attacked them in their dreams, and afterwards Kate and her flatmates talked about whether it was possible to interpret meaning from dreams. Emma told them she'd been dreaming about the book from the National Library. She'd been back to read it that afternoon, going through the ceremony of filling in the forms, then slipping on the white gloves and placing the book on its protective cushion. She'd spent hours lost in it, enjoying the smell and touch of the old pages, and the vividness of its stories and characters.

'How did you know it was there?' asked Kate.

'I didn't. I just asked if they had anything about gypsies and they brought it out.'

'Is it going to help, though? With finding Nash's sister?'

Emma shook her head. 'I just like reading it. When it's open in front of me and I'm taking notes – I don't know how to describe it – it just feels important. But the search is going nowhere. The council promised us a meeting but we're still waiting.'

Brian clapped his hands. 'I've got an idea. Let's consult the Ouija board.'

'Be serious,' said Emma.

'I am,' said Brian. 'It's real. There's good magic and bad.

I've been reading up on it.'

Soon they were all knelt around the coffee table as Brian set up the board. He explained that he would be the conduit for the spirit and that they needed to be serious and respectful. Others could ask questions but he had to repeat them or else they wouldn't be heard in the spirit world. He lit candles and said a few words of an incantation.

'Dear entity – we call on you in peace and positivity. We mean you no harm and bid that you bring us no harm. We have in our presence, a dear friend, Emma Lacklow, looking for a relative cruelly taken from the bosom of her family by agents of the fascist state many years ago. So we ask you...' He flicked a glance at Emma. 'What is it you want to know?'

'Oh...is Jenny still alive?'

'We ask you: is Jenny Lacklow still of this earthly realm?'

Brian shut his eyes and placed a finger on the upturned glass. He told everyone to focus and put their fingers in a stack on top of his. He asked the question again and the glass quivered and began to shift; just a tiny, side-to-side movement.

Emma hissed, 'Jesus, Brian, it's obvious it's you doing that.'

'I swear. I fucking swear, it's not me.'

'How's it doing that?'

'It's us,' said Brian. 'Our collective energy. We're channelling the entity.'

The glass moved in gradually bigger arcs towards the row of letters. It swung towards the end of the row, coming to a stop on letter Y, then back to E, and finally stopping at S. They gasped and gawped at each other. The candle cast flickering shadows on the wall.

'I'm actually going to shit myself,' said Emma.

'Quick,' said Brian, 'ask me something else.'

'Is there a way to find Jenny?'

Again, the glass danced around the board, spelling out the word yes.

Afterwards, Brian put a hand on Emma's shoulder. 'Ouija's all about belief. It doesn't work if you don't believe it. You believed in it. We all did.'

20

The letter of apology was propped up on the mantelpiece. He liked to stop and look at it, reading it with proudly pursed lips. There was a coat of arms in the top corner with words in Latin, and at the foot of the page was the signature of the Lord Provost of Strathclyde Regional Council. Receiving it had given Nash a sense of agency in the world but it was bittersweet that it had come only now, with so little time left. 'If I've got one regret,' he said, 'one thing I could change, I'd like to have studied. Like you, girls. It's a wonderful opportunity. Don't waste it.'

Emma and Kate sat on the sofa, nodding.

'We won't,' said Emma.

'Doesn't cost you a penny, either.'

'Not a penny.'

'Incredible. How big's the university library?'

'Huge,' said Kate. 'Books, encyclopaedias, journals.'

'Journals.' He injected reverential timbre into his voice as he said it. 'Are those like posh versions of magazines?'

'That's right,' said Kate. 'Academic. For specialist subjects.'

'And all that knowledge at your fingertips. I like a good documentary myself. Wildlife. Current affairs. I try to catch one a week. Finding out I'm dying has made me more curious about the world. You see, I've never been outside Britain. And some people would call me a Traveller. I never read much, either, but I'm making up for it these days.' He gestured at the pile of books and magazines at his side.

He'd lost weight recently and seemed to live off nothing but biscuits and tea. Physical deterioration emphasised the strain of his breathing. If there was anything powerful left in him, that was it; his efforts to breathe and control the cough.

He picked up the latest copy of *National Geographic*, with a cover story about the Awá tribe of the Amazon Basin and their shamanic ceremonies fuelled by hallucinogenic herbal drinks. 'Incredible photos,' he said. 'A group of them on a hillside. They're a good age, I'd say. Pensionable. But, Jesus, muscly wee bodies leaping about the place. Feathers and beads hanging off them. They look fit from it, too.'

Emma remembered she'd had a lecture on the topic. She dug out her notes and handed them to him.

'Access to spiritual elements... ancestral plane... opening doors to new dimensions.' He looked up at her. 'So what do you suppose they see, these shamans?'

'I think it's more about what they feel. It's a religious thing.'

'Like going to church?'

'Better than that. If you wanted to feel spiritually lifted, which would you prefer – listening to a minister for an hour or leaping about naked in the sun?'

'There's a belief they're connecting with their ancestors,' said Kate. 'With the spirit world. It's not seen as a sinister thing. It's a celebration – because we're all going in the same direction. It's like the dead are the future, not the past.'

'I like the idea,' said Nash. 'Do you think they're really making contact?'

Kate shrugged. 'There's a lot about the world that can't be explained by conventional science.'

'All those hours staring into space and chanting. There must be something in it. Why else would they keep doing it?'

'You sound curious,' said Kate.

'I am.'

'Curious enough to try it?'

'I'm too old not to be curious about things I've never tried.'

Kate went into her coat pocket and brought out a small plastic bag containing what looked like dried earth.

Nash leaned forward. 'What's that?'

'That's what we're talking about – the gateway to a new experience.' She handed it to him. He opened it and took a sniff. 'I'm at least ages with a shaman, aren't I?'

'You are, indeed,' said Emma.

Nash boiled the kettle while Kate rolled a joint. When he returned with a tray of tea and biscuits, the joint was on the arm of his chair. He lit it and settled back, with thick ribbons of smoke curling around his head.

After a few minutes, the room where he'd spent much of the last decade looked interesting and new. He felt different, too. The physical experience was just one aspect of being, and his emphysema and back pain were mere subsets of this. They weren't just bearable. They were a fraction of the whole – no big deal. He was a house with many rooms; a country mansion with sprawling grounds, walled gardens and sun-dappled apple orchards.

He smiled at Emma and Kate. 'Well, I'll be buggered if I'm not as high as a kite.'

'It's good stuff, isn't it?' said Kate.

'It's my throat,' he said, touching his neck as if to check it was really part of his body. 'My throat's warm. It's loose. I'm breathing again.'

'It's very potent,' said Kate. 'I had too much of it once. It was Brian's fault. He talked me into it. We sprinkled it in yoghurt then went to the cinema, stoned out our minds. I got *deja vu* for weeks afterwards.'

'Like flashbacks?' asked Emma.

'No, I didn't feel stoned or anything like that. This was straight forward *deja vu*. I'd be walking down the street and see a woman in a yellow hat, walking a poodle, and it would feel like I'd already seen it in a dream or something. Have you had it much?'

'Maybe a couple of times,' said Emma.

'Same here – until that night. Man, oh, man. Then I had three or four of them in a month. That changes your perception of reality.'

'So do you think you were seeing the future?' asked Nash.

'Maybe I was seeing the past, present and future all in one moment. Maybe there's no such thing as time. It's something we invent, that helps us process life.'

The concept was a little too rich and magical. Nash shook his head as if trying to dislodge it from his brain. He passed the joint back to Kate. 'I think I'll leave it there, thanks.'

'Do you remember that plane crash in the North Sea?' asked Emma.

'Last year,' said Kate.

'The night it happened – before it was in the news – I had a dream about seeing an explosion over water. That was all I could remember; dark water lit up by flames. Then in the morning when I switched on the news, there it was.'

Kate absorbed this, blinking slowly and heavy-lidded. 'Like I say, there's a lot that can't be explained by conventional science.'

'Wait a minute,' said Nash. 'How many people are in the country?'

Kate scratched her head. '50 million. 55 million. Something like that.'

'So that's 55 million people dreaming on any given night. And what are the chances of someone dreaming about fire and water?'

'Very high,' said Kate. 'And we dream lots each night. Like, hundreds of times.'

'Okay,' said Nash. 'So we're talking hundreds of millions of dreams each night. Chances are, somebody's going to dream about fire and water. I mean, those are like natural things.'

'Elemental,' said Kate.

'Right. It would be the primitive part of your brain at work.'

'But I'm not talking about millions of other people,' said Emma. 'I'm talking about me. It was vivid. It was there, fresh in my head when I woke up.'

They were quiet for a while then Emma said, 'You know, the librarian told me the last person to read it before me was ten years ago.'

Kate stared at her for a moment. 'What are you talking about?'

'The book. The old book. Remember, I told you.'

She'd been at the National Library again that afternoon when she should have been in a lecture on primary research methodologies. 'The woman at the desk told me the last requisition before me was ten years ago.'

'Lonely old book,' said Kate.

Nash asked, 'Is that what they call it in the library trade, a requisition? When you ask for a book.'

'Yeah,' said Emma, 'you fill out the form and they get the book and bring it out to you.'

'Why don't they keep it out on a shelf? That'll be the reason nobody reads it. Nobody knows the damn thing's there.'

'They can't do that. It's too old.'

'Must be worth a few bob,' said Nash.

'Probably. You need identification and a letter from university just to get in the place. No bags allowed at the desk, and you have to fill in two request slips.'

Nash smirked. 'You mean requisitions. You need to fill in two requisitions.' It may have been because he was stoned but his adoption and use of the word to correct Emma was, to him at least, highly comic. 'Next time I'm at the library for my detective stories I'll tell them I'd like to make a requisition. *Please, Madam, I'd be much obliged.* They'll be well impressed.'

Emma thought about Nash's name in a requisition file at his local library, listed many times against the trashy detective novels, and she wondered about its final entry; when that would be and which title would be listed as his last requisition.

21

It was a big house a few streets from Carluke town centre. Ivy had been stripped from its white painted stone, leaving a pattern like grey veins spreading across the front. Kate sat in the car, staring at it like she didn't trust it not to move. 'I'm not sure this is a good idea.'

Emma switched off the engine and turned to her. 'Why? What's the matter?'

'It just feels wrong. We could get into trouble.'

'This is arranged. We've got an appointment.'

'Under false pretences.'

'It's not that much of a lie.'

'No, it is. It's very much a lie.'

It had been weeks since Strathclyde Council promised to refer Emma's enquiry to the head of children's welfare but she'd got fed up waiting.

'If the manager asks, just flash your student card. He's not going to look that closely. It worked a treat at the town hall.'

'Yeah, but this is a children's home.' Kate looked at the house again. 'What sort of kids do they have there, anyway? Where do they come from?'

'I don't know.'

'Could some of them be dangerous?'

'Would you relax? We're just going to look at files.'

'You're sure?'

'That's what I told the guy. You don't have to come but it'll be a lot quicker if we both go.' Emma checked her watch. 'I told him two o'clock. Are you coming or not?'

Eddie Reilly was crew-cut and stocky. Emma imagined him running evening Judo classes in cold community halls. He'd been manager of St Augustine's for five years and was a prison guard before that. Working in care homes was more rewarding, he told them.

He stood at his desk and searched through papers. 'I've got you here somewhere, girls. Remind me what it was about.'

'Children's welfare between the wars,' said Emma.

'You'd think I'd remember. It's not like we get a lot of researchers visiting. You were writing something.'

'My PhD thesis.'

'Now I remember. Edinburgh?'

'That's the one.'

'Soup, girls?'

'Pardon?'

'Have you eaten? I've made soup. Carrot and lentil. I make it by the vat load.'

'We're good, thanks. Ready to get down to business.'

He opened a hatch in the floor and led them down rickety steps into the basement. 'All this shouldn't really be here at all.' He gestured at stacks of boxes. 'It's a mix of junk and old records.'

Emma said, 'The council told me everything had been centralised.'

'Most of it has. Believe me, there was a hell of a lot more than this. But they left these behind, probably because they couldn't be bothered sorting it out.' He tapped a box with his foot. 'Clothes, toys, comics, mixed with files, letters, whatever else. It's not in any sort of order but you're welcome to take a look.'

'We don't mind, do we Kate?'

Kate forced a smile. 'As long as it's old then we're happy.'

'Well this stuff's from way back,' said Reilly. 'I'm not exactly sure when but it looks old – certainly smells old.'

'Why have you kept it?' asked Emma.

He picked a child's shoe from one of the boxes and examined it. 'I just haven't got round to dealing with it. But I suppose it can't stay down here forever.' He tossed the shoe back in the box. 'Make the most of it while it's here, girls.'

He went back up through the hatch and Emma looked inside one of the boxes. It was a jumble of ragged clothes and books, with loose papers mixed in with it. There were cobwebs speckled with tiny dead insects and husks of spiders tangled around flies. She fished out a paper; an admittance form from

1940. Kate leaned over her shoulder and frowned at the form's indecipherable hand-writing. 'We'll be down here for hours,' she sighed.

'I thought you wanted to help.'

'I do but, still...needles, haystacks, you know?'

'Were you expecting it to be neatly indexed? We're going through every one of these.'

Under the bare lights, they searched through the boxes. Broken old toys and tatty books; the discarded fragments of unhappy childhoods. Other bits and pieces beyond identification. They pulled out papers with handwriting so faded and messy that it was difficult to know what any of it said. They'd been at it for nearly two hours when Kate pulled an envelope from one of the boxes. It was damp-stained and delicate. She peeled it open and read it. 'You better take a look at this,' she said.

Emma grabbed it and stood under the light with it.

Deer Sirs – Av no been sleepin since you took ma wee Jenny and I ken shell be missin me and hur bruthers. Wull stop travllin and setl doon and no cos nae trubl if I can get Jenny bak. Yis can inspict us any day an yell no find nae folt in how am bringin up ma weens. Am promisin tae be a good mum if yell plees give her bak. I cannae liv withoot ma wee lassie.
Mary Lacklow

Emma's lips parted but it was a moment before she spoke. 'Oh my God. She wrote to them. She could barely write but she wrote to them.' She read the letter again then slipped it inside her bag.

Back upstairs, there was a strong smell of soup and the faint sound of a television and voices from one of the rooms. They thanked Eddie Reilly and asked what it was like running a children's home.

'Come on,' he said, 'I'll show you.' He took them down the hall, to a room where a group of teenage boys gathered round a snooker table and a few others watched television. Some had big, foolish, excitable eyes and others had eyes too old and haggard for their young faces. There was a skittish energy about the place and an overpowering smell of aftershave.

'We can take up to fifteen,' said Reilly, 'but I like to keep it closer to ten. That's more manageable. Ten's okay. Fifteen's a nightmare.' He spoke in a low, confidential tone. 'Most of them have been in and out of youth detention for years – and you know what you find out if you speak to them? They liked it. They actually preferred it to being at home because it was stable. Basic stuff like they knew what time they were getting dinner and what time for lights out.'

Kate asked what happened after the boys left his care.

'They either go home again or, if they're old enough, the Social gives them their own flat.'

He went to a lad slumped in a chair and not talking to the others. He spoke quietly to him but the lad jolted forward and waved his hands around as if he wanted to be left alone. Emma couldn't hear what they said, but it was enough just to see the gestures of comfort met with gestures of despair.

* * *

Nash liked the way Arthur cut his hair and had been going to him for years. He was very regular about it too – every six weeks – but he'd lapsed in recent months. Going out was becoming more of an effort, and if he didn't go out he didn't need to worry about his appearance. But Emma had mentioned that he could do with a trim and offered to drive him.

She helped him off with his jacket as Arthur stood ready with a cover to drape over his shoulders. He hulked over Nash. The scissors were like a child's toy in his meaty hands. Yet he had a deftness of touch in the pinch and snip of Nash's hair that was all the more impressive because of his size. 'Christ, that's some head of hair,' he said, whenever there was a lull in their chat. Arthur himself had an elaborate comb-over. Emma couldn't work out where it started and ended. Up and around, over and back; a slick, black snake wrapped tightly around his skull.

She sat in the corner pretending to read a newspaper while listening to the macho talk between the three barbers and their customers. Sports talk. Health troubles. Casual swearing. Old stories of fights retold for the umpteenth time. She was good at following different conversations at once and her head swam with male triumph, worry and amusement. None of it was mundane, she'd say that for them. Whatever the topic, it was extreme or high stakes or intense. And these were old men. Was this what it was like, she wondered, to go through the world with a pair of balls? It must be exhausting.

'Wait till you hear this one,' said Nash. 'My next-door neighbour got broken into. A week ago last Tuesday, it was.'

'Wee bastards, aren't they?' said Arthur. 'It's not as if it's the dark winter nights, either. Broad daylight. They just don't care. That's the trouble. They just don't care.'

'No fear about them,' said Nash.

'Who've you got next door?'

'George Hendry.'

Arthur cast his eyes up and nodded. 'I knew his brother but not George.'

'He's a miserable sod,' said Nash.

'The brother?'

'No, George – can't stand him. Never knew the brother. No offence to him. Anyway, I was sitting about eight o'clock when the doorbell went. Two policemen, after a witness statement. They told me his house was in a state. Drawers pulled out. Cupboards emptied on the floor. I said to them, I keep the telly up loud for my hearing. Never heard a thing. One of them said that George was giving them grief. *Why didn't they get there sooner? When were they going to catch the wee buggers?* That sort of thing. These two police, they seemed like decent young lads so I told them what I thought of him. I said, we're not good neighbours. I'm not saying he deserved to get burgled – not by any stretch – but God help me he's a miserable man.'

'Did they put that in your witness statement?'

'Off the record. Anyway, the pair of them started to howl

with laughter – and I mean howl like they were going to have an accident in their pants.'

'The police?'

'Aye. Absolutely ending themselves.'

Arthur stopped cutting and stared at Nash in the mirror, waiting for the payoff.

'Turns out the burglars had done a crap in his living room. Right in the middle of the floor. The police said it happens a lot.' He turned and pointed to Emma. 'What's it called when the heart's pumping like mad and the stomach's up in knots?'

'Adrenaline,' she said.

'That's it.' He shot a finger in the air as if he'd only temporarily forgotten the word. 'They said a lot of burglars need to go in the middle of jobs because of it.'

'Ah, the nerves,' said Arthur. 'That's some occupational hazard.'

Afterwards, Nash and Emma went to a cafe, packed and dimly lit against the June sunshine. Emma asked why he hadn't told her about the break-in next door.

'You don't want to be hearing a thing like that.'

'I'll be the judge, thanks.'

'I'd forgotten about it until today.'

'You should have told me and dad. It could have just as easily been you.'

'I'd like to see them try.'

'And I thought you didn't like the police?'

'I don't. Well, I don't usually.'

'But you were having a laugh with them.'

'They were young lads.'

'Still police, though.'

He shrugged.

The afternoon soap opera was on the cafe's wall-mounted television but no-one was watching except the waitress. She set her tray down on the edge of a table and cleared the mess, keeping an eye on the drama and seemingly able to follow it amid the cafe's din.

'I went back to Carluke,' said Emma.

'When?'

'A few weeks ago. I was at the children's home; the one Nell Andrews told us about.'

'Remind me.'

'St Augustine's. The place they took Jenny. It's a boys' home now.'

'And they let you in?'

'I thought you wanted me to keep trying?'

'I do. I do. What's it they say in the detective shows – go where the evidence takes you.'

'Exactly.'

He put on a twangy American accent. 'Investigate without fear or favour.'

'The manager was a really nice man, actually. Down-to-earth and decent. He showed us around.'

Nash said, 'Must be a tough job, that. Hell of a tough.'

Her eyes scanned over him as if weighing up his readiness. 'Suppose I found something there that was hard, emotionally hard. How would you feel?'

'Don't tell me you've found something bad?'

'No, nothing bad but it might be a bit upsetting.'

He rolled his shoulders back and fixed his eyes on her. 'I'd say you're looking at a grown man.'

She put the letter on the table. 'I wasn't sure about giving you this.'

'Why? What is it?'

'It's from your mum. She wrote to them – to get Jenny back. You don't have to read it but I thought you should have it.'

'Is there anything useful in it?'

'Not exactly useful but it backs up what Nell told us. I mean, your mum must have had a reason to write to them.'

There was a long pause as Nash examined the envelope.

'It was in a box of junk,' said Emma.

'Box of junk?'

She nodded. 'Tossed in with old clothes and toys.'

She looked out the window as he read it. One of the kitchen staff was having a cigarette at the back door. He sat on an oil drum, vacant-eyed and exhausted. When she turned back, Nash's eyes had filled with tears. His hands fell to the table like he was holding a heavy weight. 'Oh Christ,' he said, stifling a sob. He looked at it again, very briefly, then flicked it away.

'What am I meant to do with this?'

'I don't know. I just thought you should have it.'

'Not exactly a nice keepsake, is it?'

'But maybe it shows we're in the right ballpark.'

'You think? There were hundreds, maybe thousands of children's homes back then. Maybe she wrote to all of them. Maybe there's letters like this from her all over the country. She was a desperate woman.'

Emma picked up the letter and looked closely at it, all the misspelt words in an unsteady hand. 'She was a brave woman.'

'Brave. Desperate. What difference does it make? A fat lot of good it did her. I think we should take this as a sign. Spence was right. All this is doing is raking up old heartache. We should write to the council and tell them to forget it. Forget the whole thing.'

'We can't do that. This could mean something. It could mean we're close.'

Nash shrugged and said nothing.

'I couldn't just leave it there,' said Emma.

'I suppose not.' Nash picked it up and tucked it inside his jacket. One more piece of heartache for the collection.

22

'I've not broken any rules, have I? You guys should have taken those boxes a few years ago.'

'Did you get their names?'

'Look, the issue here is that you people didn't do your job properly. That's not my fault.'

Eddie Reilly, manager of St Augustine's children's home, was on the phone to Richard Ash, head of records at Strathclyde Council.

'Did you get their names?' repeated Ash.

Reilly paused and scratched his neck. 'I did but I'd need to dig them out.'

'These two girls, what were they looking for?'

'Something about children after the war or between the wars. Can't remember which.'

Ash straightened the angle of the letter opener at the edge of his desk and leaned back in his chair. 'I really do want their names.'

'Look, pal, what is this? They showed me their ID. I'm the manager here. I'm allowed to let people into the place and I don't need you people breathing down my neck about it.'

'You let them look through records. I'm the head of records for the region, so I'd like to know if these two girls you let into your facility had appropriate supervision.'

'This is getting way out of proportion. I could have thrown those boxes in the tip years ago and you'd never have even known about it. But I'm trying to do the right thing here.'

Reilly had finally got round to phoning Strathclyde Council about the boxes in his basement. The office junior had taken his call initially but felt out of his depth so sent it up the management chain. Eventually, Reilly found himself speaking to the head of the department and mentioned that what prompted him to call was a visit a few weeks earlier by two researchers from Edinburgh. Two girls. It was no more than a passing comment, just a bit of context. Reilly couldn't see why

Ash was now so fixated on it.

'I'll send someone to collect the boxes,' said Ash. 'Now these two girls, what did they look like?'

'What the hell is this? I told you. They showed me their student cards. They were legitimate. End of story.'

'So you took their names?'

Reilly cursed under his breath and rifled through the papers on his desk. 'What do their names have to do with anything?'

'I need to know if they were legitimate,' said Ash.

'Why else would they spend hours in a stinking basement going through old boxes?'

'Well, I hope for your sake they were who they said they were.'

'Are you threatening me?' Reilly's heart rate was up now but Ash sounded just as calm as he had at the start of the call.

'I'm checking that you've done your job properly,' said Ash. 'What's the world coming to when a man follows due diligence and is accused of threatening another man? Now, are you going to give me their names because if you can't, I'm going to assume you don't keep appropriate visitor records, which wouldn't be good for someone who's supposed to be the manager of a secure facility.'

'Have it your way, pal. Let's see...' still searching his desk, 'here it is. Lacklow. Emma Lacklow. A sociology researcher. She said she was doing her PhD. Nice young woman. Didn't get the other's name.'

Later that day, Professor Andrew Miller was in his office marking papers when the phone rang. Richard Ash got straight to the point. 'I'm wanting to check about a PhD student. Emma Lacklow. She's one of yours, I believe.'

The name was familiar but Miller had a lot of students. He checked the records. 'Ah, yes. Emma. But she's not postgrad. She's still in first year.'

'That's interesting because she was at one of our children's homes a few weeks ago and told the manager she was doing research for her PhD.'

'That can't be right.'

'That's what I'm told by the manager.'

'There's probably been a mix up.'

'Well I'm sure you can help clarify. St Augustine's is a home for boys from very hard backgrounds. Nut jobs, to be frank. We can't have researchers – or anyone else for that matter – turning up at places like that without the right permissions.'

'Which would be?'

'Permission from me, here at the central office. I'm head of records for the region. The manager of the home let them in. He shouldn't have. I've spoken to him and clarified the procedures. Miss Lacklow had unsupervised access to records for a few hours, and it's me who's accountable – just as it's you who's accountable for Miss Lacklow.'

'I'll speak to her,' said Miller. 'Like I say, I'm sure it's just a mix up.'

'The strange thing is, she came to see me months ago about getting access to our archives but it was a private family matter – nothing to do with her studies but it did involve looking into children's records. That's quite a coincidence, isn't it? She's a rather feisty young woman. She brought a protest to the council offices a few weeks ago. It turned ugly.'

Miller remembered now that Emma was the girl who asked him for advice about tracing a long-lost relative. Something about her family being Travellers and that she was doing it for a dying grandad or uncle. Miller had sent her to the General Registrars with a warning of slim chances of success. If what Ash was telling him now was true, there was no question about it – she'd be expelled. Miller cleared his throat. 'Like I said, I will speak to her.'

'This was a major breach of the rules,' said Ash. 'You'll understand why I'm concerned.'

'You wouldn't have phoned otherwise.'

Miller was about to wind up the call when Ash asked him another question: 'How are the standards on your course these days?'

'I beg your pardon?'

'You know her family are Travellers? If this is what they do when they get an education – use and abuse their institution's good name – they'd be better off not getting an education at all, don't you think?'

'What I think is that I've heard enough of this call.'

'Then let's get to the crux of the matter. Before you hang up, can I clarify, as her supervisor, you were aware of her visit and she was there to do university research?'

Miller paused. 'I've got a lot of students to look after. I'll talk to her and get back to you.'

'Who should I write to in the meantime?'

'You don't need to write to anyone.'

'Of course I do,' said Ash. 'There needs to be a proper record of this. Time and date – and the nature of the discussion. Not that I'm saying I don't trust you, but two men chatting on the phone isn't a record. I'll need to notify the right authorities at the university. I'm assuming you have a boss.'

'Look, if you'd give me a week, I'll talk to Emma and get back to you. I'm sure we can sort it out.'

'I'm sure we can but I'll still need to send a record of my concerns. I'll write to the principal.' A click then the line went dead and Miller sat for a moment, frowning at the receiver.

23

Next morning, Emma wandered into the kitchen, scratching and yawning. She tied up her dressing-gown and switched on the radio. Spence was in the middle of a phone call but watched as she clattered around, making breakfast: cornflakes poured into a bowl with some scattered over the side, onto the counter-top. She fished a teabag out of her mug, shook it and tossed it in the sink. Now only half listening to the man on the other end of the line, Spence grabbed a dish towel and threw it at her, gesturing grumpily at the counter. 'Right then...I will...I'll let her know...she'll be in touch. Bye.' He hung up and stood for a moment, picking at the grouting between the tiles on the wall.

Emma asked, 'Was that for me?'

'I thought you'd gone out already.'

'I was working till 12.30 last night. Busy one.'

'Fair enough. No classes this morning?'

'Later on. Are you okay? You look tense.'

He nodded towards the phone. 'That call.'

'What?'

'It was some professor from your university.'

'Which?'

'Miller. Something about you being at a children's home in Carluke. He's had some bigwig from Strathclyde Council giving him grief. They're saying you fibbed your way in to look at records.'

Emma rolled her eyes. 'I got fed up waiting for those muppets at the council to get back to me. Might as well do their job for them.'

'Well the professor wants a word with you. Apparently, the principal of the university has his knickers in a flap about it.'

'Ah, bollocks.'

'I did warn you.' She waited for him to get angry but it never came. He actually looked semi amused as he took off his jacket and sat down. 'He said you've been late with a few assignments and missed classes too.'

'I've maybe gotten a bit distracted recently but I'll catch up.'

'Hey, listen. Don't worry about it. We all make an arse of something at some point in our lives. Maybe going to university just isn't for you. If you're struggling, why don't you pack it in?'

'I'm not – I'm not struggling.'

He gestured for her to sit down. 'There's no point putting up a front with me. The professor told me all about it. You're in it up to your eyeballs. He wants a meeting with you. You've to call him back.'

She took a breath, running through different scenarios; what Professor Miller might say and how she might respond to wiggle out if it. 'Look, I'll talk to him. It'll be okay.'

'You want my opinion? Bugger them. Bugger the lot of them. Why don't you leave and work with me? We could build up a business together.'

'Are you joking?'

'Emma, I wouldn't be saying any of this if you were making a success of university, but you're not, are you?' His tone was soft and reasonable. 'I'm not religious or superstitious or whatever, but some things happen for a reason.'

'I told you; I've been distracted but I'll catch up.'

'I'm talking about everything we've been going through recently. Mum leaving and the bad news about Nash. Then there was what happened with Archie, God bless him, and now this. It could be a sign.'

She stared at him. Where was he going with this? 'Dad, it's not a sign of anything. It's just life. Things happen.'

'Hear me out. I need a reliable partner, right? Someone with their head screwed on the right way. Someone I can trust. It doesn't matter how good I am – I'm still just one man. Maybe that person's been under my nose this whole time?' He smiled and gestured at her.

She let out a nervous laugh. 'I'm not listening to this.' She got up to leave but he got up too, and put his hand on her shoulder.

'Wait a minute,' he said. 'I've found a cheap industrial

unit. It just needs a lick of paint and it'll be fine. See, I've been thinking – what's holding me back is the lack of premises. It just doesn't look good to be trading out of a van these days. So we'll go up market. No more cleaning rags and hoover bags.' He was animated now, talking quickly, eyes wide, and hands waving. 'If we're going to do it, we'll do it right. We'll go for it. It'll be a proper family business. Something to be proud of. I'll be out on the road with deliveries and you'll be in the showroom dealing with customers and...'

Emma cut him off. '*Showroom*? Dad, this is delusional.'

'This place I've found – it's ideal. I'll arrange an appointment for you to see it. You'll love it. It's perfect. All I need is the first three months' rent up front and it's ours.'

'Dad, I know what happened with Archie was a big shock – and really unlucky with the money and everything else but, seriously, what the fuck are you talking about?'

He put his hands on her shoulders and faced her square on. 'You've got to be bold in life. I've spent 30 years being timid and it's got me nowhere. This time it's going to work but I need you on board. Why don't you get another loan from university? Drain them for every penny then leave. I'd see you right within six months. Father to daughter, I promise.'

24

Nash was in the armchair, unshaven and uncombed, propped up with extra pillows from the bedroom. He put on the mask, turned on the cylinder, and sat back with the stream of oxygen tickling his face. Behind him, Spence clattered around in the kitchen. After a few minutes, he brought him his lunchtime pills on a tray with a plate of pie and beans. Nash pulled the mask from his mouth and let it fall to his chest. 'I'm feeling *shan* today. *Awffy shan.* I have to think about every breath.' He made a fist, pressed it to his mouth, and closed his eyes tight as his body shook in the grip of a dense, multi-layered cough.

'How do I look?'

'Braw,' said Spence. 'Still a heartbreaker.'

'You effin liar. I feel just about done with it. You hear me? Done with everything.'

'Stop it with that nonsense. I need you here.'

'Make use of me while you've got me.' Nash paused. 'Something's bothering you.'

'It's not an issue as far as I'm concerned,' said Spence, 'and nothing I didn't see coming.' Another pause. 'Emma's got herself in a jam at university.' He pulled up a footstool, sat down, and told him about the phone call from Professor Miller. 'I tried telling her. I said, this shows you what matters in life. Family. It's the only thing you can depend on.' He patted Nash's hand. 'I'm sorry about the way I acted before when you asked her to find your sister. It's been a good lesson for her.'

'You've changed your tune.'

'I've been reflecting on it,' said Spence. 'It's shown her what I've been trying to tell her since she was wee – family are the only people you can trust in life. You think back to when she first started at university. Starstruck with it. And now look; they've turned on her. And for what?' Spence pursed his lips and shook his head bitterly. 'For trying to do right by her own family.'

'So now it's our turn to support her.'

Spence only shrugged.

'You're not too bothered if she gets thrown out, are you?'

'Sometimes it's best just to let things run their course.'

'And sometimes it's not a bad idea to think about things in advance. Plan ahead. We're not the beasts of the field. So let's say she does get thrown out – then what? She ends up where exactly? Working at the racetrack or in a rusty van with you? Bit of both, maybe?'

'It is possible that she found it harder than she was expecting. The way I see it, it's like the big fish in the small pond.'

'Fish? You talk a load of rubbish sometimes, you really do.'

'I'm serious. I've been thinking about this.'

'Thinking too much. Your brain's gone haywire.'

'Hear me out. She was always the smartest in class all the way through school. But now she's at a fancy university where they're all smart buggers. Right?'

Nash nodded reluctantly.

'They can't all be top of the class, can they?' continued Spence. 'Some of them are going to struggle to keep the pace. Maybe she's just one of them.'

'No way,' said Nash. 'She's clever – a *fly gouri*. I knew she was smart from the day I put her on my knee to read her a story.' He broke off to cough, hunching forwards, his baggy blue shirt unbuttoned to midway down his scrawny chest. His shoulders curled forwards and his head hung down. The effect was like a wilting flower. It was a long coughing fit. When it seemed to have stopped, it started again, with his body shaking as if being driven through by rivets till he slumped back, his eyes bloodshot and streaming. He wiped his mouth with a napkin. 'Spence, you did talk to her, didn't you? As her dad, you sat down with her and told her not to give up? We're her family. Do right by your own – your words.'

Spence tapped the edge of Nash's plate. 'Eat up. Your food's getting cold. She's always going on about us respecting her independence, her rights. So I reckon she's grown up enough to steer her own course.'

'I thought I was a man at twenty but still had plenty to

learn about life. Come on, she's had a rough ride in the last few years, what with Fran leaving the way she did.'

'We've all had rough rides,' said Spence. 'I was fourteen when my dad died and...'

'Spence, Spence, Spence – sometimes you're like a broken record, son.' Nash held up his fork and gestured angrily at him with it. 'She's the first Lacklow to do anything like go to university. You could at least have asked for a meeting with her lecturer.'

Spence tipped a couple of pills into his hand and passed him a glass of water. 'It sounds like it's too late for that. Anyway, if she gets a lesson in what it's like out in the real world, it'll be good for her.'

* * *

The Department of Sociology was a warren of dark corridors, burrowing deep through the building. Staff criss-crossed the hall, going between rooms. A janitor walked with Nash, gripping his elbow, guiding him to the right office. A secretary showed him in and Miller got up to shake hands. They smiled and took the measure of each other – the sociologist and the ex-labourer and sometime-artist. They read their clothes, mannerisms and accents.

'This is just between me and you,' said Nash. 'You won't tell Emma I came to see you?'

'I'm happy to respect your wishes,' said Miller. 'I'm seeing her tomorrow. Please, take a seat.'

Nash sat down and set his walking stick to the side. 'I'm not sure what she'll tell you but she's been going through a lot over the last year.' He opened his hands, spreading out gnarled fingers. 'Her mum upped and left. Gone to live in one of those – what'd you call it – a commune in the middle of nowhere.'

'Emma's father never mentioned that when we spoke.'

'He wouldn't. Spence is very private. That's why I wanted to see you.'

Professor Miller leaned back and knitted his fingers, flexing thin wrists back and forth. He was silvery stubbled and softly spoken and had risen in the ranks of the university

152

but was now privately disillusioned and lacked the appetite to go any higher. He loved sociology and felt childishly resentful of his management responsibilities, as if they drained his intellectual creativity. 'I need to be honest with you,' he said. 'This is a serious situation. She could lose her place on the course. Are you and Emma close?'

'I've seen her grow up,' said Nash. 'She's like a grand-daughter to me. We've been spending more time together recently since I got my diagnosis.' Nash told him about his limited life expectancy. 'So you see, all this stuff about Emma at the children's home, digging around in their records – whatever that was. That was me. I asked her to do it because there isn't much time left. She was just trying to help.'

Professor Miller looked at him but didn't speak. He was at ease in the chair beside his desk. He made small, delicate movements around the space. Things were exactly where he needed them to be. Books, pens, stacks of papers on the desk and on the floor.

'Look at me,' said Nash. A chuckle and disdainful gesture at his shrunken body. 'I'm in no fit state to travel across the country and root about in a basement. I could barely make it in here to see you. I'll be paying for this tomorrow.'

Miller cupped the side of his face, pressing his arm into his body and wrapping the other one around his stomach. 'When I spoke to Emma's dad, he said he'd give her a kick up the backside.'

'See, now, that's Spence to a tee. No nonsense.'

'When did her mum leave?'

'Last summer. Just before Emma started university.'

'And you think that might have affected her?'

'Of course it has,' said Nash. 'It's made things harder at home. Don't get me wrong; Spence's heart's in the right place, but he's stubborn. Fixed in his ways. He's all about working and making money for the family.'

'Nothing wrong with that, is there?'

'No, absolutely not. That's how he was raised. It's all he's known.'

'That's very admirable.'

'Of course it is, but his line of work doesn't bring in a lot of money.'

'What does he do?'

'Hawker. He sells carpets and rugs – when he can. We're of Traveller stock, you see, and Spence is from a line of carpet hawkers. I'd never say it to him, but there's no future in it these days. He's got grand plans about building a family business and wants to rope Emma into it. He never thought it was a good idea for her to come to university. He can't relate to it.'

'He'll have a different set of values,' said Miller.

'Exactly. Her coming here was her mum's idea but Fran's gone now and she's only got Spence. I'm not going to be here much longer. You see what I'm saying?' Nash paused and dropped his voice, as if fearful of committing the words to the air. 'She's not got the right support – at home.'

'What would she do if she wasn't at university?'

Nash studied his hands, turned them over, back and forth, then ran his thumb across the knuckles of his other hand. 'Prospects? I really don't know but I'm worried about the influence Spence would have on her, with her mum not being around. Look, I know she shouldn't have done it – gone to that place – but please, can you see what you can do for her? She's a good lass.'

'I'll do my best.'

Nash leaned to one side and took his cigarettes from his jacket. 'Sorry, do you mind if I...?'

'Please go ahead.'

He angled the open packet towards Miller. 'Smoke yourself?'

'I shouldn't. I'm trying to stop, but...' He got up and took one. He looked again at Emma's file but didn't seem concerned with it. 'I remember Emma telling me your family are Travellers. Fascinating.'

Nash nodded and straightened up. 'The Lacklows hail from Dumfriesshire. We're from a line, a well-known line. There's a queen away back somewhere, according to Emma.

154

But in my time it's been horse dealers, basketweavers and hawkers.'

'What was it like?'

'Growing up?'

'Yes, as a Traveller.'

'Hard. It was very hard.' Nash spoke about his life and Miller sat transfixed, wishing he had more time to research the experiences of people like Nash. Cigarette smoke drifted around the room. They could have been two men in a bar somewhere.

When they finished, Nash took his walking stick and got up. 'Sorry about giving you chapter and verse there, about the family situation. I just wanted you to hear the full story. You know what it's like with families.'

'I do indeed,' said Miller. 'We all have families and all have hinterlands.'

'Och aye,' said Nash. 'Heartbreak doesn't discriminate. We're all helpless against it.'

25

The train was stifling in the summer heat. Warehouses and fences streaked past then gave way to fields and hills as the carriage pitched and rocked gently over the tracks. Nash watched out the window and told Emma about a documentary he'd seen a few nights earlier. 'It was about two brothers who'd been orphaned during the war. There was a lot of stories like that during the war. Kids left without parents. It would break your heart, so it would.' He wiped his glasses and blinked in the sun's glare. 'These two brothers, they were put into separate care homes and lost contact with each other till, years later, one of them decides he wants to trace the other. This was just a few years ago. He was in his fifties by then. And guess what? He found him. Tracked him down in Australia. Australia! Opposite side of the bloody world.' He looked out the window, his eyes following the flickering run of the landscape. 'I'm glad we didn't give up,' said Emma. 'We've been working so hard on this, we're due a bit of luck.'

They arrived in Glasgow just after lunchtime and got a taxi to the council headquarters on India Street. Back again, thought Emma, looking up at the ten-storey block. The windows caught the light and vibrated as buses and lorries rumbled past.

A tall woman in a floral-patterned smock met them at reception and introduced herself as Elizabeth Foster, Head of Children's Welfare. She took them up to her third-floor office where Nash cast unsettled eyes around the room. He'd been expecting a 'suit', a pinstriped pen-pusher. More than that, he wanted a man so he could talk sternly and not mince words, but Miss Foster and her pleasant office made him less inclined to anger. There were plants, tapestries on the walls and bookshelves lined with titles about modern parenting and family matters.

'Please,' she said, gesturing to a table by the window. 'Your case was referred to me by Councillor O'Grady.'

'He apologised,' said Nash.

'I want to say sorry too, for what happened to your sister and how we've dealt with your request.' She sat next to him and wrung her hands. Her voice was gentle and reassuring. 'It might have been a long time ago but that doesn't excuse what happened. What was your sister's name?'

'Jenny. We called her Wee Jenny.'

'What was she like?'

'I wish I could say. I remember a grin but maybe that's just wishful thinking.'

The secretary brought tea and biscuits and Nash allowed himself to relax. As he recounted what was by now the well-rehearsed story of his sister's removal, Elizabeth Foster listened with her head cocked and a mildly-pained expression.

He brought out the old family photo and showed it to her. 'That's the only picture of us all. That was the year before my father died. The ugly wee runt there, that's me. The wee one there, that's Jenny. She'd have been about five when it happened.'

'I gather you've been doing a lot of your own research,' said Miss Foster.

'I've done hee-haw,' said Nash. 'It's Emma who's done all the work. She's the brains of the outfit. She goes to university. She's right into this sort of thing; protests, causes, getting on her soapbox.'

'So I heard,' said Miss Foster.

Emma handed her a piece of paper with the details for St Augustine's children's home. 'We're pretty sure this is where they took her. It was a receiving home back then so kids didn't stay there too long.'

'That's very helpful. I'll pass it to our archivist.' She turned to Nash. 'Mr Lacklow, I'm grateful you've come forward about this. Really, I am. It helps us understand more about our own historic practices. But please understand this case is very old. So the chances of you being able to find your sister now, after...'

Emma cut in: 'No offence, but every official I've spoken to

has said the same thing – that it's impossible. We won't find anything.'

Miss Foster leaned across the table and touched Nash's hand, her brow creased, her voice hushed. 'Don't get me wrong. What you've gathered is impressive and it'll certainly help when we look into it but I don't want to get your hopes up. That's all I'm saying. We'll try our best but there's still a strong likelihood we won't find anything.'

'It's all right,' said Nash. 'God knows this all happened way before your time. I'll cope. I've gone this long not knowing what happened to her so the worst case scenario is I'll just carry on not knowing. But I'll tell you what I don't understand about it all...' He hunched forwards, resting his arms on his knees. 'How? How could anybody do that, actually tear a child away from their mother's arms?'

'I can't imagine.'

'Why did somebody think that was for the best?'

'I'm sorry,' said Miss Foster, 'I just don't know how to answer that.' She got up and took a couple of leaflets from the shelf. 'You've been very brave in revisiting this.' She laid them on the table and nudged them towards him. 'Have you considered speaking to anyone about this, about how it's affected you?'

Nash stared at the leaflets. 'What are those?'

'Psychological therapy.'

He looked up at her, horrified at the implication. 'A head doctor. No, no, no. There's nothing the matter with me, hen.' Straightening himself up, he tapped the side of his head and narrowed his eyes. 'The only way it's got to me is I've never been able to stand looking at photos – family photos. I mean, that one there...' he gestured at the old family picture. 'Emma will tell you what I was like when she pulled it out from a pile.'

'Like he'd seen a ghost,' said Emma.

'I hadn't seen it in decades. But I don't even like seeing photos from years later, when me and my brothers were older. I'm talking about when we were grown men. Long after she'd gone. Weddings, birthdays – whatever the big occasion was –

if I look at those pictures, I don't see us. I only see her. Jenny's not there, of course, but she sort of is, like an invisible presence. I see it in our eyes. A sort of sadness, I suppose.' Transfixed by the thought, Nash's gaze fell to the floor. 'It's just the guilt, you know. Tremendous guilt. It comes at me when I realise I've forgotten about her, forgotten that she was even there in the first place.'

Miss Foster finished her coffee and stared into her cup. 'I'll speak to our archives department. I'll make sure they have a thorough search but please remember – the chances are slim.'

'But you will make sure they try?' said Emma.

'I promise.'

'What a sweetheart you are,' said Nash, taking her hand and squeezing it. 'You're breaking the mould here, you really are. I'm very much obliged.'

They stayed a while longer and Miss Foster spoke to them about emotional pain and family trauma. It was, she believed, an area that would become better understood as brave people like Nash came forward with their personal experiences. As they were leaving, she reassured them that children's welfare was what got her out of bed each morning and kept her up at night. Every case mattered. There really was no faulting her, thought Nash.

On the train home, his thoughts channelled into gulfs of doubt and uncertainty. 'Have I been foolish with all this?'

'If you've been foolish, God knows what that makes me,' said Emma.

'Back there – Miss Foster was right. I know I'm probably not going to find her. I do know that. But as long as she ended up somewhere better, that's all that matters. She was probably just as well shot of it all. The old life. Once she was a bit older, she probably wouldn't remember any of it. Sometimes I forget we were dirt-poor. No shoes. Surely it wouldn't have been hard for her to move up in the world after that?' He scratched his neck and mulled this, trying to reason with himself whether he'd done the right thing. 'Remember, months back, when you were telling me about your university course. You said something about the class system – people moving up and bettering themselves.'

'Social mobility.'

'Aye, so maybe getting taken off us gave her a leg up the social ladder. It might have done her a favour in the long run.' He took the photo out of his pocket and looked at it. 'I see her ending up with a nice family. She was about the right age for it. Still an adorable wee thing.'

'No doubt about it,' said Emma.

'They probably put her with one of those poor couples, you know, the ones who can't have kids of their own. A wee one like her would have brightened their lives. Just because the Social took her the way they did, doesn't mean she didn't go to a good family. You know what I'm saying?'

'It's how her life turned out in the end that matters,' said Emma.

'That's what I'm going to hold on to after this. What was it Miss Foster said back there about what I was looking for? What was the word?'

'Closure,' said Emma.

'That's it. I'm looking for closure. Maybe I just need to find it in myself.'

The sun glinted off Nash's glasses as he drummed his fingers on the table. He turned to her and said, 'The American Indians got their bairns taken off them, too. I've been reading a book about it. You'll like it. It's right up your street. Not an easy read but powerful, I'd say. Do you think there could be, like, how would you put it – some sort of connection there?'

'How'd you mean?'

'Between all the poor buggers of the world who've been shat on by governments.'

'Like a connection between persecuted minorities?'

'I'm talking about something that passes down through the years, through generations, across the continents. Some-thing spiritual, almost.'

'There are theories about collective psychological trauma.'

160

Nash screwed up his face. 'Nah, something more hopeful than that.'

'An affinity?'

'That's the one. An affinity.' He pinned his shoulders back and threw a proud look at the world. Pylons waltzed past the windows as the land softened and colours deepened in the afternoon glow. Purple shadows streaked the hills and peaks and crags persisted and repeated themselves from a gradually-changing angle as the train moved along the bend of the tracks.

26

The old woman stood, squinting and sun-dazzled, in the door of her cottage. 'So you're Andy Miller's naughty girl,' she said with a wink. 'He told me you've been stirring up all kinds of trouble.' A Golden Retriever went berserk at her side and she cursed at it to be quiet.

'The trouble wasn't intentional,' said Emma. 'Not really. It was more like accidental trouble.'

'It doesn't matter,' said Dr Dorothy Chester. 'Andy likes you so hang in there. According to the gossip, the principal was spitting tacks but Andy got you off the hook.'

'There's gossip?'

'Oh, yes,' said Dr Chester.

'I didn't know it was that big a deal.'

'Academics are a sad little bunch. We take our thrills wherever we can get them. You're an ivory tower rebel. But with that surname, I'm not surprised. Not really.'

Emma wasn't sure what she meant.

'Your lineage, my dear. Your rebel blood.'

Still, it took a moment for the penny to drop. 'Ah,' said Emma, 'you're talking about Queen Lacklow.'

It was a week since Emma sat down with Professor Miller for what was recorded in her student file as a disciplinary meeting. She received a formal warning for what she did in Carluke. The university recognised that it was a first-time offence, so she wouldn't be expelled but she was left in no doubt about the seriousness of what had taken place. Privately, though, Andrew Miller didn't care. In fact, he admired her tenacity. Weren't faculty always being told to encourage students to use their initiative, to think outside the box? Of course, he said what he was required to say about the student code of conduct but speaking off the record, he understood it was exceptional personal circumstances that led her to bend the truth to get into the children's home. At the end of their meeting, he gave her the details of a retired colleague who might be able to help with the search.

'What did he tell you about me?' asked Dorothy Chester.

'That you're an expert and I should get in touch.'

Inside, they went to Dr Chester's study and, without fanfare, she handed Emma a thick sheaf of typed pages and told her she could take it home with her. Emma's lips parted in surprise as she read the manuscript title – *The Never-Ending Road: A Contemporary History of Gypsies in Britain*.

'I finished it a few years ago. Something to keep me out of mischief in retirement. Now, if I could only get some bugger to publish it before I die that would be ideal. If I'd been a man, you can be assured it would have been published by now. Without doubt.'

They went out with the dog, cut down a lane, and were soon on a dirt track that skirted the edge of a field behind the cottages. Dr Chester told Emma about her career. She'd taught history in Edinburgh for 30 years but had never been made a professor, for which she blamed what she called a club of silly little men.

She was broad and bowlegged, walking with a hunch and purposeful pace, all the time alert to the land, as if soaking up its energies. Mostly, her manner was brisk and she laughed in quick, nervous snorts.

Emma told her how she'd hit a brick wall in the search for Jenny and that she'd become very frustrated.

'What age was Jenny?' asked Dr Chester.

'Around five.'

Dr Chester sucked her teeth and grimaced as she strode along. Emma got the impression that she bore some discomfort, perhaps a sore knee or hip that she wasn't about to let get the better of her. Emma said she was working on the assumption that Nash's sister was put up for adoption.

'Well now,' said Dr Chester, 'if we're talking about Traveller children, it certainly wasn't many who got adopted. You could say those who did were the lucky ones.'

Emma asked what she meant.

'There were three options that depended on the child's

age. The oldest girls were sent away to be servants, the oldest boys sent to the navy. The youngest – those five and under – were sent for adoption. But the five to twelve year olds were less fortunate.'

Emma blinked and her eyelashes caught blurred sparkles of refracted light. 'Less fortunate?'

Dr Chester's pale, alert eyes settled on her. 'They got stuck in children's homes. So in your case, with a five year old, it could have gone either way. She might have been adopted or…'

Emma turned to her. 'Kept in a children's home – at five years old?'

'Those were hard times. You need to understand that nobody really wanted Traveller children. They were seen as dirty and wild.' She said it plainly and unflinchingly, like a doctor delivering a bad prognosis.

Emma threw the ball for the dog and its tongue lolled and became flecked with dirt. A low hum of contentment came off the land as tiny flies zipped about.

'There's no point lying to you,' said Dr Chester. 'Children's homes were harsh, sometimes cruel places. If kids weren't already on a bad path in life, growing up in a children's home was sure to put them on one. They'd get out at fourteen or fifteen and, well, the best thing I can say is that their prospects weren't good. Alcohol, violence, crime – that tended to be how their lives panned out.'

Emma stopped and put her hands on her head. She swallowed the urge to say – no more. Please, no more.

'There were many types of homes,' continued Dr Chester. 'It was quite an industry – reformatories for young criminals, orphanages, convalescent homes for the sick, receiving homes and working homes. You name it. All run by religious organisations. They thought they knew best, of course.'

The Ettrick Hills were sun bleached and sinuous in the distance. Emma's skin turned slick and prickly in the afternoon heat and she began to feel sick. She rubbed her brow and it reddened and wrinkled under the pressure of her fingers. 'I never thought…I never stopped to think that I might find out something I didn't want to know.'

Back in the cottage they went to the kitchen where Emma met Dr Chester's husband. He'd set a lemon, a knife and three glasses on the counter. Dr Chester glanced at her watch. It was approaching six o'clock.

'Now Richard,' she said, 'you're not allowed to go to the drinks cabinet until precisely six. Do you hear me? Six on the dot.'

His eyes twinkled at Emma. 'This is what she does; she teases me. Tortures me!'

'Oh, Richard, stop being melodramatic.'

The clock struck the hour and Mr Chester brought out the gin. He filled the glasses with ice and poured, and the drinks fizzed on the sunlit counter top. Over dinner, Emma noticed the way the Chesters acted out a playful sort of pantomime annoyance with each other yet still showed tenderness. There was a tug of sadness inside about her mum and dad splitting up. Flushed with gin and the heat of the day, she tried to make conversation but Dorothy Chester's earlier words kept coming back. The children who got adopted were the lucky ones.

It was a knot of her own making, with no-one to turn to for help. Despite warm words from the council, the chances of them finding anything were still remote. So why drop this news on Nash now? But what if, one day the phone rings or an envelope drops through the door. What then?

* * *

Next day, she drove to the village of Roslin on a tip from Dr Chester. She followed the bend of the road to a church overlooking the glen. She went inside and sat below the light of a stained-glass window. She heard the echo of a door closing behind her then footsteps coming closer on the flagstone floor. The minister smiled and said good afternoon. She asked if he knew anything about an exhibition. He led her up a narrow staircase to a door with a sign: Gypsy Curiosities.

It was a small room, lined with glass cabinets displaying paintings, photos, ornaments.

'It's okay to look around?'

'Yes, yes – that's why it's here.'

'I'm a descendant of Queen Lacklow.'

The minister nodded and smiled but it meant nothing to him.

There were pictures of a tiny cottage in the village of Yetholm known as the Gypsy Palace. A faded print of Charles Faa Blythe, a handsome old man on a throne in the middle of a field. He was high cheek-boned and wiry in a crown and robes for his coronation as King of the Gypsies on 30 May 1898. There were coins, postcards, rusty horseshoes and a wall-mounted fiddle said to be owned by Scotland's finest gypsy musician. Then she noticed a copy of the book *A History of Scottish Gypsies* by Charlotte Harris. It sat angled forward on a box in the centre of one of the cabinets.

She asked the minister who owned the collections.

'The family of the lord of the glen,' he said.

She told him how a copy of the same book was held in the rare collections at the National Library and that she'd been reading it recently. 'I seem to be following it around,' she added.

'Or it's following you.'

27

She always told him it was a safe area because of all the students but she didn't know there was a notorious neighbourhood not ten minutes' walk away. Back in the fifties and sixties, you'd take your life in your hands going anywhere near it. And at this hour on a Saturday night, the streets around the nearby homeless shelter would be strewn with drug addicts and drunks. Spence squeezed his eyes shut to block out the ugly thoughts and tried to distract himself with the radio. It was approaching 12.30 and Emma was almost half an hour late. Where the hell was she? He got out and walked up and down the street then went back to the van and rifled around in the glove compartment, sorting out papers that didn't need to be sorted.

Nightmares bulldozed through his mind – she was murdered or lying raped in an alley. Someone had got her drunk then given her pills and she'd done something stupid like going up on a roof – then slipped. He couldn't stop thinking about terrible scenarios. He could barely comprehend it, but these things happened. Nightmares could become reality. He didn't follow the news but these types of stories had a way of coming to his attention. Usually it would be Nash, waving some horrid headline at him and prodding it as if to say; lightning bolts are out there, hanging in the atmosphere, waiting to strike. Please God, not our Emma.

Recently, there'd been news stories about a man murdering young women around the north of England. He was still on the loose and the newspapers had given him a nickname, but Spence tried to avoid the details. What he knew of the cases was more than enough. Victims would be abducted coming home from nights out, walking in the street, or waiting for a bus. Some of the girls weren't even far from home but they'd just disappear. *Last seen saying goodnight to her friends.* The police would be at a loss and parents would be bereft. Then a few weeks later, the discovery of a ragged body, dumped miles away. When he allowed it to take hold, the idea that the person he loved most in the world could suddenly and irreversibly cease to exist was unbearable.

He sighed and checked his watch again. She was now almost 45 minutes late. He could understand her being a bit late. It was her birthday after all, but this really wasn't like her.

It was 12.45 when she finally showed up. She was with Kate and they were coming down the road arm in arm, laughing and swaying under the amber glow of the street lights.

He twisted the key in the ignition, choking the engine into life. Emma stopped in the glare of the van's headlights and did a little jig, then grabbed Kate and spun her round in a playful foxtrot. Right in front of him. His grip on the steering wheel tightened. They were laughing and Emma's head lolled back in a giddy swoon.

'I was worried sick,' he fumed when she opened the door.

Her brow furrowed over bleary eyes as she checked her watch. 'Am I late? Oops.' She slurred an apology and started to explain how she'd lost track of time.

'Just get in,' he said. 'You're drunk.'

She pulled a comically grumpy face and told him to calm down.

He said, 'I had you lying dead somewhere.'

'Okay, okay. Jesus. Okay. I'm sorry.' She held up a hand as if to stifle his concerns. 'We were at the pub but then we met some friends and they said they knew this guy who was having a party...'

'Emma, I've got to be up early tomorrow so would you just get in the van.'

'She could have stayed at mine, Mr Lacklow.' Kate smiled and draped an arm over Emma's shoulder.

'Excuse me,' he snapped, 'this is between me and my daughter.'

Emma swayed and gripped the van door. Her words came out on a woozy mudslide of drunkenness. 'Hey, don't you talk to her like that. This lady here...this lady...she's my best friend. The best. She escorted me through the streets...' She gestured at the van and put on a theatrical posh voice. 'To my awaiting carriage.'

'Well, I daresay it was your pals who got you into this state.'

'It's called having a good time,' said Emma. 'You should try it sometime.'

Spence switched off the engine. 'What's that you're saying?'

'It's good to get a break from all the grief.'

'Oh really. What grief would that be?'

'Domestic. Trouble and strife on the homefront.'

'Your mum shipped off and left you but you reckon I'm the one giving you grief? Me? Who's working hard to give you a home, doing the job of two parents. That's grief? You don't know you're born, you silly wee lassie. Get in.'

She shook her head but Spence reached across and grabbed her arm. She slapped a hand over his, trying to prise it off, and they were locked briefly in an awkward tug of war till Kate pulled her away. She shouted, 'Don't you fucking dare touch her.'

Spence's face fell as he lurched back. His eyes flashed wide and panicky, like he'd just woken from a nightmare. 'Fine. Go on. Get out of my sight.'

The van door slammed shut and Spence watched them walk away. Then he sat for a long time, staring at the empty street. He muttered to himself and rubbed his fingers, cursing sporadically through gritted teeth. He caught himself going through cliches about hard hard-working, under-appreciated parents and their ungrateful children. Of course, he never had wild teenage years. He'd been pulled out of school at fourteen and put to work for his family. Grief? Emma didn't know the meaning of the word. He replayed parts of what had just taken place but changed his reactions and things he'd said, making them more measured, and in this version, Emma wished Kate goodnight, got into the van, and he drove her home.

Spence visited Nash a few nights later. On television, the rerun of a seventies sitcom. A man of slight build paraded in a floral-patterned shirt, firing out innuendo and waspish humour. Canned laughter over high camp oohs and aahs.

Mock outrage from the other characters. A vicar, a middle-aged man of military bearing, and a woman who looked like she'd chair a village committee of some sort.

'God save us,' groaned Spence. 'Can we put this nonsense off?'

'What's the matter?' said Nash. 'I like this one. It's not been on for years.'

Spence grabbed the remote and switched to another channel. A music show. On stage, a band fronted by an androgynous singer. Make-up and teased-out hair. Hips and arms swinging amid lights and dry ice.

Spence nodded at the screen. 'You ever wonder what it's doing to the youngsters?'

'Bloody awful,' said Nash. 'Bleeps and whistles. It's not real music. More like a computer on the blink.'

'I mean the way they're dressing these days. Some of them, you wouldn't know what you're looking at.'

Nash squinted at the screen. 'That's a lassie.'

'It's a laddie.'

'A lassie.'

'I'm telling you, it's a laddie.'

'So what's your point?' asked Nash.

'Maybe it's confusing for youngsters to see this kind of thing.'

'How would you know?'

'I'm a parent, aren't I? I'm allowed to be concerned.'

'Are you still peeved about Em cutting her hair?'

A frown and shake of the head. 'I'm just saying, this type of thing...' he gestured again at the television. 'Ach, it doesn't matter.'

'Where is she, anyway?' asked Nash. 'Not seen her for a while.'

'She's hitting the books. Lots on at university.'

'Never does anything by halves, does she?'

The truth was Emma hadn't been home since the night of the argument.

* * *

He pretended to browse the shelves but kept an eye on the counter and waited for an opening. When it was clear, he approached, handing over a pile of paperbacks. 'I think he's just about read the entire library by now,' he joked. The librarian was a thin woman with an inscrutable face and huge, bouffant fifties hair-do. She smiled and began return-stamping the books as Spence continued: 'He's read so many of those detective stories, I reckon he could write his own.' The librarian nodded, having got the joke the first time. She asked about Nash. Was he recovering all right and would he be back at the library any time soon? Then she asked how Emma was getting on at university.

'Oh, she's giving me grey hairs.' Spence gave her a weary smile that said – you know what kids are like these days. 'While we're on the subject, I was wondering if you have any advice books. You know, like guidance for parents.'

'What's the issue?'

'Oh, just kids growing up, getting into boyfriends and girlfriends. The usual carry on.'

The librarian asked if he could be more specific.

'Never mind,' he said. 'Have you got any books on parenting at all?'

The family section was a couple of shelves of books about adoption, fostering, and bringing up troublesome teens. Front covers with muted colours and willowy fonts whispered of sensitive issues, calmly discussed. He took one off the shelf and flicked through it – challenging behaviour, nurturing independence, avoiding smothering. He gave up, picked up more crime novels for Nash, and returned to the counter. The librarian asked if he had found what he was looking for.

'Not exactly.'

'I could call one of the other libraries. They might have what you're after.'

'I've troubled you enough.'

He thanked her and went quickly to the exit but stopped at the door. He took a deep breath then forced himself back to the desk. 'It's my daughter,' he said. 'She's making new pals at university and getting all kinds of ideas in her head.'

'Sorry, I'm still not sure what you mean.'

He checked no-one else was within earshot then leaned closer. 'She's got a girlfriend,' he whispered. 'We've had a fall-out and I said some things I shouldn't have. I'm on my own, you see. My wife's gone and I'm needing some help. Bit of advice.'

The librarian smiled and patted his arm. 'I've got three of my own. I know what it's like.' She took a leaflet from a wall rack behind the desk. 'The meetings are every Thursday at seven o'clock.'

A few nights later, a group of women sat in a circle at the local community hall. Next to them, a table with a plate of biscuits, a kettle and a jar of coffee. Jeanette, the group's leader, had just started the evening's discussion when the door creaked and she became aware of a figure lurking at the entrance. She held up her hand. 'Welcome. Please, come in.' Spence hurried in and took a seat, avoiding eye contact with the others.

'We've been talking about change,' said Jeanette, 'and how finding out your child is gay or lesbian represents something beyond our control.' Jeanette looked and spoke like she'd never be in a rush for anything. Her voice was low-wattage and she slumped in the chair, legs stretched out and crossed at the ankles. She invited Spence to say a bit about himself and why he'd come to the group.

'Well, it was a shock,' he said. 'It was a big shock finding out about my daughter. She has a friend who'd been at the house for dinner. Nice enough lassie. Then I found out they were more than friends.'

Jeanette said, 'Things had changed, right?'

'You're telling me.'

'How did it happen?'

'I found out by accident,' said Spence.

There were nods and understanding smiles around the group. Jeanette said, 'That's often the way.'

'I was going to speak to her about it.'

'Good,' said Jeanette.

'I had it all planned out, what I was going to say. I'm no good with these types of things, but I was going to tell her I respect her. That she's a grown up. That sort of business.'

Jeanette gave him a thumbs up. 'We're cooking with gas.'

'I was even going to make a joke about it because when she was wee I was always saying how I wouldn't let her have a boyfriend. How I'd chase the boys away. I've always hated the idea of her bringing a laddie home. Going upstairs to her room. Closing the door. Putting a record on.' The thought made him shudder still. Hands on her body, testosterone coursing to the fingertips. 'And I was going to say, she's saved me the torture. But then she was out on her birthday and I was meant to pick her up. She wasn't there at the time we agreed.' His eyes passed round the group. 'What else do you do but worry? My only child. I won't go into the details, but when she turned up – her and her girlfriend – they'd had a few drinks and I lost my rag. It was late and I was tired. I said a few things I regret. She's not been home since.'

'A lot of things happen out of the blue,' said Jeanette. 'But sudden change doesn't always have to be negative, does it?'

'Some lucky sods do win the pools, I suppose.'

'So how would you react if you won the pools?'

'Me?' He laughed and turned to the others. 'I'd probably think, I can't believe it. Must be dreaming.'

'Really? What about this is amazing? I'm going to be so happy and rich. See, even in a situation that would be undeniably positive, you had a negative response.'

'Did I?'

'Think about what you just said. I can't believe it. I must be dreaming. Now think about how we react to bad luck. We say things like – this is typical. Why do things like this happen to me? The point is our natural reaction to sudden change is to be on guard. We're responding to a new situation with wariness. It's a survival instinct. There's logic behind that but it's easy to let negativity take over.' She asked if he could talk about any other experiences of sudden change.

'There's been a few. My old man dropped dead when I was fourteen. Then, when I was in my twenties, I got into trouble for selling stolen goods that I didn't know were stolen. That's still hanging over me. And, last year, my wife left me. Ran off to live with one of her old university friends. Never saw that one coming.'

'Yet here you are, a fine man raising his daughter. Once we get over the shock of sudden change we adapt. We survive. But the first step is acceptance.'

Jeanette was about to move on to someone else but Spence wasn't done. He was primed and in salesman mode. Talking about his problems to strangers felt surprisingly good. 'Now my uncle's dying. He's the only family I've got left. I'm not sure if I've got my head around that yet. Oh, and a few months back, my business partner died in the middle of a job. I had to deal with that. I mean, actually deal with his body. Then there was a delay with getting paid and I got beaten up by loan sharks, but who doesn't have money worries?' He shook his head and chuckled. 'One thing after another, eh?'

* * *

Kate's essay was going nowhere. She'd been working on it since Emma left a few hours earlier and only managed to write half a page. It had been an afternoon of coffee breaks and standing at the window, watching the street. When the Ford Anglia finally pulled up outside she rushed out to meet Emma in the stairwell.

'I'll come down and give you a hand,' she shouted over the banister.

Emma looked up from the dimness of the first floor landing. 'It's okay, this is it.' She was carrying only a couple of bags.

'Where's the rest of your stuff?'

'I didn't bring it.'

'Why?'

'Give me a sec. I'll talk to you inside.'

In the kitchen, Kate stood at the counter, arms folded, and

Emma sat at the table, avoiding her eyes.

Kate said, 'I got a bottle of wine. I was looking forward to making our first dinner together as official flatmates. Do you want to tell me what's going on?'

'I just need more time to think about it.'

'Was he there?'

'Yeah.'

'What did he say?'

'That he was sorry,' said Emma. 'He said sorry a lot. He was scared I wasn't going to speak to him again.'

She'd gone home that afternoon with the intention of clearing her room and telling Spence she was moving out. He stood like a ghost at the door of her room, apologising and asking if they were still pals. There was no excuse for the way he behaved that night. All he wanted was a second chance. She couldn't help laughing when he joked that he hadn't told Nash about their fall out because he was scared of what he would do to him. 'Emphysema or no emphysema, he'd be out of the chair and strangling me.' He followed her around the house, seeming more crumpled and beaten as she packed her bags. It was painfully reminiscent of when Fran left. In the end, she couldn't do it. She said she'd stay at Kate's a few more nights to consider his apology. She wanted to teach him a lesson.

'But we spoke about this,' said Kate. 'I thought we'd decided.'

'I thought so too but I don't know if I can do it to him, not so soon after mum leaving, and not with Nash being ill.'

'But the way he spoke to you that night...the way he spoke to both of us.'

'He said sorry about that.'

'He was going to get violent.'

Emma's eyes hardened. 'No he wasn't.'

'He grabbed you.'

'I was legless. He was worried something had happened to me.'

'Do you realise what you're doing? You're making excuses for his behaviour.'

'Just drop it, okay. I know my dad. He might be a lot of things but he's not violent. He knows he was out of line and he said sorry. I'm allowed to give him a chance.'

'This is about you, though. This is a chance to get out of Tranent.'

'Edinburgh isn't the centre of the universe, Kate. Life does go on elsewhere. Besides, if I moved out now it would be like I was leaving Nash as well.'

Kate's eyes narrowed. 'Did he say that?'

'No!'

Kate sat down next to her. Her voice softened as she stroked Emma's fringe. 'Listen, sweetheart, I hate to say this but Nash isn't going to be with you much longer – and then what? You're going to feel even more chained to your dad. I can see it coming. You'll say he's lonely and won't want to leave him on his own. You'll want to stick by him because you're a good person.'

Emma thought about her mum. It was her fault she was in this position, like a caretaker for Spence. But it wasn't just that she'd left. It was the way she did it, acting like there was some noble and complex reason behind it that Emma was too young to understand. She might understand it one day, but not for a long time.

She angled her head away from Kate's hand. 'I told you, now's not the right time.'

'So where does that leave us?'

'What d'you mean?'

'Me and you. Living together. I thought that was the plan.'

'He was crying, Kate. Begging. What was I supposed to do?'

Kate got up and went to the window. 'Jesus, Emma, it's only moving out. It's no big deal.'

'Have you been listening to anything I've said?'

'Yes. I think you've got Stockholm syndrome. You're seeing this all from your dad's point of view.'

'Oh, for God's sake.'

'I'm serious.'

'Really, really patronising, Kate.'

'You're twenty years old. It's time to live independently. Take the grown-up step.' Kate gestured out the window at the street, student central, with all the protest signs and pot plants in the dirty windows. 'We've all done it.'

The way she said it struck some deep chord of aggravation in Emma. A long moment of silence then she said, 'Okay, fuck it. I'm just going to come out with it – and I really hate sounding like my dad – but don't talk to me about independence. None of you here have a job.'

'What's that got to do with anything?'

'It's easy to be independent if you're getting a helping hand from mum and dad.'

'Why are you doing this? Don't turn this into a class issue.'

'This is all about class from where I'm standing.'

'Maybe you've got a chip on your shoulder.'

'Yeah, I do,' shouted Emma. 'I don't like privilege.'

'Neither do I.'

'It's not the same.'

They stood either side of the kitchen table, eyes alert and hearts pumping. Emma searched for something to say, something that would lift the ugly feeling, but found nothing.

Mr Tate was covering her tables when she arrived at work. The restaurant was heaving and he gave her a ticking off for being late and for her appearance – dishevelled and red-eyed, like she'd been crying. As punishment, he quickly filled up the rest of the tables in her section. She was getting orders wrong and customers were complaining. She was waiting at the hotplate when he stuck his head through the kitchen door and told her he'd just given her an extra table of six. 'Rich-looking business men,' he added. 'So for God's sake put on a smile.' The door swung shut but Emma's eyes lingered on the spot where his face had been a few seconds earlier. She wiped her brow as the chef put two plates of spaghetti under the hot lights. She picked one up, feeling its weight and the burn of hot porcelain. She turned to the door and raised the plate. Then a scream and twist of the shoulders as she hurled the plate and her hand was free of the burning pressure. The kitchen fell silent and she stared wide-eyed at the splatter of sauce dripping down the door and lumps of spaghetti mixed with white shards on the floor. A kitchen porter jumped up and down, squealing with excitement, and a chef let out a long, high-pitched whistle.

The house was empty when she got home. She went upstairs and took a shower with a song stuck in her head – mournful Manchester lyrics of heartbreak over a delicate keyboard harmony. She hummed it, then sang. She'd heard somewhere that singing was all about breathing control, engaging the diaphragm, and she thought about this as she tilted her head back and soaped her body, running her hands up and down over her stomach, squeezing in and pushing out. Her voice held steady over the verse but went off key at the chorus, going up and down through a spectrum of wrong notes. It annoyed her that she couldn't sing – like, really couldn't sing, not a single note. Spence was the one who would wander around the house, humming and whistling then, smoothly, seemingly without awareness, segue into song.

Later, in the kitchen, a discussion was on the radio about psychoanalysis. She half-listened as she made dinner. The debate had a languid air about it that seemed in harmony with the unusually warm night. One of the panellists said, '*Single-mindedness. Recurrence of thought and preoccupation. Monomania. The point I'm making is that these terms are often associated with mental imbalance – worry and neurosis – but they can be very helpful in focusing our minds and blocking out distraction.*'

Spence arrived home, shocked but over the moon to see her back. He hugged her tight and said she'd lost weight then insisted on taking her out for fish and chips. They sat in the van with greasy wrappers open on their laps, as the air filled with the heady richness of deep-fried haddock and chips. She told him what happened at work and showed him the scold marks on her palm. 'Mr Tate didn't know whether to sack me or feel sorry for me.'

'Bugger them all,' said Spence, though he resisted the urge to sermonise about the benefits of self-employment. 'I'll get you some cream for that burn.' Then he took her hand and gave it a gentle kiss.

Emma said, 'If I'm going to move back home I want you to get the car fixed. It's making weird noises again.'

Spence had been delaying for months but it wasn't just about the money. Once the car was fixed that would be another step on the way to Emma's full independence. Now he didn't have a choice. He nodded solemnly. 'I promise. I'll pay the money. I'll fix it. But please, if you're going to be driving back and forth to Edinburgh, promise me you'll take care on the roads.'

'That'll be a lot easier if the car's not falling apart.'

'I'm talking about other people. Idiot drivers. And I don't want you going out joyriding with your friends.'

'Dad, they're students. They're not like the teenagers around here.'

He smiled and shook his head. 'You know, sometimes I wonder how you've turned into such a snob.'

'I hear them at nights,' said Emma. 'Engines roaring into the distance. It's sad seeing flowers by the roadside. Why do they do it?'

'Speeding? Boredom. Wanting a thrill.'

'But why's it called joyriding? I wouldn't get joy from a car. To me, joy means you're in an elevated state. It's love or sex.'

'Maybe it depends what sort of speed you're going at.'

'You're talking about driving, right?' She nudged him in the ribs and they burst out laughing. They ate in silence for a while then Emma said, 'There's something I need to tell you.'

He touched her arm. 'It's okay. I already know.' He told her about finding the photos of her and Kate in her textbook.

'Were you snooping in my stuff?'

'Emma, you left it on the sofa. I sat down and it poked me in the arse.'

'Were you going to talk to me about it at any point?'

'I could ask you the same thing.'

'I'm asking first.'

He rubbed his ear and shrugged. 'Quite honestly, I'm just

not bothered. I know it's selfish but I've never been able to stomach the idea of you having another man in your life. To think about you getting married and having kids means I need to contend with you going on dates and having boyfriends until eventually you'd find someone to marry. Some Barry, Michael or Steve. It wouldn't make any difference to me. He'd have flaws, of course, because we all do. And I'd be the first to see them and I'd hate him for them. Then, later, you'd be pregnant and there'd be the horrors of childbirth and all the sleep deprived months with a new baby and a strained marriage. Steve or Barry would be feeling sorry for himself that he wasn't getting out for a drink with his pals anymore, and I'd have to watch you, my girl, worn down to a husk.'

'Jesus,' she laughed, 'why didn't you tell me sooner? I'd have put you out of your misery.' She hugged him. 'So it's okay?'

'If you're okay, I'm okay.'

Ghostly figures move around behind the takeaway's steamed windows. Customers smoked outside, waiting on their food.

'I'm going to call mum and arrange a visit,' said Emma. 'It's been a while.'

Spence nodded and carried on eating.

Emma asked, 'When was the last time you spoke to her?'

'A few weeks after she left.' His eyes flashed at her. 'We're not needing anything from her, mind. We're doing fine.'

'Relax, it's just a visit. I need to see her sometime.'

'I'm not standing in your way.'

'When are you going to speak to her?'

'What do we have to speak about?'

'Getting divorced.'

'That would mean speaking to a lawyer and that would cost money. She can ask me for a divorce if she wants but I'm not asking her.'

'So you're never going to speak to her again?'

'Emma, how would I, even if I wanted to? I thought that was the whole point of her being away up there – to shut herself off from everything.'

'I don't think that's how she sees it.'

'She has a history of running away from things.'

'Her family?'

He nodded. 'I'm not sure whether she disowned them or they disowned her, but, either way, it was because of me.'

'So you never met them?'

'No, but I don't think she was in contact with them much by the time she met me. You might say I was the straw that broke the camel's back.'

Emma asked how they met.

'She was at the Appleby Horse Fair with a load of friends in a big trailer. Not Travellers, but sort of hippy types. She had an idea that Travellers were very romantic.'

'So you proved her right.'

He poked around in his fish supper, searching for the fattest chips. 'Let's just say things moved fast. She was expecting you before I could blink. I suppose we both had a wild streak. She was rebelling against...whatever it was. And me going with her, a non-Traveller girl and getting her pregnant, turned me into a rebel among the Travellers. So there we were, two rebels from opposite ends of society, expecting you.'

Some people might have thought he was after Fran's money, but no. To Spence, old money was dead money. The thought of it accumulating without being spent made him suspicious. It had to be earned and in your pocket to mean anything. It came in and went out.

'I knew your mum had money but it was as if she wanted to live like she was poor,' he said. 'She thought it was romantic or some nonsense. It's strange, but those were the sixties. There were plenty stranger things happening.'

He knew life with him wasn't what Fran was expecting. She wanted campfires and open roads but he was moving away from all that. After the upheaval of the war, there were swathes of fresh and affordable housing across the land. His whole family was settling down and he wasn't any different. He'd grown up hearing too many awful stories about Travellers

181

being moved on from their traditional stopping places. And, of course, there was what happened to Jenny. It haunted the family, echoing through the generations. Was it unreasonable for him to want a stable family life for Emma?

But Fran was restless. She had a go at writing for a while; a semi-autobiographical story of a woman living on the road – but never finished it. Then she made garments. Scarves, hats and bags. Spence took them out on his hawking rounds. He even managed to sell a few. 'I remember her seeming very happy around that time. But the problem was she was never going to be accepted as a Traveller. Never in a million years.'

'It doesn't make sense,' said Emma.

'Why?'

'They wouldn't accept mum as a Traveller even though she was your wife, but they see me as one because I'm your daughter.'

'It's all about blood. She was an outsider. We managed fine for a while but there was a point in the early seventies when her old friends started going off to far flung places to set up communes or cooperatives, or whatever you call them. They had big ideas about living off the land and living like they were in some…some fairytale world.'

'Utopia,' muttered Emma.

'And your mum felt like she was missing out on something. Who wouldn't want utopia? That was a turning point for us because, I've got to tell you, there's no way – absolutely no way – I was doing that.'

'She asked you to go?'

'You'll remember those holidays we took up around the Highlands and Islands, staying at those big houses?'

'Sure. She was catching up with old friends.'

'Aye but she was also testing the waters, seeing if I'd come round to the idea.' He shook his head bitterly. 'No way. Can you imagine me? Up there with that lot? They weren't my people. I remember one commune up near Wick – the far end of Scotland and I never heard a single Scottish accent. Every one of them spoke as if they'd gone to one of those posh private schools. I was never going to fit in that sort of place. That one was run by her old university friend.'

'Robert?'

A flick of his hand. 'Whatever he's called. You know what he once told me? Wait till you hear this; he wanted to live without money. Self-sufficiency, he called it. Live without money?' He threw back his head and laughed.

They had reached the bottom of their fish suppers and their greasy fingers gathered up the dregs of chips and sodden lumps of battered fish. For a while, they watched the bright lights of the fish bar then Spence said, 'I know she stayed in touch with him after that. They sent letters. I opened one of them once. He was boasting that they had a waiting list – people writing to them from all over the country – and he said it was a shame she hadn't come in at the start but it wasn't too late to join them. I've got to hand it to him, it's a hell of a sales pitch.'

'How did she tell you?' asked Emma.

'Here, in the van. She was sitting where you are now. She said she couldn't stand living in a built-up area anymore. She was worried about what living near a main road was doing to her health. Her lungs. Her moods, too. She wanted to live a simpler life, closer to nature, and she thought everyone should be living that way but society was going in the wrong direction. I asked her – what will you do up there and she told me she'd be part of something meaningful.'

'She didn't think life with me and you was meaningful?'

'Maybe you should ask her when you visit.'

The windscreen steamed up and Spence rubbed his sleeve on it so he could keep an eye on the street. 'By the way, Nash showed me the letter from his mum. The one you gave him. You might as well have handed him a hand grenade. It's devastated him.'

'Don't be dramatic. I mean, yeah, he got a bit upset when I gave it to him but he's fine now.'

'He's putting on a front for your sake. But I'm telling you, he's devastated. Absolutely devastated.'

Emma rolled her eyes. 'Okay, you don't need to say it. I

know – you warned me. It would only dig up a load of hurt. But I couldn't just keep it.'

'Of course you could,' said Spence. 'Or even better, you could have left it where you found it.'

'Lying in a box full of crap? Nice suggestion, Dad. That letter might be as much as we ever discover. He had to see it.'

'I know what I'd have done with it. Ripped the damn thing up.'

'You know what's going on here? Sexism. You act like it's me who's doing it, and it's got nothing to do with him. Nash wanted me to look into it. He asked me, so that's what I did. Okay, so he got a little upset but he knew what he was letting himself in for. The issue here is that you can't handle anything emotional – ever. Mum left and...'

'Please, not again.'

'See, you're doing it now. You're actually doing it right now.'

'Fine. Okay. Say your piece.'

'Mum left and you carried on as if nothing happened. Tonight's the first time we've spoken about it.'

'Good, because I'm trying to be more in touch with my feelings. But back when she left, what did you want? Did you want me going to pieces? I was being strong for both of us.'

'You're scared of emotions. And, quite honestly, sometimes I think you're scared to act.' He was the one who'd brought up hand grenades so she thought, fuck it, let's blow the walls off. 'I phoned a lawyer.'

'About Nash's sister?'

'No, about you and mum.'

'You did what?'

She brought out a slip of paper with a number on it. 'Just call and speak to him. He thinks you might have a case. Money, Dad. I'm talking about money.'

He closed his eyes and pinched the bridge of his nose, rubbing at the skin. He laughed a hollow, helpless kind of laugh, like he had nothing left inside. 'You never stop, do you?'

It was late when Emma lay on her bed, clutching Jenny's one-legged doll. Its fabric carried the grime and smell of decades. It had been in the world since before World War Two, even since before the Great Depression. She'd been covering it in one of her classes. In Glasgow alone, there'd been nearly 100,000 unemployed. Inner-city slums emerged. Industries went into permanent decline. The pall of it hung over the city, still. Not that a global economic slump made an ounce of difference to Nash or the rest of the Lacklows. The family photo of them ragged and shoeless was proof of that.

She picked up the book Kate had given her on the meaning of dreams. She read how dreams were a filter for our daylight worries, hopes and preoccupations – a sort of waste disposal unit for the mind. But go back only a few centuries and it was a common belief that dreams foretold the future.

Finally asleep, she dreamt she was at the edge of a forest with trees outlined against a clear night sky. There was movement from the trees and out rode Queen Lacklow in a green cape fringed with gold. Wearing a shining broach and leather boots, she was off her horse, walking slow and light-footed. They communicated without words. Her eyes were cast in shadow below the brim of a cocked hat. Whispering voices came through the air like a hidden audience, muffled and conspiratorial.

28

The year was at a point where it could safely be said that it had been a good summer; one for the garden and the park bench. Radios blared from open windows all around the estate. Nash was on a deckchair, elbow propped on the plastic arm, holding a cigarette and cup of tea. 'You know, for all the years I've been living here, I've never taken the slightest interest in that game.' Across the park, cricketers in white stood out like beacons on the yellowed grass.

Emma was next to him, crouched on his back door stoop. She shielded her eyes from the sun and squinted at the players. 'I don't have a clue how it's played,' she said.

'Aye but you'd think we ought to take an interest. I mean, here we are, watching from the comfort of my garden. For all we know, that's a riveting match going on over there.'

'Doesn't look riveting.'

'Neither does a game of chess. You see my point? We don't know how it's played.'

'Now I get you. We could be witnessing a classic game.'

'And we're sitting here none the wiser, like a right pair of ignoramuses.' He watched with a sort of relaxed concentration, a folded newspaper at his side with his cigarettes tucked into its pages.

'So what do you make of it?' asked Emma.

'Bowling. Batting. Back and forth. I've got that much.'

'Some of them look bored. There's a lot of standing about, doing nothing.'

'True, but if you keep watching you'll see that every wee while something happens.'

'Someone whacks the ball, right?'

The match ebbed and flowed, with the cricketers alternating between holding themselves tense and ready for action then loosening their arms and legs, their baggy trousers bright in the sun.

'Keep an eye on that fellow there...,' Nash pointed at the bowler. 'Look – here he goes.'

Emma watched the bowler's slow build up. His short steps became faster and longer. Head down, the ball held close to his body. Then a sudden shift across his shoulders and his bowling arm came sweeping up and over and he launched the ball at the wicket, with flailing arms and legs left in its wake. The batsman lunged forward and hit the ball across the park.

'What a crack!' said Nash. 'You wouldn't want that coming at you.'

Behind them in the hallway, the phone rang. Nash groaned and got to his feet. He picked it up but didn't speak for a long moment, then said, 'I wasn't expecting to hear from you.' A shift in his voice. 'What's that?...I didn't catch what you said...' Another pause. 'Really? *Really*? Right.' Emma got up and stood in the doorway, listening and watching. Nash grabbed a pen and scribbled a number. 'I will...I'll do that. No, don't worry, I won't get my hopes up.' He hung up and turned to her. 'That was Elizabeth Foster. They found records from the children's home.'

'Are they going to look?'

'Better than that. We can go ourselves. We just need to make an appointment.' His hands trembled as he showed her the piece of paper. 'I've got the number – see. We just phone and make an appointment.'

A nod and a brittle smile. 'So this is it. We'll go.'

'It's all thanks to you, Em. You got us here.' He laughed and hugged her.

Back out in the sun's glare, she knew there was no dodging it. Now was the time. 'I need to tell you something...before we go. I found out that a lot of Traveller kids...the ones who got taken by the authorities...a lot of them were put into homes.'

He nodded, as if to say *I know. Why's this news?* 'Aye. They got new homes. Homes with new parents.'

'No, homes, like care homes. Children's homes. Permanently.' She spared him the unpleasant details but still his face slackened.

'They didn't get adopted?'

Her eyes fell to the ground but met the sight of his shadow

stretched across the grass – much bigger than the real Nash – his hunched back and craned neck. 'Some did,' she said, 'but only the youngest.'

'How young?'

'No older than five.'

'How do you know all this?'

'Someone told me. An expert.'

'Right. I see. That puts a different complexion on things. I see why you didn't want to tell me.'

'I did, I just didn't know how. I want you to think about it because if we do find anything – once you know – that's it. You can't undo that.'

'You want me to turn away from this – to sit here and do nothing – because I'm scared of bad news?'

'Just think about it.'

'There's nothing to think about. There's still a chance. That's the bottom line. There's still a chance.'

'I'm sorry. I wish I hadn't found out what I did.'

He grabbed his cigarettes and pulled one out. 'What's there to be sorry about? It's the way things go. This is my fault, anyway. I should have seen it coming. Society didn't want adult Travellers so why would they want the kids? Stupid. I'd convinced myself that...ach, you know what I thought. You're probably sick of hearing it.' He sighed and smoothed back his hair. 'I'm a sentimental old *eejit*. You know, I even had a daft notion that we might find her and she could be a new woman in your life.' He looked sheepishly at her. 'After your mum going.'

'You really thought that?'

'I told you it was daft.'

'You don't need to do any of this for me,' said Emma. 'I'm fine. Bugger it. We don't have to go.'

He shook his head as if trying to get a bad taste out his mouth. 'No, no, I want to know. If there's anything in those records, whatever it is, I want to see it. I want to know. They might have destroyed my family but they won't make a coward out of me. I'm not running away from anything – not now.'

Afterwards, Emma dropped Nash off at the local shop so he could get something for supper. She offered to drive him home again but he wanted to walk. It was a nice evening, and not many left now summer was on the turn. The shopkeeper was away from the counter and the place was empty apart from two teenage lads over by the magazine rack. 'Dinnae, Kieran,' shouted one of the lads. 'You'll gie the old man a heart attack.'

Nash ignored their sniggers and stage whispers and carried on browsing the tins of baked beans and spaghetti hoops. They stood with their backs to him, a tall one and his runty sidekick, flicking through the pages of a dirty magazine taken down from the top shelf. Kieran, the taller of the two, groaned out of the depths of his loins and puffed his cheeks at the pictures.

'Ha ha! Nae luck,' squawked the scrawny sidekick. He pointed at one of the pages. 'That one looks like your sister, by the way.'

'Aye, they thought yours was too much of a boot,' boomed Kieran. 'She gave them an audition but she cracked the fucking camera lens.'

Nash glanced around for a fellow shopper, someone to exchange a tut and shake of the head with, but he was still alone. He made do with a loud sigh and a few muttered words of disapproval. This only made things worse.

'Whoar! Fuckin hell,' roared Kieran, now practically waving the magazine in the air. He checked over his shoulder to see if he could catch Nash's attention and shouted, 'Look at the size of them! Have your eye out, like.'

'Kieran, I'm no kiddin',' said his runty sidekick, 'the old boy'll keel over if he sees that. He'll have a heart attack. You'll get done for murder.'

Nash scraped his teeth over his bottom lip, almost biting into the flesh. Remember you're the adult, he told himself. They're just daft laddies. It was mid-summer. Hot weather always made young lads act up. It was the hormones raging in the heat.

Kieran grabbed more dirty magazines off the shelf and stuffed them inside his bomber jacket. 'Leave some for the old man,' said his runty pal.

That did it. Nash spun round and pointed at them with his walking stick. 'Hiy! Yous,' he shouted. 'Thieving wee shites. Put the magazines back.' It was their grins, their cackling – the downright brazenness – that made him snap.

Kieran stepped forward, his thin lips teasing up at the edges. 'Are we takin your favourites, mister?'

A rustle of bead curtains from the front of the shop and the shopkeeper appeared. 'Get out,' he shouted at the lads. 'You're banned! I told you before – banned!' He waved his arms and came marching down the aisle. 'Get out! I'll call the police! Go on, bugger off!'

Here was the thrilling climax of impending trouble and the animal need to escape. All squeals, grins and flapping arms – like they were having the time of their lives – the lads broke for the door. Nash stood in the middle of the aisle, inadvertently blocking their exit. They threw the magazines in his face and rammed him into the shelf. He dropped his walking stick and reached out to steady himself but succeeded only in pulling the carefully arranged tins off the shelf. The tins clattered down around him as he fell backwards on the grimy black and white linoleum. He let out a gasp as the air was knocked clean out of him, and his face wrinkled horribly at a stabbing pain in his hip.

The shopkeeper chased the lads out then helped him sit up and rest against the shelf. Nash took out his inhaler and puffed on it. A woman with a gaggle of children came in and picked up his glasses. She handed them to him then noticed the floor strewn with a collage of tinned food and pornographic magazines. The scattered pages showed women in a variety of positions. Some on their backs with their legs open. Others on all fours, looking over their shoulders towards the camera – all glossy-lipped and open-mouthed. The woman with the children looked aghast at Nash and he looked back at her. His mouth was open but before he could offer any explanation she withdrew in disgust, guarding her children's eyes against the sight on the shop floor.

The shopkeeper helped Nash to his feet then put the tins back on the shelf and tidied up the magazines. At the counter, Nash tried to pay for a tin of beans, a bottle of beer and the evening newspaper but the shopkeeper wouldn't take his money. As a gesture of thanks, he gave him one of the magazines recovered from the floor.

'I'm too old for all that,' said Nash. 'Really, I wouldn't know what to do with it.'

'Please,' said the shopkeeper. 'It's for helping. You're a brave man. We need more people like you.'

Not wishing to seem ungrateful, Nash took the magazine and slipped it inside the newspaper.

'Are you okay to get home?'

'I'll manage,' said Nash.

'I can call a taxi.'

'Really, I'm only five minutes along the road. I'll be all right.'

Outside, he stopped in front of the shop's graffitied shutters, tucked in his shirt and neatened his tie. There was no sign of the lads so he started hobbling homewards. He was halfway up the street when somebody behind him whistled. It was the two from the shop coming towards him with a bunch of other lads. Kieran shouted, 'Hiy, you auld wheeze bag, that was top quality wanking material.' The grinning pack caught up and closed in around him.

'The mouths on you,' said Nash. 'You're a disgrace.'

'Please accept my apologies, sir,' said Kieran. 'Allow me to rephrase: That was educational gentleman's reading material that you cost me back there. That's caused me and my associates a bit of – what'd you call it – inconvenience.'

'Get away or I'll stick my foot up your arse.'

Kieran stepped up to him and tapped a finger against his chest. 'Get your lame arse back to that shop and get me those mags.'

Nash no longer noticed the splitting pain in his hip or the creeping tightness across his chest. His heart pounded with a rage that was transcendental. It had taken over his entire being and its focal point was Kieran's grin. Like all good punches, it started by dropping his weight to his back foot. He twisted his shoulders to the right, then, as power flowed up through him, he swung back around and planted his fist directly into Kieran's sneering mouth. There was an explosion of blood and spit as the big lad dropped to his knees and slapped a hand over his mangled mouth. In the same moment, Nash felt something like an explosion in his chest. This quickly became an unbearable tightness and he fumbled and pulled at his jacket as if searching for a way to release the terrible inner pressure. Ashen-faced, he pitched forwards on top of Kieran then collapsed onto the road.

29

Hours later, he came round to the sound of voices coming and going from his bedside and the steady beep of the heart monitor. The sensation was of coming up through himself, pushing away layers of vague and unpleasant recollections and of light breaking into darkness. His eyelids quivered, fluttered and eventually opened.

When the doctor checked on him, he explained it wasn't officially a heart attack. The correct medical term was a *cor pulmonale*, caused when the arteries pumping blood through the heart stop working because of poor lung function. 'It was probably triggered by the overexertion of your confrontation with the youths,' he said. Twenty blood-crusted stitches ran the length of his forehead and a large bruise blotched his left cheek. Nash pursed his lips and nodded. So he'd wiped the grin off Kieran's mouth and lived to tell the tale. It was almost worth it. He'd be a local hero after this. Then came less welcome news. The doctor explained that it was common for patients to have a full blown heart attack soon after a *cor pulmonale*, so they needed to keep him in for observation.

The police came to take a statement and the other patients listened and quizzed Nash about it afterwards. They spoke about social decline and how young lads weren't being raised properly. It was the parents, or lack thereof. It was television. Videos. Drugs. Schools. Unemployment. 'It's not as if you can just give them a cuff round the ear anymore,' commented the man in the opposite bed.

'Well,' chuckled Nash, 'I did and look where it got me.'

Next morning, a nurse took him for tests; blood samples, x-rays and breathing into tubes connected to machines to measure oxygen and lung capacity. The doctor came back while Nash was eating lunch. He sat on the end of his bed, leafing through the results. There'd been a sharp decline since his last set of tests. 'It's hard to be certain,' he said, 'but you might only have a few months left.'

'Will I see the end of the year?'

The doctor held up Nash's chunky medical file. 'To be honest, it's a miracle you've made it this far.' He clapped him on the shoulder, gave him a brisk smile, then joined a group of junior doctors waiting for him at the ward entrance.

Nash watched him lead the juniors from bed to bed, showing off his clinical expertise with the sick and dying. The doctor flirted with the female trainee – not much older than Emma – and ridiculed the males. Watching it made Nash feel confined to some hidden place of irrelevance, not really living anymore but not dead either; just waiting and watching the world go on around him. Here he was, stuck in a hospital bed while a middle-aged doctor used patients to make himself feel more alive and in command of the world. It was primal, like all that mattered was relative virility and robustness. He watched with mounting disgust and eventually lifted his hand and called out, 'Hiy, you.'

The doctor looked across the ward, frowning, with an uncertain smile.

'I'm talking to you. You're supposed to be my doctor.'

The doctor broke away from the juniors and came to Nash's bedside.

'Are you my doctor?'

'I am.'

'And your name?'

'My name?'

Nash gestured, drawing him closer as if to whisper to him but then propped himself up and shouted, 'What's the matter, are you deaf? I said, what's your name? You told me I'm dying and you never gave me the courtesy. Don't they teach you manners?'

He was asleep when Spence and Emma visited that evening. He had that awful look of having been arranged while unconscious, with his hands clasped neatly on top of the covers as if to give him some dignity. But it was seeing him stubbly and grey, messy-haired, and without his tinted glasses that upset Emma the most. 'He looks like a corpse,' she whispered to Spence.

194

She hated the smell of hospitals; the starched bed linen and bleached floors fighting to overpower the stench of sickness. She looked around the ward at the other beds and the family members clustered around sick relatives; they held stilted conversations and cracked jokes as if everything was normal.

Nash stirred and half-opened his eyes. He was very groggy, mumbling something about being given a magazine as a reward and not wanting anyone to think of him as a dirty old man. Spence and Emma assumed it to be gibberish from the bump on the head and strong painkillers. They just nodded, patted his hand and told him not to worry about anything. Eventually, he put on his glasses and took a sip of water but remained subdued for several minutes. Spence put a bottle of diluting juice and a large bar of chocolate on the bedside table. He crouched down and began taking out paperbacks from a bag.

Nash squinted at the back of his head. 'You know, you've got a wee bald patch coming on at the back there, son.'

'Have I?' A flash of panic across Spence's face as he patted the crown of his head.

'Too bad you've not got my genes. Now, I'm telling you, don't bother with those adverts you see in the magazines for miracle cures and what have you. Don't waste your money.'

'What d'you take me for?'

'Some men get desperate.'

'Not me.'

'Good, because there's no such thing as a cure for baldness – and I'll tell you why...' he held up a hand to focus their attention. 'Because if there was, Sinatra would've had it, that's why.' He nodded slowly, as if accepting gratitude for imparting great wisdom.

'Hang on,' said Emma, 'what about the actor off that detective series that you like?'

'Telly Savalas?' said Nash. 'That bald head's part of the man's look. It's made his career. No, no, no – it's Sinatra. The man's obsessed with finding a cure. I was reading about it. He's spent a fortune. They reckon he's blown $50,000 over

195

the years. $50,000! He's been to every clinic, seen every specialist, tried everything. Obsessed.'

'That's not obsession,' said Emma. 'That's someone with too much money.'

Nash picked up the magazine and leafed through it. 'I've been thinking, I want you to go to Glasgow to see those records.'

'To the archives?'

'Aye, I want you to go soon.'

'I thought we should wait till you get out of here and we could go together.'

Nash put down the magazine and knitted his fingers together, spiralling his thumbs around each other. He stared at her as if to make plain his displeasure at having to state the obvious: 'Are you having a laugh? I'm in no fit state.'

'Yeah, but once you get out. You'll eat, you'll rest. Get your strength back.'

He shook his head. 'Em, my strength isn't coming back. Besides, I wouldn't know what I was looking at. Papers. Documents. That's your area. You'd be going on my behalf. You'd be going as my...representative. I wrote the number down. It's next to the telephone.'

'I know.'

'So call and make an appointment.'

She shrugged. 'Okay, I will.'

'Soon,' he said. 'I want you to go soon.'

'No problem. I will. I'll call.'

A sternness came over him. 'Em, I might not have a lot of time left.'

She patted his arm. 'Don't worry about it. I'll go.'

'Because I'm drowning in my own filth here.' He tugged at the flimsy breathing tube that hung around his neck.

'Hey, enough of that,' said Spence. 'You'll get back on your feet.'

Nash looked around the ward as if he'd ended up in there by some mistake. 'I don't want to go this way,' he said. 'Not in here.'

30

A few days later, Emma came out of the train station and crossed George Square to Glasgow City Chambers. A doorman in a top hat and long coat opened the door and directed her to a reception with arched ceilings and marble pillars. The archivist was waiting there for her. He was overweight, with a thick head of wavy hair and ruddy cheeks. They descended to a dim-lit basement of thick walls and heavy doors. Going from reception to this reminded her of the National Library, with its grand entrance then the fusty rare collections room with the worn carpet. Funny how history seemed to house itself in the shabby corners of these grand places.

She asked, 'What sort of stuff do you keep down here?'

'Oh, just about anything we can get our hands on.' The archivist gave the impression of someone who'd just woken from a long sleep, and she wondered if he'd acquired his soft manner and slow movement from working with delicate old documents. 'Building plans, maps, deaths, births, church records, ships.' Then, with playful malice, he said, 'I know all the city's secrets and juicy gossip. As a matter of fact, you're one of our most recent entries.'

'Me?'

'The newspaper story about the protest. Your riot. That was a cracker. It's strange to think that somebody could be down here in a hundred years, standing where you are now, looking for it. They'll have your name on a piece of paper.'

He led her down a long hallway, past narrow rooms lined with shelves of boxes, and to a larger room with a table and chair. His tiny office was in a corner recess. A radio played and there was a strong smell of cigarettes despite a no-smoking sign. 'It's just me down here usually,' he said.

He gestured to a table with nothing more than a box on it. Another two boxes were stacked on a chair by the wall. 'Here it is. All ready for you.'

She looked around hesitantly. 'I don't have to fill in any forms?'

'The message that came to me from on high was to let you come in and have a look. Absolute free rein. So here you go.'

'What happened to the man I dealt with? Mr Ash. He was in charge of all the records.'

'He's gone. There was a review. They moved him to some other department, I think.'

'Oh. Oh dear.'

The archivist looked at her and laughed. 'Yeah. Exactly. Senior officer for paper clips or something like that.' He removed the box lid and the smell of old papers rose up at them. He leafed through the first few sheets. 'This is something to do with children, is that right?'

'My great-uncle's sister,' said Emma, and gave him the details – the date, the place, by now as well implanted in her memory as the details of her own life.

'The message I got was to look for anything from Lanarkshire children's homes in the late twenties, early thirties. St Augustine's in particular.'

'That's right,' said Emma. 'That's where they took her.'

'Well, here it is,' he said. 'It's all a bit of a mess. I'm not sure where I'd begin with sorting it.'

'Maybe I can give you a head start,' she said.

'Very kind. Oh, if you find anything in there other than papers, can you let me know?'

Emma shot him an apprehensive look. 'Like what?'

'You'd be surprised what can turn up.' A chuckle and shake of the head, and he disappeared into his office alcove.

She leafed through the first few grimy sheets and scanned the dense lines and columns. Names, places and dates. The handwriting was elegant and difficult to read; the language of old officialdom, documenting young lives cut off from their families. There were admittance papers, work records and adoption forms. A punishment record, meticulously detailed – an ugly rendering of some poor child's life: wetting the bed; refusing to eat dinners; poor manners; walking with a slouch.

Punishments for all of it.

A file came to hand for a boy named Anderson, admitted to St Augustine's in January 1926. There was a behavioural record – all satisfactory – and a record of duties carried out around the home. Again, all satisfactory. Then, in April of the same year, there was a release form for his adoption by a family in Renfrew. The father was a banker. The mother, a teacher. Perhaps there was hope yet.

Emma spent the next hour sorting the papers into categories. She noted dates and cross-referenced forms. She wanted to be sure not to miss anything. After coming this far, doing so much, it was important to draw a firm line under the matter and leave knowing that was the end of it.

After a while, the archivist checked on her and was impressed with the stacks of papers. 'You'll have me out of a job,' he joked. And it was true that by the time she was near the bottom of the last box she was in a quick and efficient rhythm, identifying admittance forms, behavioural records and release papers, then placing them into neat piles on the table. Perhaps she was just tired or rushing to get finished but the file caught her off-guard. Right under her nose yet it took a second or two before she noticed the details. A registration form dated 29 October 1929. If anything, she was expecting to spot a name crammed in among a list of other names, or some tiny, tantalising clue. But this was plain as day – the cover sheet of a file comprising several pages.

Tinker girl, six. Father deceased. Lacklow. Refuses to speak.
First name not known. Not suitable for adoption.

The archivist heard her gasp and stuck his head out from the alcove to ask if she'd found something.

'Just a dead spider,' she said. 'I hate them.'

A sick feeling gripped her stomach. You knew to expect this, she told herself. It was always a possibility.

More sheets were attached with notes and dates.

11th February, 1933 – five lashes of the belt for running away.

She made a mental note that Wee Jenny would have been around eight. She flicked through the rest of the papers.

8th August, 1934 – Belted and locked in for attempting to run away.
15th May, 1935 – Reprimanded for talking back to the house master.
21st September, 1935 – extra cleaning duties for stealing food from the kitchen.

There was more but she couldn't go on. Sitting there, cocooned inside the thick walls cast in poor light, she was like some secret adjudicator. The judge of how far this information would be allowed to seep into the outside world. She checked the papers again. There might have been a mistake. She was tired and it was possible, after hours in a gloomy basement scanning hundreds of documents, that she'd misread some of the words. She checked again but the information remained as stubborn as an old stain.

* * *

A game show was on the television in the hospital day room. A beaming contestant had just won a holiday to Spain and £5,000. Emma found Nash alone in there, sitting listless in front of it, his hair without its Brylcreem sheen and his eyes naked and tired without his tinted specs. It was his second week in hospital, though the doctor said he could go home at the weekend.

'Well?' he said, without looking up.

Spence used to say to her that people could always tell when you were fibbing; little giveaway gestures, unconscious yet impossible to hide. She felt this as a great pressure building up inside just before she spoke. She smiled thinly and shook her head. 'I didn't find anything, sorry.'

He turned to her and arched his eyebrows in delicate scrutiny. 'No? Nothing at all?'

'Nah, not a bean,' she said. 'I went through all the boxes. Nothing. You'd have been wasting your time if you'd come. I mean, the files...they were from the right time and all that, but there was nothing. Just a load of old junk.'

The afternoon sun shone through the blinds, streaking their faces with shadow and light. The end credits were rolling on the gameshow and Nash turned back to the television, to the music and grinning presenter and contestants showered by glitter and waving at a non-existent studio audience.

'Just a load of junk?' he said.

'And they pay a man to look after it. Absolute waste of taxes. They really need to sort it out.'

'But you checked? I mean, that's why I asked you to go, because I can trust you to be more thorough than some stuffed shirt.'

She squeezed his hand and smiled. 'Swear to God, I was very thorough. I checked all of it.'

'And there was nothing?'

'I swear.'

She apologised again but Nash raised his hand in a slow, dismissive gesture. 'No matter,' he said. 'You did your best. That's the end of it.'

31

The delicate chime of the mantle clock signalled that another hour had passed in the rare collections room. Emma sat with the book, reading about her ancestor, Queen Lacklow. She'd decided that this connection to the past was the real prize of her search for Jenny Lacklow. She was enriched by it and proud to be a Lacklow woman. After Nash was gone, she'd still have the book. It would always be there for her, safe in the archives, and a signature on a requisition slip away from being in her hands.

She yawned and stretched, and her thoughts drifted back to the previous week's visit to the archives at Glasgow City Chambers. Down in the basement, after finding Jenny's file, she had checked over her shoulder a couple of times before slipping it inside her coat. She held her hand firmly against it as she thanked the archivist and left. On the train home, she thought about ripping the pages up and scattering the pieces out the window but somehow that wouldn't have been enough. Next morning, after Spence had gone out, she took the papers to the garages behind the house. It didn't matter if Nash lived two more weeks or two more years, she wouldn't let the papers share the world with him. There had to be no possibility of him ever seeing them. She flicked through them one last time then put a match to them. They were so old and dry and it was a relief that they burned quickly, as if they were waiting for just such a release. Black wisps spun around in the morning air and soon became tiny specks and she watched them till they were gone completely. She thought about the many times during the search that she'd been told by officials there was no requirement to keep records. In this way, she didn't feel like she was doing anything wrong.

A reader at one of the other desks sneezed and blew his nose. The disturbance brought her back to the here and now, to the rare collections room and the book open in front of her. She read how, after decades as the outlaw leader of Scotland's gypsies, Queen Lacklow was eventually caught in March of the year 1735. There was speculation that she was betrayed by a member of a rival gang who had lured her close to Edinburgh on the promise of a lucrative horse deal. But on arrival at the agreed location, she was ambushed by royal guards and taken into custody. She and her gang were sentenced to hang from trees on the city's southern outskirts as a warning to other gypsies.

On the day of the execution, a crowd gathered and guards were positioned around the area to protect against any attempt to rescue the gang. It was said that Queen Lacklow chewed tobacco as the charge sheet was read out and responded in mocking defiance:

I've run rings around you for all these years and you would've been chasing me yet if it hadnae been for treacherous help from my own kind. You've looked under every rock, behind every door, under every bed but you've shown yerselves incompetent at every turn. Well, for the sake of the crowd's entertainment, let us pray you can get this one task right.

Emma read a passage that described Queen Lacklow's appearance and from this she made a quick sketch of how she imagined her: lavishly cloaked, with flowing hair and defiant eyes.

When she was sure the librarian wasn't watching, she slipped off the white handling gloves and touched the soft leather of the book's cover and smelled a century and a half of musk on her fingers.

She considered the book's age and wondered how long it had been part of the library's collections. She thought about all the people who must have handled it over the years. But didn't the librarian say that nobody had requested it for ten years before her? You're keeping it company again, she'd joked about Emma's visits. Her curiosity became intense and she looked over her shoulder towards the requisition desk. The librarian was nowhere to be seen. She waited a few moments longer but the desk remained unattended. She got up and approached, pausing to check behind her at the room's only other reader. He sat facing away from her, snuffling into a tissue over a stack of dusty books.

The hatch lifted with a slight creak as she slipped behind the counter and took the book's file out of the pigeon hole. She opened it and saw her name listed on many dates over recent months. The last requisition before that was from 1972, by L McLeod. There was an address in Glasgow. She took a note of it and shut the folder.

Behind her, the storeroom door opened and the librarian reversed out balancing a pile of books. She banged into Emma and the books tumbled to the floor, their brittle spines splintering and breaking off from their covers on contact with the polished hardwood.

'Oh shit!' cried the librarian, and dropped to her knees.

'Shit – I'm so sorry.' Emma crouched down, fumbling at the broken pieces.

'Jesus Christ!' hissed the librarian. 'What are you doing? You're not supposed to be back here.'

'I was just checking...' Quick, she thought, come up with something. 'I couldn't remember when I first visited. I was just making a note of the date.'

The librarian picked up one of the broken books. She examined it, the cover hanging off, its pages drooping. She whispered, 'What the hell am I going to say about this?'

'I'm so, so sorry. I'll pay for the damage.'

A manager had heard the commotion and came to see what was going on. Hands on his hips, eyes popping, he demanded, 'Who is this and why's she behind the counter?'

In the pause that followed, Emma's life as a student flashed before her. This was it. They had her details. It would be reported to the university and she would be expelled.

'It's my fault,' said the librarian. 'I was carrying too many books. She's just helping me pick them up.'

Emma mouthed thank you then made a hasty exit. On her way out, she smiled at the security guard then ran across the road, cutting between cars and buses as they sounded their horns. At the end of the street, she looked over her shoulder with a hunted feeling like the guard might be coming after her, running between shoppers, one hand on his cap to keep it in place, the other pointing as he shouted at her to stop.

She turned down a cobbled road into Edinburgh's Old Town and stopped under a bridge where the air was cool and traffic rumbled overhead. Under the black, dripping stonework, she took out her scribbled note from the book's requisition file and stared at the name and address of L McLeod, then tucked it back into her pocket.

With a strange sense of detachment, she wandered through the Grassmarket and from there up to Westport where, among the strip bars and pubs, she found herself standing outside a tattoo parlour. It was tiny and neat inside, with walls covered in pictures of tattoos. All the classics – hearts, daggers, skulls. Love, hate and death.

The tattooist was a skinny man with slicked-back hair, wearing a white coat. His hooded eyes moved slowly in the lamp light, as if they had gone that way from all the time spent inking people's bodies. Emma showed him her sketch of Queen Lacklow.

'Can I have that please, on my left arm.'

'Gypsy?'

'Yeah.'

'So how'd you want her done, then? You want her buxom?'

Emma's face soured at the question. 'Please – she's an ancestor of mine. Make it tasteful, eh? Make her look proud.'

She sat down and rolled up her sleeve and her skin became fiery and pulsed at the rub and scratch of the needle's tip. Afterwards she smiled and blew on her pink and freshly-tattooed skin and pressed around it as if to verify that it was now part of her body.

* * *

A solitary man wandered the patch of grass in front of the looming tower block. He walked with his hands in his pockets while his dog sniffed around clumps of litter and a discarded sofa. A tribe of kids went tearing across the grass, some on bikes, others on foot.

Emma checked she was in the right place. The note she'd taken from the requisition book definitely said Queen's Park West. She looked up at the laundry hanging from the balconies and reprimanded herself for thinking this wasn't the sort of place where an academic would live. For that's who she hoped to find; someone to expand on what she'd learned from the book and open new avenues of research.

She'd told no-one she was coming here. Nash and Spence would burst blood vessels if they could see her standing at a high-rise estate on the southern outskirts of Glasgow about to enquire at the door of a stranger. The assistant at the National Library had once remarked to her how they got their share of oddballs visiting the rare collections. This really could be anyone, she thought. Still, she entered the tower block and took the lift to the ninth floor. At the end of a long corridor, she found the door and forced herself to knock.

There was nothing to the woman who answered. Silvery hair pulled back tight, with alert eyes blazing out from a hollowed face. Skinny hands hung out the sleeves of her oversized fleece.

Emma explained she was looking for someone called L McLeod who lived there or may have lived there a few years ago. The woman's eyes narrowed and she pulled back from the door. 'Who's asking?'

Emma hurried through an explanation: she was a student doing research into Travellers and had found L McLeod's name in a file at the National Library.

The woman hesitated then said, 'That was ten years ago.'

'So it's you?'

A cautious nod. 'Aye, that's me. Lilly McLeod.'

'I'd love to talk to you, if you've got a few minutes.'

In the living room, Lilly's pet terrier was up on her chair, sniffing at a half-eaten sandwich on the armrest. 'You wee bugger! I'm out of the room for one minute! Get down from there!' She reclaimed her seat and the dog jumped up next to Emma, snuffling her hand and wagging his tail.

Emma said, 'I'm the first person to look at it since you – the book, I mean.'

'Just the two of us, eh?' Lilly leaned back and scratched her chin. 'Not much of a library book if no-one ever reads it. A wonder it's not ended up in the rubbish tip.'

Emma brought out her notepad, filled with passages transcribed from the book. 'I'm still in first year but I'm hoping to specialise in Traveller history. Carry on and do a PhD or something like that.'

Lilly took the notepad and flicked through its pages. 'Well, I'm not sure I'll be much use to you. I'm no scholar, love. Mine was what you'd call a personal interest.'

The dog jumped down from Emma's side and sat in front of Lilly, staring at her until she gave him a piece of sandwich. Lilly explained that she was recently retired and her husband had died a few years ago, so it was just her and the dog. 'I shouldn't but I spoil him.' She sat back and pulled her fleece tight around her body. 'So, how can I help?'

'I was wondering how you found out about it?'

'It was my daughter, Esther. She had a friend who worked in the library and told her about it.'

'What's the connection?'

'I'm not sure,' said Lilly. 'That's the problem. I've got a few memories. Not very clear ones. Maybe they're not even real but they've been with me a long time. Esther heard about this book and thought looking at it might help me. Stir up my memories. She was a hippy back then, like they all were.' Lilly sat forward and lowered her head. 'I never knew my family, you see, and I'd got a bit down in the dumps about it. Esther was into all this mumbo-jumbo stuff. Past memories. Past lives. Whatever it was. I'd got to a point where I thought all the memories – fields and forests, moving from place to place – were made up. Wishful thinking from spending so long stuck indoors. So Esther thought it would help. She said: *Come on, Mum, we'll go see this book. Better than getting pills from the doctor.* So we went to see it. I'd have tried anything at that point because it had become very hard for me, not knowing where I came from. It's like looking in the rear-view mirror when you're driving and getting the sun in your eyes. You know something's back there but you can't make it out. I tried to find my parents a long time ago but got nowhere. This was back in the sixties. See, I'd been brought up in care homes. That was all I knew, so I wrote to the authorities about it.' She shook her head. 'They were as much use as a chocolate teapot.'

Emma told her about Nash and the search for his sister.

'So this wee lassie,' said Lilly, 'when was she taken?'

Emma gave her the date. Lilly nodded but said nothing. Emma asked if she could remember anything about being taken into care but Lilly said she didn't like to think about it. Her voice thickened with emotion. 'I remember being smothered. Pushed and pulled around, my mum screaming after me. I used to dream about it a lot. You know in the films when someone wakes up screaming, all covered in sweat. That was me. I'll be honest, I've had bad spells. Been at the doctor about it more than once but I'm better these days.' She turned to Sammy and ruffled his chin. 'Isn't mummy better now? Yes, she is.'

Outside, clouds parted and unblocked the afternoon sun. A pure and intense light came flooding in and fell across Lilly's face. It was like a picture coming into focus. The more Emma looked, the more she saw. But she told herself she was mistaken. Seeing things. Becoming like Spence, with his carpets and crazy schemes. Not grounded in reality. Still, familiarity persisted. A movement of Lilly's eyes, a twist of her mouth.

Suddenly Emma was on her feet, picking up her bag. 'I'm sorry. I shouldn't have come. You don't even know me and I'm barging into your home, asking about personal stuff. I'm so sorry.' She sobbed into her hands. 'It was a stupid thing to do. I don't know what's wrong with me.'

Sammy wagged his tail and licked her hand. Lilly got up, took her bag, and laid a hand on her shoulder. 'Sit down.

You're not leaving like that.'

'When I saw your name at the library, I thought you'd be an academic or teacher, or something like that. I thought you'd be able to help with...I don't know what. I just need to stop now. I just need to stop.'

Lilly made her a cup of tea and told her she was getting it with two sugars whether she took it sweet or not. They sat down again.

'Well,' said Lilly, 'you've got me talking now so I might as well carry on. I don't have a birth certificate. The only reason I know my age is because that's what it said on my file when I got out. That's all my childhood was – a file. If you misbehaved or didn't work hard, it would go in your file. That's what they used to say. They used it like a threat, like something that would be with you forever.'

'Did it work?'

Lilly smiled and shook her head. 'I ran away a lot. I was like Steve McQueen in *The Great Escape*. Tried and tried but never learned.' But around the time she was twelve, Lilly was transferred to a new care home and things changed. 'Not far from here,' she said. 'You might say that was my salvation. The home was run by a decent man – Mr Nichol. He taught us the basics we'd need in life. Reading, writing, numbers. This would be, what, the late thirties? I was nearly into my teens, but better late than never.' She patted Sammy then took out a cigarette. 'I think about Mr Nichol a lot. That's all it took – one good person.'

Emma had by now regained composure. She opened her notepad and held a pencil at the ready. 'Did you ever see any information about where you came from?'

'I remember someone at Auggy's said my mum was in jail for not taking care of me, but they said nasty things like that all the time.'

Emma cocked her head. 'Auggy's?'

Lilly held up a hand in clarification. 'Sorry, that's what we always called it. St Augustine's children's home – we nicknamed it Auggy's.'

Lilly was still speaking, unpacking the difficult memory, but Emma didn't seem to be listening. She had put down the notepad and was searching around in her bag. Lilly's voice trailed off as Emma brought out the one-legged doll and passed it to her. They sat in silence as Lilly studied it, turning it over in her hands, and pressing into its worn and familiar fabric. 'Damned ugly thing,' she said. 'How could I ever forget this?' She looked up from it. 'How did you know?'

'Know what?' asked Emma.

'To look in the library file? How did you know I was there?'

Emma frowned and stared at the floor. 'I can't explain it.'

32

It was months before they got round to it. The house had stood quiet and empty over autumn but the council needed it back by the end of the year. Each day came with a cold, seasonal shift, and it was as if this was the signal that it was time to do what needed to be done. They came with the van to sift and sort, pack and remove.

Memories came at Emma in the turn from one room to another. Moth-eaten clothes, kitchenware thick with greasy dust, rusty tins of food, cheap ornaments. Most of it was destined for charity or the tip so it felt important to see, touch, and take mental note of it all. Stiff drawers and fusty cupboards crammed with boxes and tins – like Russian dolls of storage – faded photos, letters and knickknacks. Going through it all in the peace and quiet, without having to rush, it didn't feel like he was gone.

She thought back over the last few hospital visits and tried to recall something he'd said – a remark she could treasure, a grand observation on life or advice on how to deal with its challenges – but there was nothing that stood out.

The hospital had phoned early one September morning. They dashed to get there but Nash wasn't conscious when they arrived, so they just sat and held his hand, occasionally whispering that they were there with him. If he heard them, he showed no sign.

There was a breathing tube under his nostrils but it was no longer needed and he had been disconnected from a monitor. He lay like some old, redundant piece of machinery as the nurse came in occasionally to check on him. Gradually, his breathing slowed and became more faint, to the point where there was a short period when Spence and Emma couldn't be sure one way or the other. She wondered what he was experiencing in that fleeting state between life and death. When he'd got stoned with her and Kate, they talked about the possibility that shamanic ceremonies opened gateways to ancestral worlds. Perhaps this was his travelling time, on his way to becoming one of the ancestors. He could carry himself proud and look forward to a place in the firmament. In his final months, he'd wrenched his demons from the dim past and into the light, a big gamble for a dying man. He might kill them off or they might resist and torment him more than ever. But he'd won.

The rooms were now mostly clear and Spence patted her arm, signalling it was time to go. Without meaning to, they'd left Nash's armchair and side table till last. It was as if once these were removed then he'd truly be gone. Emma gathered up the books and magazines and put them in a bag. As they hunched down to lift the armchair, she noticed a piece of paper wedged between the cushion and armrest. A letter from Lilly, saying how nice it was to meet him and proposing another visit soon.

It took some coaxing to get them together; a few weeks of Emma going back and forth between the two of them. It was as if now, suddenly confronted with it, Nash was scared. What would she be like? What would they talk about? What should he call her, the woman introduced to him as Lilly McLeod but who he knew as Wee Jenny?

They met a few weeks before he died. Lilly came with her daughter, Esther. They stood in a knot in his living room, eyeing each other. Awkward movements and nervous words, like someone would come along and tell them what to do. But there was no advice book or blueprint for such an event; a miraculous reunion; 50 years in the making. Decades suddenly condensed and they were back, next to each other, a little worn around the edges but alive and within grasp.

Something hung in the air, an expectation that couldn't be met by polite chat over tea and sandwiches. They were strangers yet there was something familiar between them; all the flashes of similarity Emma had noticed at Lilly's home were on display again – a sort of confirmation.

'Maybe we could do tests,' pondered Lilly. 'To find out for sure. We could ask a doctor. They might know a way.' Nash smiled and nodded but knew he wouldn't be around long enough. Besides, he'd had enough of medical professionals poking and prodding him. He was happy just to meet. He showed her the old family photo, and the more he told her the more she remembered. Sometimes the conversation flowed. Sometimes it lapsed back into awkwardness. Then, at the end, when they said goodbye, a hug.

Spence locked up and they drove to the rubbish dump and waited in a queue of cars. Emma had taken Nash's paintings and easel. Spence took a few books and old copies of *National Geographic*, vowing to take a greater interest in things beyond selling carpet. There was also £2000 in a jar under a loose floor board in the hall. Nash had been told to put his affairs in order and that's what he did. He'd rolled back the carpet and showed Spence the loose floorboard.

As they neared the front of the queue, Emma watched the men who worked at the rubbish dump, lifting, carrying and sorting through unwanted goods. They yelled at people in their cars, directing them to units for metal, units for wood, and so on. They threw quick, indecipherable jokes and comments at each other, like a band of wild-haired brothers whose only sphere of existence was there among the rubbish. One of them, bearded and grizzled, wore a cap with artificial bird crap on it, with the slogan – Damn seagulls! It was tatty and old and Emma wondered if someone had thrown it away and he'd taken a shine to it and claimed it as his own.

A man got out of a car near the front of the line. He opened the boot, pulled out a roll of carpet and made his way towards a skip with it balanced on his shoulder. Spence spotted this, jumped out of the van and ran over to him. A brief exchange with Spence asking questions and gesturing enthusiastically at the carpet. The man looked puzzled, then shrugged and handed it over. Spence brought it back, smiling like he'd found £1000 on the ground.

Emma asked, 'Would you ever stop?'

'Stop what?'

'Hawking carpets.'

He studied and pressed the flesh of his leathery hands as if the ups and downs of all the years were written into their wrinkles and gnarled lumps. 'Throw the towel in? Nah, it's going to have to finish with me, you know. I'll not be finishing with it.'

* * *

Trees and bushes scraped the paintwork as Emma took the Ford Anglia slowly along the dirt track. The main road was far behind by the time the track swung right and the big house loomed into view. She got out and stretched, and tried to shake off the six-hour drive. She knew she was in the right place because of the broken down Bentley painted with peace slogans at the edge of the drive. The house had been grand once, too, but nature was closing in around it; its roof spotted with moss and its gutters cracked and choked with weeds.

The front door swung open and Fran came tearing out and threw her arms around her. 'My baby,' she cried. 'Oh, God, my baby. It's so good to see you. So good.'

'Good to see you too, Mum.'

It had been almost a year since she'd seen Fran. Her mum was only forty years old, and Emma noticed how, despite the clean air and open countryside, the skin under her eyes still had that overworked look. Emma asked how she was doing.

'Focusing on my diet. Lots of whole foods. We try to grow what we can here.'

Robert appeared on the doorstep, laughing and rolling his eyes as Fran squealed and tried to swirl her around like she was still a toddler. He came down the steps and hugged her. She'd forgotten what he looked like; gangly and bearded, with an ever-ready grin.

'So, how's it going?' she asked, gesturing at the lumbering house.

'Still a bit of a pile,' said Robert, 'but we're getting there.' He smiled and shook his head in a way Emma imagined as a gesture of endearing foolishness, one that said he must have been out of his mind to take on such responsibilities, such lofty ambitions. But where would we be without dreams?

Inside smelled of incense and damp, and all the rooms had bead curtains instead of doors. In the kitchen, a group of women prepared a stew and baked bread. Looking out the window, she saw caravans and campers towards the back of a huge lawn and squealing children chasing chickens across the grass.

Emma dropped her bag in one of the rooms and joined the residents for dinner. There were about twenty of them gathered round a long table in the kitchen. The stew was bland and stodgy but was compensated for by good wine.

When her mum asked about Kate, Emma said they'd split up then changed the subject, asking Robert about the commune. He explained how he regarded the household as one big family and that they were at the forefront of something exciting; a new way of living that was also a very old way of living. 'When you think about it, it's really quite ironic,' he said. 'I suppose it's a sign of how twisted society has become that what we're doing is seen as subversive.'

'At the end of the day, the nuclear family is an artificial construct,' added Fran. They had that way of finishing or continuing each other's sentences; locking eyes, and nodding and smiling in mutual pleasure at their unity of thought.

'That's right,' said Robert, gesturing at the residents around the table. 'This is how our ancestors lived centuries ago. Lots of tribal societies have prospered this way – the Native Americans, African tribes. It's a very simple, very pure way of life. It's just a shame that we in this country seem to have forgotten it.'

Emma set down her glass and ran a finger around its rim. She studied the rich, oily darkness of its contents and brought her eyes up to meet Robert's. 'Actually, there was more trading and interdependence between tribal societies than a lot of people realise. The idea that it was all about self-sufficiency is a little...well, wrong.'

Residents kept interrupting to ask Robert questions on aspects of the commune's running; electrics, plumbing, damp ingress, food supplies. There were thoughtful pauses and lots of beard-stroking, but Emma sensed the uncertainty and mutual lack of specialised knowledge.

Fran asked how Spence was doing and Emma said he was fine, but he'd been obsessing over his business and trying to make a success of it. 'It happened after Nash told us he was dying. I think it was a reaction. Control. It was about control.'

Fran wasn't surprised. 'It took a long time for me to realise that all your dad wanted was to make money. It was depressingly small-minded but I don't blame him. He's a victim of the system. That's why I had to get away. Up here, you understand what's important. Nature's always there.'

She thought about the time Fran told her she'd like to be a beautiful vase in an empty room. She was eight years old and Fran was showing her pictures from an art book with paintings of elegant Dutch interiors. Even as a little girl, she felt it was a strange thing for an adult to say. The image stuck with her and she remembered it now not as an expression of calmness but one of frustration and despair.

She told her mum about Nash dying and Fran shook her head and asked if he'd smoked till the end.

'Like a chimney,' said Emma. 'He refused to quit. It was kind of admirable.' She told them how she'd traced Jenny and that, despite all the phone calls and letters and meetings with the council, she found her through an old library book.

'And now they hold all that information on you,' said Robert.

Emma shrugged. She was happy to be part of the record on this chapter of the Lacklow's fortunes. Like the archivist said, maybe one day someone would find it useful.

'We had a census taker at the door a couple of weeks ago,' Robert continued. 'We told everyone to hide, especially the kids. We didn't want them knowing there were kids here.'

'No, absolutely not,' said Fran.

'All the Tory bullshit about wanting a small state – that's a lie,' said Robert. 'Thatcher's just a puppet. There's government – and then there's *government*. You know? The corporations

216

and bankers. The business networks. I was at school with them. It's intergenerational. International, too. There's not many places left to get away from them.' He'd never let an agent of the state onto his property if he could help it.

'What do you think they want?' asked Emma.

'Our freedom,' he said without pause. 'It's all about control. The system doesn't work without mass control. Propaganda. They say democracy is freedom but it's slavery. People need to wake up and realise.'

Fran looked at him and nodded solemnly. 'Freedom's what they're most scared of,' she said. 'That's the real threat. People like us, living like this. They want to use us like fodder for the system. They want us trudging out the door every morning, like drones.'

After dinner there was pot smoking and music from a guitarist and fiddler. The evening wound down as a woman sang a sorrowful ballad in the soft glow of candlelight. A couple of dogs had gone to sleep in the corner and the indefatigable squad of pink-faced children ran in and out, squealing and grabbing chunks of bread from the table.

In the morning, Fran gave her a pack of leaflets and booklets to take home. There was a mail order form with a personality test to send to an organisation in America. 'It's actually a church,' said Fran. 'But you learn a lot about yourself.'

They went for a walk. Above them, huge clouds banked up messily, densely shifting and dwarfing the sprawl of the land. They strolled through the garden and to the edge of a field. Fran showed Emma inside a polytunnel where she was growing vegetables then, back outside, pointed out features around the field where she said Robert was making progress in cultivating the land. All Emma could see were mounds of dirt and stone.

She turned to Fran and asked, 'Why did you leave the way you did?'

'There wasn't any other way. What you need to understand is that I realised I needed to reclaim something I had lost – and I was running out of time. I'd want you to do the same.

That's why I raised you the way I did.'

Emma knew that was an attempt to guard against accusations of selfishness. She could also sense her mum was trying not to sound regretful but the wind had picked up and brought cold darts of rain down on them. There was no disguising that she'd opted for a life of hard toil in a dilapidated house in Scotland's sparse north-easterly tip.

As they walked back to the house, Fran said, 'I was very young when I met your dad. Very idealistic and romantic. If I'd taken things more slowly maybe I'd have realised sooner that we weren't soul mates. But we had you very quickly so that was me...' She stopped herself but Emma knew she was about to say stuck. 'So that was me committed. I put all that idealism into raising you.' She cupped Emma's face and smiled. 'You're a wonderful young woman. I'm very proud.'

END

TIPPERMUIR BOOKS

Tippermuir Books Ltd is an independent publishing company based in Perth, Scotland.

PUBLISHING HISTORY

Spanish Thermopylae (2009)

Battleground Perthshire (2009)

Perth: Street by Street (2012)

Born in Perthshire (2012)

In Spain with Orwell (2013)

Trust (2014)

Perth: As Others Saw Us (2014)

Love All (2015)

A Chocolate Soldier (2016)

The Early Photographers of Perthshire (2016)

Taking Detective Novels Seriously: The Collected Crime Reviews of Dorothy L Sayers (2017)

Walking with Ghosts (2017)

No Fair City: Dark Tales from Perth's Past (2017)

The Tale o the Wee Mowdie that wantit tae ken wha keeched on his heid (2017)

Hunters: Wee Stories from the Crescent: A Reminiscence of Perth's Hunter Crescent (2017)

A Little Book of Carol's (2018)

Flipstones (2018)

Perth: Scott's Fair City: The Fair Maid of Perth & Sir Walter Scott – A Celebration & Guided Tour (2018)

God, Hitler, and Lord Peter Wimsey: Selected Essays, Speeches and Articles by Dorothy L Sayers (2019)

Perth & Kinross: A Pocket Miscellany: A Companion for Visitors and Residents (2019)

The Piper of Tobruk: Pipe Major Robert Roy, MBE, DCM (2019)

The 'Gig Docter o Athole': Dr William Irvine & The Irvine Memorial Hospital (2019)

Afore the Highlands: The Jacobites in Perth, 1715–16 (2019)

'Where Sky and Summit Meet': Flight Over Perthshire – A History: Tales of Pilots, Airfields, Aeronautical Feats, & War (2019)

Diverted Traffic (2020)

Authentic Democracy: An Ethical Justification of Anarchism (2020)

'If Rivers Could Sing': A Scottish River Wildlife Journey. A Year in the Life of the River Devon as it flows through the Counties of Perthshire, Kinross-shire & Clackmannanshire (2020)

A Squatter o Bairnrhymes (2020)

In a Sma Room Songbook: From the Poems by William Soutar (2020)

The Nicht Afore Christmas: the much-loved yuletide tale in Scots (2020)

Ice Cold Blood (2021)

The Perth Riverside Nursery & Beyond: A Spirit of Enterprise and Improvement (2021)

Fatal Duty: Police Killers and Killer Cops: the Scottish Police Force 1812-1952 (2021)

The Shanter Legacy: The Search for the Grey Mare's Tail (2021)

'Dying to Live': The Story of Grant McIntyre, Covid's Sickest Patient (2021)

The Black Watch and the Great War (2021)

Beyond the Swelkie: A Collection of Poems & Writings to Mark the Centenary of George Mackay Brown (2021)

FORTHCOMING

William Soutar: Collected Works, Volume 1 Published
Poetry (1923–1946) (Paul S Philippou (Editor-in-Chief) &
Kirsteen McCue and Philippa Osmond-Williams (editors), 2024)

William Soutar: Collected Works, Volume 2 Published
Poetry (1948–2000) (Paul S Philippou (Editor-in-Chief) &
Kirsteen McCue and Philippa Osmond-Williams (editors), 2024)

William Soutar: Collected Works, Volume 3 (Miscellaneous
& Unpublished Poetry) (Paul S Philippou (Editor-in-Chief) &
Kirsteen McCue and Philippa Osmond-Williams (editors), 2025)

William Soutar: Collected Works, Volume 4 (Prose
Selections) (Paul S Philippou (Editor-in-Chief) & Kirsteen McCue
and Philippa Osmond-Williams (editors), 2026)

The Black Watch From the Crimean War to the Second Boer
War (Derek Patrick and Fraser Brown (editors), 2024)

The Perth, Dundee, Angus & Fife Murder Book: Notorious
and Noteworthy Cases from the Sheriffdom of Perth – The
Sequel to Perthshire's Pound of Flesh (Mark Bridgeman, 2024)

A Most ~~Unsuitable~~ Beautiful Game: Celebrating Scottish
Women's Football Fifty Years After the Ban
(Karen Fraser, Julie McNeill & Fiona Skillen (editors), 2024)

The Lass and the Quine (Ashley Douglas, 2024)

The Royal Edinburgh Military Tattoo: 'The Show Must Go
On' – Travels of the Tattoo Producer (Brigadier Sir Melville
Jameson, 2024)

Balkan Rhapsody (Maria Kassimova-Moisset,
translated from the Bulgarian by Iliyana Nedkova, edited by
Cara Blacklock and Paul S Philippou, 2024)

A Wildlife Guide to Edinburgh (Keith Broomfield, 2024/5)

The Road to Mons Graupius (Alan Montgomery, 2024/5)

The Whole Damn Town (Hannah Ballantyne, 2024)

All Tippermuir Books titles are available from
bookshops and online booksellers. They can also be purchased
directly (with free postage & packing (UK only) –
minimum charges for overseas delivery) from

www.tippermuirbooks.co.uk

Tippermuir Books Ltd can be contacted at
mail@tippermuirbooks.co.uk